OTHER BOOKS BY KATE L. MARY

The College of Charleston Series:
The List
No Regrets
Moving On
Letting Go

Zombie Apocalypse Love Story Novellas:
More than Survival
Fighting to Forget
Playing the Odds
The Key to Survival

Anthologies:
Prep For Doom
Gone with the Dead

NEW WORLD

Book Five in the *Broken World* Series

KATE L. MARY

Twisted Press

Published by Twisted Press, LLC, an independently owned company.

Copyright © 2015 by Kate L. Mary
ISBN-13: 978-1518896729
ISBN-10: 151886723
Edited by Emily Teng
Cover art by Kate L. Mary

NOVEMBER

CHAPTER ONE

JON

The clank of metal jerks me awake, and I open my eyes to a room cloaked in darkness. I don't need the light to know what the sound is, though. It's the same noise that wakes me more often than not these days.

On the other side of the room, Ginny thrashes and moans, causing her bed to slam against the wall. I should be used to it by now, but the erratic thump of my heartbeat tells me I'm not. When a cry pierces the darkness, the pounding grows even more intense, and I roll out of bed so fast my legs get tangled in the sheets. I kick them off and scramble across the floor as Ginny's whimpers grow more insistent. Every whine she lets out makes my gut clench tighter.

Dammit. I'll never forgive myself for what I put her through.

"Ginny," I whisper when I reach her side.

I run my hand over her head, but her hair is so damp it clings to her moist skin. When she lets out another sob, her whole body jerks. I don't stop whispering her name though, doing my best to ignore the painful squeeze in my chest. It usually takes a few seconds to bring her out of the dream.

Suddenly, she gasps and bolts upright, knocking my hand away and shaking the entire bed again. Her eyes are so wide that even through the darkness, the whites are visible. She has the sheets knotted around her fists, and she's gasping for breath, shaking. I pull myself up until I'm sitting next to her on the bed and run my hand down her arm, trying to ease the tension in her body while I wait for her to realize she's safe. Because she is. Even if I have to die trying, I am going to make sure nothing bad ever happens to her again.

"It was a dream," she finally says, but the stiff muscles of her forearm seem to tighten even more.

"It was. You're okay."

Ginny swallows and nods twice, then without another word, she scoots down until she's as close to the wall as she can get. I crawl into the tiny bed at her side. My arms wrap around her small frame, and her body trembles against mine.

I can't wait until we have a bed big enough for both of us. Ginny only sleeps well when my arms are around her. Of course, I don't have a damn clue why she needs me so much. God knows I don't deserve her trust. Not after what I did.

When the weight of the guilt feels like it's going to crush me, I kiss her temple. Of course, that only makes me feel guiltier, because the gesture has more to do with easing my own pain than hers. Some of the tension in Ginny's body eases, taking my own pain with it, but we both know this will be with us until the day we die. It will always hang over our heads. A cloud of guilt and pain so thick that if anyone could see it they'd think it was the end of the world. Again.

"Don't leave me." Ginny's voice seems impossibly tiny in the silent room.

"Never," I say, pulling her closer. Holding her tighter.

Damn you, Jon. Why the hell did you have to drag someone else into your problems? Why couldn't you be a man and take care of things on your own? Damn you.

I'm still cursing myself when Ginny's body relaxes. Then, not too long after that, her breathing slows until it's nothing more than a quiet sigh. When I'm certain she's finally out for the night, I allow my hold on her to relax a little. But not completely. If I ease up too much, she may start to cry in her sleep. It's happened before.

The morning sunshine wakes me next, penetrating the thin layer of skin covering my eyes. Ginny's body is still pressed against mine, but she isn't as relaxed, and I don't have to look to know she's awake. When I finally manage to pry my eyes open, I find her staring at me.

"It happened again," she whispers, but it isn't a question.

I nod because I don't know what to say. We've had this conversation, more than once. She doesn't want me to apologize and she doesn't blame me. It was a hard thing to believe, even harder to accept, but I finally have. Now, I just have to work on forgiving myself for what I did.

I'm not sure that's possible, though.

Ginny turns her gaze to the ceiling and lets out a long breath. "Thank you."

I want to tell her not to thank me, but again I remain quiet. She doesn't want my apologies or my sympathy. All she really wants is to move on and leave that person behind. Only I'm not sure it's really possibly. We're doing better, but the sadness Ginny carries with her is never very far away, and sometimes it comes back so suddenly that it leaves me feeling breathless. And helpless. Especially at night.

After a few seconds of silence, Ginny twists her body like she's trying to force it to wake up. "I guess we should get moving so you have time to eat before you have to head out."

"Sounds like a plan," I say, stretching my sore back before I roll off the tiny mattress.

Being crammed into the twin bed every night has taken a toll on my body. Or maybe I'm just getting old. I feel old. Older than thirty-one, that's for sure. It's hard to believe it's only been a few months since the world changed. It feels like a different lifetime, and I'm a different person. Sometimes, I even find myself wondering if the life I had before all this was just a dream.

I twist and my back pops, which makes Ginny cringe. "Don't suppose they have a chiropractor around?"

She snorts and pushes herself into a sitting position. "Doubtful."

"Well, hopefully we find one soon. Otherwise, I'm going to get you a book as soon as we clear the street the library is on. You need a new career, right?"

"And you think chiropractor is a good place to start?" Ginny arches an eyebrow my way as she eases off the bed.

"Why not? We can grab a few zoms for you to practice on. Maybe you'll be able to fix this whole mess with a simple spinal adjustment." I flash her a smile, and when she returns it, something in me tightens in a familiar and comfortable way. There's never going to be a time when I get tired of seeing her smile.

We get ready for the day, moving around each other effortlessly like it's always been just the two of us. She doesn't bother with makeup, and the clothes she throws on are simple and baggy. Warm.

My first wife, Carrie, was always well dressed. She never left the house without doing her hair or spending some time in front of the mirror, and I have a strong feeling Hadley Lucas was the same way. But Ginny likes to keep it simple, and I'm okay with it. Even with almost no hair, she's beautiful in my eyes. She's put on some weight since we arrived in Hope Springs, and her face is fuller now. Healthier. When it's chilly her cheeks turn pink, making the freckles on her nose stand out. It's her eyes I really love, though. They're big and round, and greener than seems humanly possible. Like a spring meadow. Every emotion she feels is clearly visible in those eyes. The hopefulness that passes over her when a group comes back from a run, the fear she feels after one of her dreams, the joy of being in a safe place. The love when she looks at me.

I'd almost given up hope that I'd be able to make her feel that way.

Breakfast is quick. Steaming oatmeal with canned peaches. We don't have a lot of fresh food, but when spring comes, it will be different. The people of Hope Springs have plans in place for everything. The livestock we have now isn't being slaughtered; instead, they're working to increase numbers. Breeding while we still have canned goods and nonperishable items to go through. In the spring we'll plant crops, and hopefully hunting will be better. If nothing else, we'll be able to start killing a few animals.

They've tried sending out hunting parties, but there hasn't been much success. It seems the animal population got hit just as hard as the human population did. Every time someone brings it up, my mind wanders to Axl and the others. Wherever they are, if they're as low on food as they were the last time we saw them, winter is going to be rough. They depend on Axl and Angus's hunting skills to get the protein they need to keep going. If they're still in the area, it isn't going to matter how straight the brothers can shoot. Not when there's nothing to shoot at.

If they're still alive, that is.

Ginny walks in front of me, carrying her plate toward a table already occupied by Gretchen, the teen we picked up after getting separated from the others. The guard she's been spending time with, Mark, is already with her, and the two seem to be more interested in staring at each other than eating. I'm not positive, but I'm pretty sure they're sleeping together. The condoms I had in my backpack have disappeared, and it makes sense that Ginny would have given them to Gretchen. It's not like we need them anymore.

"Morning," Gretchen says, smiling when she tears her eyes away from Mark.

Her hair and makeup are perfect, and as usual she looks like she's dressed for a day of shopping or something equally unrealistic. Mark sits so close to her that he might as well crawl into her lap. Their public display of affection usually makes Ginny uncomfortable, so I'm not surprised when I find her gaze focused on the bowl of oatmeal perched on her plate.

"Morning," I say for the two of us.

"You ready for a day of clearing?" Mark asks when I sit across from him. "Should be able to make some real progress out there soon. The bastards are getting slow."

"Let's hope so," I say with a nod. "They haven't frozen completely just yet, but a little more snow and a little more time, and I think we'll have them. For the time being, though, we still have to be careful."

"Once they do freeze it will move faster. Right?" Gretchen asks, her blue eyes growing bright as they fill with hope.

I nod, but I'm just guessing. So far we've come across a few zoms that seemed to be so cold they could barely move, but not all of them are like that, and the ones still up and moving around are as determined as ever to bite our faces off. Things have been easier to take out than they were when we first got here, but we still have to be cautious.

"We'll have the city cleaned out before spring," I say firmly. "Don't worry about that."

Gretchen smiles and glances toward Mark, who's grinning back. I can just imagine the thoughts going through their heads: a house of their own where they're free to screw as much as they want without having to worry about anyone hearing them. It's the same thing I would have been thinking at their age. Not now, though. Now all I want is a house for Ginny and me before the baby comes.

"Morning," Richard says as he slides into the empty chair on the other side of Gretchen. He grins at the teen, making the skin around his eyes crinkle, and she returns it. He's still smiling when he turns his gaze on Ginny. "How's the hope for the future doing?"

Ginny rolls her eyes. "I wish everyone would stop saying that."

"Can't," Richard says, scooping up a huge bite of oatmeal. "You and that baby are going to prove that we can start over."

Ginny shakes her head and her cheeks grow pink, but she's so focused on the bowl in front of her that I doubt anyone other than me can see the hesitation in her eyes. Even though she doesn't usually bring it up, I know she's still torn about this baby. I can't blame her, not really, but I can do everything in my power to make her feel comfortable and safe—and loved. For me, though, this baby is a new beginning. One I never thought I could have after I lost my first family, that's for sure.

"Right now we're just trying to take it one day at a time," I say, giving Ginny's hand a pat. "What about you guys? Is the weather going to stop you from going out there?"

Richard scratches at his gray beard. "Not sure about that just yet. I'm thinking we've done 'bout all we can in this area, and with winter coming, we aren't going to want to go much further." He frowns and shakes his head. "Dax has other ideas, though."

"He wants to keep going out?" Ginny says, perking up.

Richard nods, and I give her hand another pat, knowing that—as usual—she's thinking about Vivian and Axl and the others. Every time a scouting crew goes out she gets her hopes up, but so far there's been no sign of them. With winter coming and the snow getting deeper, there have been talks about putting those trips on hold for a few months. Guess Dax decided the risk was worth it.

"Isn't that dangerous?" I ask.

"Dax doesn't seem too concerned with that," Richard says. "He's not really a cautious person."

I shake my head as I scoop more oatmeal from my bowl. "Sounds like a dangerous way to live these days."

Richard snorts but doesn't say anything. He shakes his head, and I can't help wondering what it means. He acts like Dax is a fool, but there's something else there too. Only I'm not totally sure what it is.

I glance toward the clock and scoot my chair back. "I have to get moving." No time to figure out what's going through Richard's head now.

I'm still chewing when I stand, pausing just long enough to kiss Ginny on the cheek.

"Gross," Gretchen mutters. "At least swallow your food before you do that."

I grin around my oatmeal as I pick up my bowl. "Have to seize the day. Take advantage of every moment. Can't let a little oatmeal get in the way of showing someone how we feel."

Gretchen just rolls her eyes, making me laugh.

"Be careful," Ginny says, just as I turn away.

"Always am," I call over my shoulder as I head across the cafeteria.

THE BUS IS ALREADY RUNNING WHEN IT COMES INTO view. I zip my leather jacket as I jog toward it, my boots sliding on the icy pavement. The few guys standing around climb on, so I pick up the pace. Don't want them leaving without me.

I'm still a good fifteen feet away when Jim sticks his head out the open door. "Come on! We're ready to go!"

I jog faster, and by the time I get there, I'm gasping. Every breath I let out sends a burst of steam up in front of me. It's so cold out that the tips of my fingers are like little icicles. I shove my hands in the pockets of my jacket as I reach the bus. I hate winter.

Less than a second after I climb aboard, the door shuts behind me. The bus lurches forward before I've even made it two steps, and I have to brace myself on a seat to keep from falling. Guess they really were ready to head out.

"'Bout time you showed up," Jim says, slapping the seat at his side.

I drop down next to him, fighting back a shiver when the cold vinyl somehow manages to penetrate the three layers I'm wearing. "It's fucking cold out there."

He throws his head back and laughs like I just told the best joke he's ever heard.

"I'm serious," I mutter, rubbing my hands together.

"Oh, I know, which means you're in for a big surprise. It's only November. We got the whole winter ahead of us."

He shakes his head and chuckles as the bus drives through town. Thanks to the steel plates welded to the sides, we can't see a thing unless we look out the front window, but it doesn't really matter. Right now everything just looks white. I feel like someone picked me up and dropped me in Antarctica, although I'm told it's much colder there. I can't imagine. It's times like this when I really start to miss the desert.

I yank my hat lower, trying to cover the tips of my ears, and then pull on my leather gloves. They're thickly lined and warm. Everyone on the cleanup crew has a pair, but it's less about keeping us from freezing and more about making sure our fingers don't get bit off. I feel like a biker every time I head out to work. Or some badass hero in a futuristic post-apocalyptic movie—which isn't too far from where we are. Leather jackets and gloves and pants are distributed to anyone going into the city to clear, and they're all big so we can layer them over our regular clothes. They must have raided a Harley Davidson store somewhere.

We drive through town in silence. Jim smokes while the people around us talk. The leather suits him better than it does me. His shaggy blond hair and messy beard make him look like he stepped straight out of *Sons of Anarchy*, but I'm not sure what he was before all this. He's tight-lipped about his past, and whenever I ask, he just shrugs and tells me it's all behind him now. It kind of adds to the biker persona, though. He's younger than I am, probably by a good five years, but for whatever reason, it feels like he's lived more. Seen more, done more, been around the world in ways I can't even imagine.

"You have family before all this?" I ask even though I know he's not going to give me more than a few cryptic answers.

"Everybody has family." He grins and blows smoke out of the corner of his mouth, away from me.

"You know what I mean."

"Was I married? Yup."

"Kids?"

"Never had the pleasure."

"There's still time."

Jim chuckles again. "Have kids now? In the middle of all this shit? No thanks. It's hard enough keeping my own ass safe."

"I'm going to have one, you know."

"Then God help you." He blows more smoke out as he shakes his head, and we go back to sitting in silence.

The bus turns right, and only a block later it lurches to a stop in front of the gate. Conversation slows as the people around me get ready. Zipping jackets and pulling on gloves. Checking weapons. I touch the knives strapped to my belt without giving it a second thought. One was given to me my first day of clearing, but the second knife I borrowed from Axl. It has a wooden handle and blade so long it could probably go clear through a zombie's skull and out the other side. He was always cleaning the thing. Took special care of it. I grabbed it the morning we left, not realizing it was his until we'd already gotten separated from Angus and Darla. Hopefully one day I'll be able to give it back to Axl. Until then, it's going to keep me safe.

The gate opens, and a few gunshots break through the air as the bus lurches forward. Jim drops his cigarette on the floor and snuffs it out with the toe of his boot. When he slips his hands into his gloves, the expression on his face reminds me of someone going off to war.

"You ready?" he asks, just like he does every morning.

"Yeah."

"Keep your eyes open and stay alert. Don't think about that woman you got back there, or that baby you got coming. Think about you and me, and keeping our asses safe. They're slower, but they can still rip your throat out." He twists to face me, and his icy blue eyes are harder than steel. "Got it?"

I nod once.

"Good."

This time when the bus stops, we all get to our feet. No one says a word. The door opens and Shep, our crew leader, jumps out with his gun drawn. Row by row, we file out after him. I step into the aisle ahead of Jim, but he's so close that when he exhales, the scent of tobacco fills my nostrils.

We reach the door, and behind me, Jim lets out a deep breath before sucking another one back in. He does it a few times, working to calm his pounding heart before we step out into the battlefield, just like he always does. Seems like a waste of time to me. Even if I managed to calm down before heading out there, my adrenaline would skyrocket the second I set foot outside.

"Ready?" I ask, pausing at the door.

"Ready," Jim says firmly.

I'm too focused on what we're about to do to feel the cold when I step outside, and my knife is drawn before my boots have even crunched against the freshly fallen snow. In front of us, the dead have moved in, and the people who were sitting closest to the door are already busy fighting them off. Jim and I jog forward, moving as a team. Side by side with each step we take until we've joined the others. The icy ground is already littered with bodies, but I don't stop to take count.

"This way," I bark, moving to the left, just past our team leader.

Jim keeps pace with me like he's a shadow as we rush toward the advancing dead. It's a bigger group than usual, but they're just as slow as they've been since the temperatures dropped. It makes our job easier.

"Red jacket!" I call once I've set my mark.

Jim doesn't say a word, but I don't need a response to know he's got my back. I reach the zom and wrap my gloved hand around his neck. The tips of my fingers dig in, and even through the layers of leather and wool, his decaying skin is cold. He growls and opens his mouth, giving me an eyeful of crystalized saliva. It shimmers in the early morning sun. The bastard's eyes have frosted over too, and his skin has taken on a white tint like he's covered in a layer of frost. He reaches toward me, but the movement is slow, and before he can do any damage, I slam the blade of Axl's knife into the creature's temple. His arms drop as fast as his body does, landing in a pile on the ground. I do a quick survey of the area before turning my attention to the dead man at my feet and pulling the knife free.

"Overalls," Jim says when my guy is down.

He takes off, and I'm right behind him. This time, my focus is different. Jim is my concern, not the dead man we're charging. My partner makes contact while I watch his back, scanning the area to be sure no other bodies get too close. Watching the zombie in front of Jim to be sure the bastard doesn't get the upper hand. Doing everything in my power to make sure my partner is safe.

The zombie falls and I'm already looking for my next target. All around us, moans and growls ring through the air, mixing with the crunch of snow as men rush forward and the clash of blade against bone. The thump of bodies hitting the ground. On the buildings above us, archers and snipers sit, ready to take the zoms out if they get too aggressive. At our backs, the men guarding the line move the barricade forward as we work to clear, blocking the way for any more zombies. The system is intense, but intricately planned out and executed to perfection. It has to be, or we fail. And failure means death.

Jim and I work as a unit, taking turns killing the zombies just like we do every day. Today, the process is particularly gratifying for a couple reasons. At the end of this block sits a row of businesses, one of which is the OB/GYN. I've been waiting to clear this street since we got here, knowing it will mean better prenatal care for Ginny, as well as an ultrasound. It means giving our baby a better chance.

But while that building is my main goal, there's another one I've got my eye on as well. I can see it in the distance. The sign is mostly covered in snow, but I know it's there.

Jim grunts, brining me back to the present. My gaze moves back to my partner—where it should have been all along—and I find him struggling with a lanky bastard who's at least a whole head taller than I am and a good seven inches taller than Jim. The zom isn't as decayed as the others either, and his movements are less erratic. Especially when he reaches out and grabs a handful of Jim's hair.

"Bastard," Jim grunts, jerking his head back.

He kicks the zombie in the stomach, and the dead man stumbles back. Based on the howl of pain Jim lets out, I'm pretty sure the dead man took some hair with him.

Jim shoots me a glare more lethal than the damn virus that started this whole thing, then charges the zombie. I'm right behind my partner, cursing myself for getting distracted. I don't know what happened when I was lost in my own thoughts, but it could have been bad for Jim. If he'd gotten bitten or scratched, it would have been all my fault.

Jim slams his knife into the zombie's head, letting out a satisfied grunt when the blade sinks in. The dead man stops moving, and my partner pulls his knife free. He barely looks at me when I move onto the next zombie.

Shit, I'm going to get an earful when we're done.

The rest of the clearing goes without incident, at least for Jim and me. A scuffle to our right makes me think someone else has a close call, but after my distraction earlier, I refuse to take my eyes off my partner. He's depending on me. I can't let him down. Not like I did with Megan. Not like I did with Ginny. Not like I did with all those other women at the Monte Carlo. I refuse to be a failure again.

We reach the end of the block, and the backers pass us, hurrying to set up the barricade while the archers take out a couple zombies that managed to break through the line. Jim and I head over with the other clearers, ready to provide backup, but things are pretty much settled by the time we get there. Still, we stand in tense silence behind the backers as they work to reinforce the barricade, claiming one more city block for mankind.

Jim spits as he shoves his knife in its sheath, then he turns on me. "What the hell was that?"

"I got distracted." I manage to look him in the eye even though the ground is calling my name. I refuse to hide from my mistakes. That's what losers do, and in this world, losers die.

"Exactly what distracted you, Jon? That little lady back there? Was that it?"

He points back toward the campus and I find myself cringing. It makes me feel like I'm a ten-year-old getting scolded by my dad, and it pisses me off, but I can't defend my actions. He's right. I let my thoughts wander, and in the process, put his life at risk.

"I'm sorry," I say even though the words hurt when they come out. I never used to be such a screw-up.

Jim takes one step closer, still pointing toward the campus. "We leave our personal lives back there. Understand? That's why I don't play twenty questions with you on the way to clearing, because it's stupid as shit and dangerous as hell. When we get on that bus, there's nothing but us and the zoms."

Other people have stopped to stare, and heat rushes up my neck to my cheeks. I screwed up, I can't deny it, and even though I'd kick myself in the ass if I could, I'm not a child. His lecture is over the top, and guilt will only keep me from beating the shit out of him for so long.

"I get it," I say, the words forcing their way through my clenched teeth.

Jim spits again and then jerks the hat off his head. He sweeps a chunk of blond hair behind his right ear and points to a bald spot on his scalp. The skin is red and dotted with blood where the hair has been ripped from its roots.

"This could have been a hell of a lot worse," he says. "Tell me it won't happen again."

"It won't," I say, struggling between the dual desires to punch him in the face and apologize again. Shit. I hate feeling like such a dumbass.

Jim nods once before pulling the hat back on his head, then slaps me on the arm. "Good. Now let's finish up."

I'm still sitting in a stew of anger and embarrassment when I follow Jim to the nearest business. It isn't until he stops at the door that I realize it's the building that had me so distracted in the first place.

Jim glances through the front window, which is amazingly intact, then turns toward the door.

When he turns the knob, he lets out a low whistle. "Somebody forgot to lock this place up. Not that it matters. Once the dead came back, this was probably the last place anyone wanted to go. Nothing useful in here."

I nod even though I don't agree. The second I saw it on the map yesterday, I wanted to get here. Maybe it would be stupid to other people, but it means something to me. I think it will mean something to Ginny too, although I'm not positive. We haven't actually talked about it, but I can't help feeling like this is something I *need* to do.

Jim shoves the door open, and a bell dings. I pull my knife while we wait to see if anything will happen. The stench that

15

floats out tells us something died in here, but the store is so silent it *feels* empty.

"Could be an actual body," I whisper when nothing comes charging toward us.

"Seems like it." Jim pulls his own knife as he jerks his head forward. "You're up."

I suck in a mouthful of fresh air before stepping over the threshold. The glass display cases are coated in a layer of dust, but for the most part, everything seems to be where it belongs. It doesn't *look* like anyone busted into this place, but the smell tells a very different story.

Jim comes in behind me, and the bell chimes again when the door shuts. My back stiffens, but still nothing happens. I take a few steps forward, feeling Jim's presence behind me with every move I make. A few seconds later, I let out a low whistle, but still nothing moves.

We don't talk as we make our way through the dark store. Jim flips a flashlight on, and the beam helps light the way as I head toward the open door behind the register. It's probably an office of some kind. Where they have the safe or where the employees ate lunch. Whatever's back there, it has to be where the stench is coming from. The front of the store is clear.

Right before I step through the door, my whole body tenses. I tighten my grip on my knife and steady it in front of me. Ready to defend myself as well as Jim. To prove I'm not a total screw-up—probably as much for myself as for my partner. At my back, Jim takes a couple deep breaths, and when I'm sure he's ready, I step inside.

The tiny room is crammed full of boxes and supplies, so it takes a few seconds to locate the source of the smell. A man, or what used to be a man, is propped up against the safe. Behind him, the door is wide open, and diamond rings litter the floor. They glitter when Jim pans the beam of the flashlight across the room. He moves the light over the dead man, but there are no obvious injuries. No bite marks or cuts or bullet holes.

"What do you think it was?" I ask, crouching down in front of him.

"Suicide? Took a handful of pills, maybe. Not sure why he'd come here to die, but that'd be my guess. He's been dead a while by the look of him."

I pick a ring up off the floor and study it. The diamond is huge, over two carats. It's square and clear and perfect. Exactly the kind of ring every little girl dreamed about before all this started.

It isn't what I'm looking for, though.

I put it down and pick a few more up, studying them while Jim looks the man over. After a few seconds, Jim lets out a grunt.

"Son of a bitch!" he growls from behind me. "Is this what distracted you? Are you fucking kidding me? I almost got my head ripped off for a damn engagement ring!"

I don't look up from the jewelry littering the floor. "You wouldn't understand."

"Like hell." Jim grabs me by the collar and hauls me to my feet. He spins me around and gets so close to me our noses are almost touching. "You're an asshole! You almost got me killed and all you can say is, 'You wouldn't understand.' Well, fuck you!" He rips the ring out of my hand and shoves it in my face. "I understand that all this shit don't mean a thing anymore, and if that's what your lady wants, then you're a damn moron for keeping her around."

I push the ring away, not even blinking when it falls. "You don't know her and you don't know me."

"I know you're holding some piece of shit rock you probably couldn't even afford to look at before all this."

"I don't want that one, and Ginny wouldn't either," I yell, shoving him away from me.

Jim stumbles back and slams into the desk, still glaring at me like he wants to shove the now-worthless diamond ring down my throat. I rip the flashlight out of his hand and pan it around until I find what I'm looking for, then scoop it up.

"This is what I wanted. Nothing else." I shove the gold band in Jim's face, and his eyes get big. "You don't know what we've been through, so you can't understand, but she needs this. It has nothing to do with jewelry or trying to act like the whole damn world hasn't disappeared, it's about me showing her I'm going to be there. No matter what. If you knew…" I shake my head and shove the ring in my pocket. "Forget it."

I turn my back on Jim, too shaky and pissed to look at him a second longer. Maybe I let it distract me out there, and maybe he has a right to be angry about that, but I'm not going to apologize. This ring means something bigger than his little brain could possible understand. Ever.

Behind me, Jim doesn't move, and as the seconds pass, the silence hanging over us becomes heavy and oppressive until I'm not sure we're going to be able to recover from this. I haven't known Jim long—don't really know him at all, if I'm being honest—but I get the impression he isn't someone who forgets easily.

Finally, Jim exhales. He crosses the room to the dead man, not once glancing my way. "Let's get this body out of here and move on to the next place."

"Okay," I say, turning to help him.

The sooner we get the stores cleared out and the bodies loaded, the sooner I can get back to Ginny.

CHAPTER TWO
JON

Jim doesn't say a word to me on the ride back to campus. He smokes and stares straight ahead, but he acts like he's thinking. Not like he's pissed off. I don't have a clue what's going through his head, though. The guy's a total mystery to me. They made him my partner the first day I went out to clear, and we've been working together every day since. Watching each other's backs. He's serious as hell when we're on the street, but in the bus he's usually pretty laid back—jokes around a lot—but he doesn't share a single thing about who he is now or who he was before all this started.

When the bus stops, I get up without telling him goodbye. I already apologized, and I refuse to do it again. He may not understand why I need this ring, but I have my reasons, and nothing he says is going to change my mind.

The little circle of gold in my pocket feels like it's five hundred pounds. Every step I take toward the dorm weighs my stomach down a little bit more, and by the time I walk through the front doors, I'm sweating even though it's only twenty degrees outside.

I find Ginny in the cafeteria washing plates. She has her back to me, and I stop for a few seconds so I can just watch her. On her head she wears a hairnet, and even though she has a red bandana under it, the elastic cuts across her forehead so tightly it's sure to leave an indentation. The woman working at her side is running her mouth off, and even though Ginny laughs, there's a sadness to her that never really goes away. There isn't a single thing about her that resembles the Hadley Lucas I remember from before this all started. Not anymore. It's like she died and was reborn as another person.

Eventually, I head over. Dinner hours are just winding down, and the cafeteria workers are busy cleaning up. My stomach growls, but I'm dirty from the clearing, so sitting in the dining hall isn't really an option. It rarely is. There's a late-night cold dinner for anyone who gets in after hours, but having someone on the inside means I usually get a hot meal. I just don't get to sit at the tables and chat like I'm back in college the way everyone else does.

I slap my hand on the metal counter when I stop in front of the food prep area. "Hey!"

Ginny spins around, holding a metal pot. Water sloshes out of it, hitting her in the stomach, but she barely reacts. Water drips from the purple gloves she's wearing, landing on her shoes. She's soaked, as usual, but she smiles when she sees me.

"Hey, yourself. You're later than usual."

I grin when I look down at my leather jacket. "And dirtier."

Ginny smiles as she pulls her gloves off and heads to the plate she set aside for me. Everything in me clenches like it's caught in a vise grip, but it isn't unpleasant. After my wife died, I never thought I'd be able to love another person like this. God was I wrong.

20

Ginny slides my plate toward me, but all I manage to get out is a smile of gratitude. She returns it before grabbing more dirty plates to be washed.

I take a big bite of processed mashed potatoes, leaning against the counter. The other workers smile my way, but by this point they're used to my hovering. I do this every night after I get back from clearing: stand in front of Ginny and eat my dinner while she washes dishes. The thought of going up to our room without her just doesn't sit well with me. I've just spent hours in the city, fighting for our lives and futures, trying to bring humanity back so we can have a life worth living. Once I get back safely, all I want to do is see Ginny. To be with her and know it will all be worth the fight.

"You almost done?" I ask through a mouthful of processed food.

Ginny's eyes move to the stack of dirty plates, and I follow her gaze. Only a handful of people are still sitting in the cafeteria, which means she'll be able to leave soon. Marge, the head cook, always shoos Ginny away before everyone else. Richard isn't the only one who sees her as the hope for the future.

"A couple minutes." She picks up a pile of plates, smiling as she does it. It makes her nose wrinkle in an adorable way that goes straight to my heart.

My team leader, Shep, comes out of nowhere and stops next to me. He's just as covered in dirt and zombie guts as I am, making him smell more than a little ripe—not that I'm under the delusion that I smell much better. No one seems to notice that kind of thing anymore, though. After months on the road, the stench has become a new kind of normal for us.

Shep shoots Ginny a wink, and her green eyes light up.

"My favorite part of the day!" he says, his voice booming through the cafeteria. "I'm not going to lie, even if it does get my ass kicked by this husband of yours. The whole time I'm out there fighting off the zoms, I think about dragging myself back in here and seeing those beautiful green eyes."

Ginny blushes as she grabs a sack dinner for him, giving her skin the pink glow I love so much. "You're just excited about the food."

"This?" Shep takes the bag from her hand and opens it, peering inside. He shakes his head. "You think this is what brings me back here? Nope. Sorry to burst your bubble, but I only eat this shit because I know I need to keep my strength up."

Shep chuckles when Ginny's cheeks get redder. This time, though, it's not as attractive. She squirms, and her discomfort is so heavy it hits me from the other side of the counter. I know Shep is harmless and he's only teasing, but the extra attention gets to Ginny. She wants to be inconspicuous, and having him single her out like this puts her on edge.

I step in front of Shep. "You may be my boss, but I doubt I'd get fired for punching you."

"Very true!" Shep chuckles as he turns away. "See you all tomorrow."

I watch him walk away just as Jim steps into the cafeteria, and my eyes lock with his. He doesn't come over to get his dinner, but he doesn't look away either. His blue eyes are glued to me as if he's trying to get a look inside my brain. It makes every hair on my scalp stand up.

"Get this girl out of here," Marge says from behind me.

I spin around to find the older woman standing behind Ginny, her hands on her hips. She scowls as she shoves her half-gray, half-black hair out of her face—she complains about her roots at least six times a day, according to Ginny.

"Standing up for hours at a time." Marge *tsks* as she shakes her head. "We're not so bad off that we need to put one of the few pregnant women here at risk."

Ginny rolls her eyes as she pulls her hairnet off. "I'm fine, Marge."

"No need to push it, that's all I'm saying." The older woman huffs.

We have this exact same conversation every night.

I spoon the last bit of potatoes into my mouth as I head

over to where the dirty plates are collected, anxious to get out of here so Ginny and I can be alone. With the way things are set up here, we don't get much alone time. When we have our own house, it will be different.

My back is still turned when I hear another woman say, "Girl, that man is pure sex. Where'd you find him?"

"You wouldn't believe me if I told you," Ginny says with a laugh.

"Well, he's yummy. I'm jealous."

"That's why I'm with him. I'm using him for his body." Ginny laughs again, but the edge in her voice is unmistakable. It makes my smile disappear.

Of course we can never tell anyone how we actually met, not even our baby. People wouldn't understand, but it's also something Ginny is trying to move past. She'd never want anyone to associate her with the horror that went on in the Monte Carlo.

I dump my plate off, careful not to make too much clatter. The sudden urge to throw the thing across the room is so overwhelming I have a tough time controlling myself.

By the time I turn back to face the others, Marge is pushing Ginny out from behind the counter. "She needs to rest her feet!" the older woman barks.

"The further along I get, the more she's going to nag me about keeping myself healthy," Ginny says when she comes out from behind the counter to meet me. "Before long, she's going to be insisting I stay in bed all day."

"She's just trying to be nice."

"No, it isn't that. It's like I have some kind of a revered status or something, and it's getting to me."

She rubs her hand across her belly absentmindedly. The little bump is so small that it isn't visible through her baggy clothes, but everyone knows about it by this point. There are a few other expecting women here, but Ginny and one other woman are the only two who got pregnant *after* the virus hit. She's important, even if she doesn't want to admit it. If our baby survives, it will mean the human race has a

23

chance of starting over. That the virus has either worn off or the babies born from here on out may be immune to the disease. It will mean life can start again.

I sling my arm over her shoulder and lead her toward the door, the whole time thinking about that little golden ring in my pocket. "If it bugs you that much, we'll get you a new job."

"It won't change the way people treat me," she says, shaking her head.

She has a point.

We pass Jim, but he doesn't even glance our way. Ginny gives him a little wave even though they haven't officially met. He doesn't return it.

"What's wrong with him?" she asks.

I shake my head, and without even thinking about it, my gaze moves to her left hand. Hopefully she'll be happy about the gesture I risked Jim's life for.

"Nothing," I say, once again focusing on her eyes. "Just a close call."

She snorts. "Tell him to get used to it. Life is a close call now."

"No shit," I mutter.

I lead her through the empty lobby and to the stairs, taking them slowly so I can buy myself a little time. It never entered my mind that I wouldn't give her the ring tonight, but the closer we get to our room, the more my nerves start to get the better of me. What if she laughs? Tells me it's stupid and I shouldn't have wasted my time? What if she doesn't want to actually be my wife? We've been telling everyone we're married, but this is so much bigger. It's a symbol that we're bound to each other, and I'm afraid it's going to scare the shit out of Ginny. She's been through so much and been so strong, but I'm constantly waiting for the one thing that will push her over the edge.

By the time we reach our room, I've started to sweat. Neither one of us has said a word since leaving the cafeteria, and she's watching me out of the corner of her eye. Almost like she's trying to figure out what has me so jumpy—because I am. I'm jumpy as hell. Knowing she's watching me only makes me squirm more, though.

My arm falls away when I push the door to our room open. Ginny steps inside, but I can barely meet her gaze. My heart has started pounding like I'm about to face a horde of the undead, and it's unnerving. I shouldn't be this nervous. I know Ginny loves me—even if I can't figure out why.

Ginny turns to face me the second the door is shut. "What's going on with you?"

I shove my hands in my pockets, fingering the ring while I take a few cleansing breaths. "I don't know what you mean."

Her eyebrow shoots up, and I almost laugh. I'm more nervous than I was the first time I asked a girl out. But I want to do this. I want Ginny to know I'm going to be here for her no matter what. Need her to understand how serious I am. To give her something more than just words to cling to.

I take her hand and I lead her to the bed, and her eyes get more narrowed as the seconds tick by. We sit, me staying close to the edge to avoid getting the blankets filthy. I tap my toes on the floor to the beat of my pounding heart, which is so fast we could have a dance party in here if we wanted to.

I force my feet against the floor and take a deep breath, trying once again to calm down. "I have something for you."

"Okay..." she says slowly, letting the word drag on for so long it seems to fill all the empty space in the room.

Ginny doesn't take her eyes off mine, so she doesn't notice when I slip a shaky hand back into my pocket. Or when I pull out the ring.

"We've been through a lot. I know you don't blame me for what happened, but there will always be a part of me that feels like I need to work to make it right." She opens her mouth to say something, but I hold my hand up to stop her. "Just hear me out. Okay?"

"Okay," she says again. This time the end of the word is clipped short, almost like someone has taken a pair of scissors and cut it in half.

"I understand now that I don't need to make the past right, which is good, because I never could. But I do need to make our future right. To stand with you. To take care of you and be a father to *our* baby." She flinches slightly, but she doesn't argue. "And those are all things I want to do. I want to be with you, but even more than that, I want everyone to know that I plan to be here for you. Including you. I don't want you to ever doubt that."

"I don't." She moves her hand to my knee despite the filth covering my leather pants. "Jon, you are the most loyal person I've ever met. I would never doubt your commitment."

"Good." I slip down until I'm kneeling in front of her. On one knee.

Ginny's eyes get huge, growing even wider when I hold the ring up. She blinks three times, and her green eyes shimmer, but the happiness in them is so clear it feels like a third person in the room. Instantly, all the fear and nervousness inside me slips away until all that's left is Ginny and me and our love.

I take her hand in mine. "I know we already tell people we're married, but I never asked you. Not officially. And I want to do that. I want to say the words out loud, to have you say them out loud. I want us to acknowledge that we are together, and I want you to have a symbol that everyone can recognize."

Her bottom lip quivers as she nods slowly, almost like she's unable to get any words out.

I take a deep breath. "Ginny Lewis, will you be my wife?"

"Yes." The word is shaky and small as it leaves her mouth, but still firm and sure and perfect.

She slides off the bed until she's on her knees in front of me, and my chest tightens when a tear rolls down her cheek. Then her hand is in mine and I'm sliding the ring onto her delicate finger. It's a perfect fit—thank God—and looks absolutely flawless. Just a slim, golden band that probably wouldn't have cost much before all this started but is now worth more than all the riches I could have accumulated in my past life.

"I love you," I say, taking her face between my hands.

"I love you."

I press my lips against hers. The kiss is brief and soft and as gentle as the wings of a butterfly. Then I pull away and close my eyes, resting my forehead against Ginny's while she quietly sobs. The sound stings even though I know they are happy tears.

I'M ON MY BED READING WHEN THERE'S A LIGHT knock on the door. Ginny is curled up on the other side of the room, the rhythmic tone of her breathing making my own eyes heavy. She hasn't been out long, though, and I wanted to make sure she was settled in before I went to bed myself.

When I get to my feet, the bed creaks, but Ginny doesn't move. Good. That means she's out. I move faster, hurrying to the door before whoever's out there has a chance to knock again and wake her. Right now she should be able to get in a few hours of deep sleep before the nightmares start, and I know she needs it. It's been tough for her to get any real rest.

I jerk the door open and step back when I find Jim standing in the hall.

"What's going on, man?" I ask, shoving my hand through my hair. Did he come to yell at me again? I hope not, because I'm seriously not in the mood.

Jim looks past me into the room, then holds up a bottle of tequila. "Your girl out?"

I glance back to where Ginny sleeps before nodding. "Yeah. Was going to turn in myself in a minute here."

"Not yet." He shakes his head. "Get your shoes. You and I are going to have a drink."

I blink a few times before turning away. If it wasn't for the fact that Jim usually doesn't want to have a damn thing to do with me, I'd argue. I can barely get more than two serious words out of the guy on a normal day, so the fact that he wants to have a drink—which means a talk—has me interested.

I keep an eye on Ginny as I pull my shoes on, but once again, she doesn't move. There's a part of me that feels bad about leaving her—What if she has a nightmare while I'm gone?—but I know if she were awake, she'd tell me to go. Which means I have nothing to feel guilty about. Too bad that knowledge doesn't stop the guilt from building in my stomach.

I step out of the room and find Jim leaning against the wall, his arms crossed and the bottle of tequila held in one hand. He doesn't say a word, and the second I have the door shut, he pushes himself off the wall and starts walking.

"What's going on?" I ask, jogging to catch up.

"I think it's about time we had a little chat. Got to understand each other a little better."

"I thought you didn't want to get to know anything about me."

He shoves some blond hair out of his face as he glances my way. "Call it an education."

I snort when the urge to call him a conceited ass hits me head-on. There's nothing I hate more than someone assuming they know more than I do. It could be true, but Jim has no way of knowing that. He's never taken the time to get to know me.

We jog down the stairs together, and I follow my partner across the lobby, where he leads me out into the courtyard. It's cold as hell, and the blanket of snow and ice coating the ground contrasts with the dark night in a way I still haven't gotten used to. Growing up in Nevada, I was never around snow before we came here. Can't say I'm a fan, either.

The wind howls, and a shiver forces its way through my body, causing me to cross my arms. It makes me feel like a little kid. Or maybe that's Jim. Something about him makes me feel like I haven't really lived a day in my life.

Jim lets out a chuckle as he unscrews the lid on the tequila bottle. "Take a drink. Get warm," he says, holding it out.

I don't argue even though I don't typically drink straight tequila.

The gulp I take is bigger than I intended, and it burns as it slides down my throat. I cough and hold the bottle out, making Jim chuckle even more. He throws some back, taking a big swig that barely makes him cringe.

"You're my second partner since I got here," he says, leaning against the frozen wall behind him.

"That right?" I accept the bottle when he holds it out to me again, taking a much smaller sip this time. It still burns, but it isn't as bad. Plus, I can actually feel the liquid warming my body as it makes its way through my veins.

"Yup."

"You going to let me in on what happened to the first guy?"

"He got distracted," Jim says. "We were clearing and the zoms moved in faster than we thought they would. Swarmed us. We should have been fine. Would have been if he'd stuck to the plan, but this guy had a wife back here and seeing the bastards all around us freaked him out. He ran instead of fighting, and then all hell broke loose. The archers stepped in to help, but by the time I had that asshole dragged back behind the barrier, he'd been bitten. Not just once, either."

"Okay," I say, "I get it. Leave your family on campus."

"It's not just that." Jim rips the bottle out of my hand and takes a long sip, his eyes on me the whole time. He smacks his lips when he's done but doesn't hold the bottle out to me again. "I get that making new connections will keep most people moving ahead, but the past is what keeps my eye on the prize. I screwed up once, and I'm not doing that again."

He pauses like he's waiting for me to ask questions, but I don't. He obviously has something on his mind, so he's going to tell me whether I ask or not.

Jim nods again, almost like he approves of me not saying a word. For some reason, it makes me feel like we're more on the same level.

"When all this shit went down," he says after a few seconds, "I was sitting in prison."

My mouth drops open, but Jim just shrugs like it's no big deal. I knew he had demons he was running from, but I thought it had more to do with what had happened after the outbreak, not before.

"Prison?" I say, my mind running through all the things he could have done as I try to figure out how much of a risk he is to me now. The world has changed, but there are some things from the past that will always matter.

"I'm not going to go into what I did," he says, then takes another swig from the bottle. "Let's just say that I had no real future. Poor life choices. That's all you really need to know. This virus gave me a second chance, and I'm not throwing it away. I'm also not going to risk my life by working with someone who plans on throwing his away. So what I'm saying is, if you can't leave your girl and baby on campus when we go out to clear, then you need to let me know. Because what I have right now, it means something to me."

I swallow, still reeling from what Jim just said. "This means something to me, too. More than you'll ever know. I can focus. What happened today, it won't happen again."

"Then we're going to be okay." Jim nods, studying me for a second before saying, "I get it. Just so you know."

"Get what?" I ask, my brain too focused on Jim and prison and all the things he could have done to be able to figure out exactly what he's referring to.

"The ring. I saw your girl today, and I can tell something's haunting her. Something big." I shake my head, ready to tell him it's none of his damn business, but he holds his hand up. "Don't worry, I'm not going to ask what happened. I just wanted to let you know that I understand. I may seem like a hard ass, but that's only because I plan on surviving this whole thing. I also know that there are bound to be places in this country where it's got to feel like hell is raining down on us. I know what men are capable of, probably better than anyone around here, and I know that with no laws, a lot of people are going to resort to things the average person can't even comprehend."

He takes another swig from the bottle, his eyes still on me. Dozens of images flash through my mind. All the things I saw at the Monte Carlo that I let slide because I was too focused on trying to save Megan. The look of defeat on Hadley's face—I refuse to think of the woman in the Monte Carlo as Ginny—when we finally got out of there. Knowing what she'd been through and that it was all my fault. I'll never be able to escape those things.

I swallow when my mouth goes dry, and suddenly the cold doesn't matter so much. I can feel the heat from the hell Jim is referring to raining down on me, and it's so hot it makes me break out into a sweat.

"You have no idea what's out there."

"Probably right." Jim shoves himself off the wall, sticking the lid back on the tequila bottle in the process. "See you tomorrow."

He's taken two steps, but I can't let him go without asking.

"What'd you do?"

He doesn't turn. "Nothing you need to worry about."

"Does Corinne know?"

"She knows what she needs to know: that I'm determined to make this life work. As far as I'm concerned, everything else is in the past."

Jim doesn't look back as he heads across the courtyard. He shoves the door open and steps inside, leaving me alone in the darkness. The wind howls, and I'm once again shivering, only I don't move.

He's my partner, and he could be a violent criminal. Murderer or rapist or one of a hundred of other crimes. Who knows what he did to land himself in prison. The real question is: does it matter? He's here even though he knows there are other places for him, which says something about his dedication to making this life work. There are tons of groups out there that embrace the baser desires of mankind, but Jim *chose* to be here. Where we have rules and goals and are looking toward the future. That means he's a changed man. Right?

Only time will tell, but I'm inclined to think so. I trust Jim with my life every single day, and he hasn't let me down yet.

CHAPTER THREE

GINNY

It's only been a few weeks, but with everything that's happened, it feels like years since we saw Vivian and the others. I haven't totally given up hope that we'll see them again, but I can tell Jon's optimism is wearing thin. He's nice enough to play along when I talk about finding them, which I appreciate, but his lack of enthusiasm makes it tough for me to cling to my own hope. Especially as more and more snow falls on the state. What if they haven't found a safe place or more food? Will they be able to make it through winter without freezing or starving?

And there still remains the big question that is never very far from the front my mind: who died at the hot springs before Jon and I got there? Which one of our friends was buried under those three piles of stones we saw?

"Ginny?" Marge says, drawing my attention to the present. "You okay?"

In front of me, the processed mashed potatoes have started to crust over. I'm supposed to be putting them in a container so we can save them for tomorrow. We can't waste anything at this point, even mashed potatoes that are a few hours past their prime.

"I'm fine," I say, pulling the tray out of the warming unit. "Just lost in my own thoughts."

"Nothing wrong with that," the older woman says. "Sometimes I get to thinking about everything that's happened, and the next thing I know I realize I've been sitting in my room for an hour or more just staring at the wall like a crazy person. Although, I think at this point we've all become a little crazy."

She shakes her head, and the little bit of hair poking through her hairnet swishes back and forth. With as long as her roots have gotten, she's starting to remind me of a skunk. I'd never tell her that, of course. She's self-conscious enough about how her hair looks. Even if I think it's a silly thing to worry about in the middle of all this, I can't help wondering if I'd be feeling the same way if the Monte Carlo had never happened. As it is, all the things that used to mean so much to me now seem ridiculous.

"When do you go see the doctor next?" Marge asks as she scrubs a large pot.

"Not until next month sometime." I scrape a spoonful of potatoes out of the tray and plop them into a metal container. "I saw him when we first got here two weeks ago, so there's no reason to go again any time soon."

"Hogwash," Marge snaps. "There's plenty reason. He should be checking in with you every week, just to make sure everything is okay."

"I have other things to do, Marge. I can't run off to the doctor every week. Especially when he has other patients."

Even though Marge means well, I can't stop a suffocating feeling from sweeping over me. She's always like this: intrusive and bossy. The worse thing about it is that she isn't alone. Everyone seems to think they should have a say in my

34

life and how hard I work and how often I go to the doctor. I'm not even showing, but everywhere I go people stop to stare at me. It's like I have the word *pregnant* tattooed on my forehead, and I hate it.

"Fine. I'll go," I say even though I have no intention of doing it.

Marge nods, obviously satisfied that she's talked some sense into me, and I scoop faster. It's time for me to get out of here.

I lug the empty potato tray over to Marge, and as she takes it, she says, "Head on out of here now. Get a glass of water and put your feet up and rest."

"Thanks. I'll see you tomorrow." For once, I don't argue when she shoos me away.

Marge shoots me a smile as I hurry out, ripping my hairnet off and charging up the stairs toward the lobby. Thank God our room and the cafeteria are in the same building. With all the snow falling from the sky, I'm not the least bit interested in going outside. It's too cold and too depressing when I remember that my friends might be stuck in this.

I'm already halfway across the lobby when Gretchen walks through the front door. She shivers as she shakes snow from her red hair, her cheeks pink from the cold. I hardly ever see her anymore, and I know why: Mark. Even though I know there's nothing I can do about it and she's capable of making her own decisions, I still feel like I should check in on them every now and then. Jon and I are the ones who found her, after all. We brought her here and she doesn't have parents anymore, so there's a part of me that feels responsible for her. She doesn't like it, but at least she took the condoms I offered her. Thank God.

"Hey!" I call, waving toward the girl.

Gretchen looks up and when her eyes meet mine, I freeze mid-wave. She hurries over, looking around like she's ready to tell me a secret she doesn't want anyone else to hear, and I can't help noticing how her blue eyes shimmer under the lobby lights.

35

When she stops in front of me, she says, "I was coming to see you."

"What's wrong?" Why can't I shake the feeling she's about to drop a bomb on me?

"A baby was born this morning," she says, eyes focused on the floor. "Mark just told me."

I suck in a deep breath while I wait for Gretchen to tell me the outcome even though I know it's not going to be good. It isn't the first baby born in Hope Springs, and even though the other one was before we arrived, I know how it ended. The virus took the poor thing. Fast.

"It died," she whispers, almost like she's afraid that if she says the words too loud it will somehow affect whether or not my baby will live.

The news hits me, but not as hard as I thought it would. I find myself twisting the gold ring around on my finger as I try to wrap my brain around it all. How does it make me feel? When I first found out I was pregnant I probably would have been relieved. It wasn't exactly welcome news. After what happened at the Monte Carlo, I knew I could never really be sure who the father of this baby is. But things are different now. Aren't they? I have Jon, and he loves me. Even gave me a ring to prove it. I look down at my left hand, still twisting the gold band. It's a promise. Jon is going to be with me through all of this, and he's excited. He wants a family and a life, and he wants to keep me safe. Knowing all that, I've not only gotten used to the idea of being a mom, but I've actually started to look forward to it a little. To what the future may bring.

Still, I'm not exactly sure what to do with the information Gretchen just gave me. It stings, but not quite as much as it should.

"The dad wasn't immune," Gretchen says, grabbing my arm and forcing me to finally stop twisting the ring. "It's not the same as you and Jon."

I nod slowly, feeling like that's all I can do. Like I'm one of those little toy birds whose head you could nudge and it would go up and down, pantomiming drinking from a bowl of water. Gretchen is trying to cheer me up, but I'm not really sure I need it, and that makes me feel worse than anything else.

"I know," I manage to get out, but the truth is, I don't know and neither does Gretchen. No one knows for sure.

Still, God couldn't be that cruel. Could He? Would He get me to the point where I've started to heal and hope and love again, only to rip it all away at the very last second? That seems like an impossibly mean trick to play on the world.

"Forget that," Gretchen says, trying to pull me toward the stairs. "Mark smuggled me a Hershey's bar. Come up to my room and we can split it."

I shake my head and *try* to look apologetic. It doesn't really work. I squirm when Gretchen won't stop staring at me, and part of me feels like she's judging me. Like she knows I'm not as upset as she expected me to be. She must think I'm heartless. Sometimes I feel heartless, but there are other times when I feel so much that I wish someone would swoop in and rip my heart out. Make it so nothing can hurt me anymore.

"No, thanks," I say, suddenly desperate to be alone.

No. Not alone. Just with someone else. Someone who can really understand how I feel and what I went through back in the Monte Carlo. Someone who will just be there to listen to me without trying to fix things.

Like Vivian.

Gretchen narrows her eyes on my face again, and I shuffle my feet. "You sure?"

"Yeah," I say, taking a step back, away from her sharp gaze and toward the door. "I need to find Richard. He and Donovan were supposed to be heading to Duncan to make another supply run and I want to find out if they came across anyone out there. Saw any signs of other people."

"Okay. See you later." Gretchen heads off, probably glad she doesn't have to share her chocolate bar. Who knows when she'll get another one?

"Bye," I murmur as I head toward the front door.

Even though I had just been feeling grateful that I *didn't* have to go outside, I find myself heading out into the cold November day. It's snowing, again, and outside the drifts have really started piling up. Soon the roads will be dangerous and most of the search crews will pack it in for the winter, focusing on cleaning the city out instead. According to Jon, the zombies are getting slower every day. Not that I would know. No one would even consider letting me near a zombie these days. All I do day after day is plop spoonfuls of food onto plates while praying the zombies will freeze the way we think they will. If that happens, we'll be able to get the city clear and move into a house.

I keep my face down and out of the snow as I cross the parking lot, heading toward the old Mathematics building. It's where they're setting up the supplies, sorting what they have by room. Clothes in one, canned food in another, boxed food in a third. There's also a room for bottled water and another for luxury food items, like the candy bar Mark gave Gretchen. They have everything catalogued and organized, and they've even turned a couple of the classrooms into greenhouses so we can try to get a head start on growing our own food. It's amazing what they've managed to gather.

I'm still a good distance away when I catch sight of the men unloading a truck. I start jogging, drawing attention my way before I've even made it halfway across the parking lot.

"You're gonna slip and fall!" Richard shouts. "Slow down. There's no fire here."

I don't listen, but mainly because I know that even if I do slip, it's not going to affect the life growing inside me. At this point, the thing is probably the size of a lemon.

Richard stops unloading the truck and crosses the snow-covered parking lot to meet me. "I'm serious. It's too slippery out here."

"I'm fine," I say, panting. "I just wanted to see how you did out there today."

"Pretty good," Richard replies, pulling his stocking cap off. His gray hair is sticking up everywhere, but I'm used to it by now. The man acts like brushes went extinct. "We finished clearing out the Sam's Club, and just in time, too. Looks like the weather is going to get real bad, real soon."

"Isn't it bad enough?" I say, mocking Jon even though he isn't here to defend himself. I grew up in Ohio, so I know a little bit about winter. Jon is clueless, though. It's actually kind of cute to hear him bitch about it.

Richard laughs. "Right. That husband of yours is in for a surprise."

"So everyone keeps telling him." I laugh too, which is still forced at times, but is starting to feel more real and relaxed. "You see any sign of other survivors out there?"

Richard puckers his lips as he shakes his head. "Not really. Lot of footprints in the snow, but that could be from the zoms. It's hard to say. The shelves were definitely picked over, but again, that could have been from when things first got bad. It's a tough call."

"Shit," I mutter.

Richard gives me an apologetic smile as he pats me on the arm. "Hang in there, kid. I'm sure your friends are okay, and who knows what will happen. Maybe come spring they'll show up at our gate shaken but having survived the long, cold winter."

"Anything can happen," I say, but I'm not sure if it's comforting or not. It's true, which we all know by this point. A zombie apocalypse was once a far-fetched scenario for late-night cable TV shows. Now it's part of everyday life.

"Very true," Richard says, frowning.

I look over his shoulder, back to where they're unloading the trucks, and catch sight of Dax and Mark and a bunch of other men I don't even know. We've grown in numbers even since Jon and I arrived. The last I heard, we had over a hundred and seventy people crammed into the dorms. The sooner we get the streets cleared and everyone into homes, the better.

"You need help unloading?" I ask.

"Not from you," Richard says, shaking his head. "Go on back to your room and put your feet up."

Why does everyone keep telling me to put my feet up?

I think about going back and a shiver wracks my body, only I'm not totally sure it's from the cold. Suddenly, the idea of going to my room without Jon is terrifying. Sometimes when he isn't with me, I feel like a boat being tossed on the waves. Jon is my anchor. What keeps me grounded and focused on the future and the hope he's trying to build our new life on.

I shake my head and head past Richard to the truck. "No. I want to help."

He throws out some weak excuse that I, of course, ignore. Then he's heading after me, cursing under his breath. He doesn't try to stop me again, which I'm grateful for. I want to help. I don't want to be trapped in my room like I'm useless, because I'm not.

I grab a huge box that weighs a lot less than it should for its size, and Richard huffs like he's watching me make the biggest mistake of my life. I peek inside the box as I head toward the building. Toilet paper. Why Richard would try to stop me from carrying a box of toilet paper is beyond me. A child could lift this.

Once inside, I let out a deep sigh of contentment. The heat is running, and the hum of warm air as it whooshes from the vents is a comforting sound. Now that the electricity is back, I'm surprised at the little things I find comforting. The ability to flip a switch and light every corner of the room or read without squinting. The chance to shower just because I feel like it or to pop a cup of coffee into the microwave when I didn't drink it fast enough. All things I never thought twice about before the virus hit but I now savor. Outside our fences the world may still be silent and lost, but inside the dorm, the old world seems to have been restored just a little bit.

"Where does this go?" I ask, grunting despite the lightness of the box.

It's big and bulky and difficult to get my arms around,

40

but I refuse to let anyone tell me I can't help. Not with something so small and easy.

"Down the hall. We have all the bathroom necessities in the last room," Richard says from my side, his face red as his fingers dig into the cardboard box in his hands. I glance at the label and the insignificance of my small contribution hits me: Campbell's. Probably cans of tomato soup or something equally heavy.

He hurries off, anxious to put the heavy box down, and I follow at a much slower pace. It's only the second time I've been in the building, and the first time it wasn't nearly as full as it now. Especially with all the people currently working to unload their recent spoils from Sam's Club.

I pass rooms crammed full of boxed and bagged food and canned goods, and another room lined with dozens of cardboard boxes. There's food in some, laundry detergent and other household cleaners in another. One room is filled with alcohol, bottles of clear and amber liquid neatly lined along one wall and bottles of wine along another. Nothing seems to have been forgotten or left out. Every tiny little need we might have has been anticipated and prepared for. Eventually we'll be able to fend for ourselves, but in the meantime, the people of Hope Springs have worked hard to make sure we're comfortable.

I find the right room and drop my box of toilet paper on top of another one. Then I scan the area, my gaze moving over all the supplies we've gathered. There's every brand of toilet paper and tissues imaginable—even the cheap stuff that would have made me cringe before all this started. On the other side of the room, there's soap and shampoo and lotions, as well as razors and shaving cream. Even makeup. Pretty much anything a person might need to keep clean. Most of it seems like a silly luxury now. Soap is good, but I don't see the point of conditioner or face cream anymore. Or makeup. After everything we've been through, I don't know why anyone would care what other people think about their looks. Who are we still trying to impress and why? All the stuff

41

that was once so important now seems as insignificant as a speck of dust floating in the wind. We have real worries now.

"Ginny?" I turn at the sound of Corinne's smooth, British voice and find her standing behind me, her head tilted like I'm a puzzle she's trying to figure out.

Maybe I am.

"Hi, Corinne." I take a step closer, the hair on my scalp prickling under her intense gaze. "I was just trying to lend a hand. I can't help feeling a little useless these days. No one seems to want me to lift a finger."

She nods slowly, her smile turning slightly stiff. It's hard to read her expression, especially with her dark eyes so narrowed. An open door to my right casts a shadow across the hall and over the other woman, making her skin a couple shades darker than it really is. More of a dark chocolate than a milk chocolate. My stomach growls, and I almost laugh. Maybe I should have taken Gretchen up on that Hershey bar after all.

"You don't like your job?" Corinne asks, stepping out of the shadow. In the light, her eyes look less harsh. Like she's trying to think of a way to help me, not judging me the way everyone else seems to be lately.

"It's fine, but everyone stares and they seem to think it's their job to tell me to take it easy."

"I'm sure it's a heavy burden to shoulder, but you are a symbol of hope to us."

Irritation prickles through me even though her words aren't accusatory or commanding.

"I know," I say, shifting uncomfortably. "It's just a lot to take once a day, let alone a hundred times a day."

Her eyebrows shoot up, and she nods. "I hadn't thought of it that way. You're right." She hesitates, but only for a second before turning and heading down the hall, away from the room I just left. "I may have the perfect job for you."

Even though I don't know why, I move after her, scurrying to keep up. I don't ask what kind of job she has for me or why I'd be perfect for it, because as far as I'm concerned, any job will be more important than the one I have. The simplicity of the cafeteria was nice at first, but now I just feel useless. Before we came here, before I found out I was pregnant, I went out on runs. I helped find food for our group and killed zombies. Contributed. Now I stand behind a counter. I want to make a real difference. One that doesn't come from my uterus.

Corinne doesn't slow. She's taller than I am by a lot, and her strides seem to be twice as long as mine. I have to hurry to keep up, but there's something about it I like. Anyone else would walk slowly, like the fact that I'm pregnant makes me an invalid they have to cater to.

She doesn't stop until she reaches the end of the hall, and her tall frame is so imposing that it blocks almost the entire door, making it impossible for me to see where we are at first. But when she pushes it open and I get a good look at the room, my shoulders drop. It's an office. A cushy office that, although on the small side, must have been reserved for someone important. The dean or a tenured professor who had published enough papers to give his name and status at the college some weight. Whoever used to reside in this office, I can't see how it would have any kind of importance to us.

Corinne flips on the light—a gesture that still hasn't lost its marvel for me—and walks a little farther in, giving me a better view of the space. The desk is big and impressive, and the leather chair behind it was probably pretty expensive. My eyes scan the diplomas and awards hanging on the walls, and an image of the person who used to work here forms in my head. Brady Sanford, professor of literature. There are a couple pictures of a blonde woman hanging on the wall and another on the desk, which tells me that whoever this man was, he had a soft spot for his wife. It's probably what made the idea of working at a larger university unappealing. His diplomas tell me he was smart and determined to succeed, and his office says he was organized almost to a fault. He was probably a student favorite who sometimes would join the upperclassmen for a drink on Friday evenings. Would

43

pick one special person to mentor every year, feeling a sense of accomplishment when they graduated with honors, a handful of job offers backing up their hard work. Of course, I have no idea if any of that is true, but it makes me like the man who used to sit at this desk.

"We found a radio," Corinne says, breaking through my thoughts.

I tear my eyes away from the desk to find her staring at me expectantly, but I don't know why. I feel like I'm missing something. What good is a radio? Even if anyone is still on the air, which they're not, music isn't going to help us survive.

"A radio?" I say, blinking. I can't help feeling a little slow.

"Yes. A ham radio to be exact. I don't know a lot about it myself, but we have a couple men on it. They're going to bring it here, and we're going to try to make contact."

"Make contact with who?"

All I can picture are little green men in outer space. It seems as likely of a scenario as being able to get ahold of actual *people*, because there aren't any. There can't be. We went from the Mojave Desert to Colorado, and the most we found—other than the Monte Carlo—were a handful of people here and there. Places like this just don't exist. They're a mirage or wishful thinking. Even now, weeks later, I'm not sure this place is real. A part of me expects to wake up at any second, groggy but sure of the fact that I can't trust anyone outside my original group.

"Other groups," Corinne says, "like ours."

"What makes you think there are other groups out there?"

"The simple fact that we're here should be enough to give someone hope." She narrows her eyes again, and I step back. It feels too much like she's trying to look through me when she does that.

"I'm not sure about that," I say, my gaze moving to the big desk so I'll have somewhere—anywhere—to look other than Corinne. "But I don't see the harm in trying." I look back, which takes more effort than it should, and find her still watching me. "What does it have to do with me?"

"You can man it. Or take a shift, anyway. We want to have someone here all day. Every day. Searching, always ready. It's the perfect job for you. It will keep you off your feet like everyone around here seems to want, and it will give you something important to do. Which is what you want. Right? You did want to go clear the streets."

She raises her eyebrows as she waits for me to respond, but it takes me a couple seconds. I never told her I volunteered to clear. After Richard's reaction, it seemed pointless. No one was going to let *me* — the hope for the future — risk her life.

"Who told you?"

"Richard. He laughed, but I knew right then you were more than you tried to make yourself out to be. When you came in with the others, you were humble about your skills, which didn't make much sense. You made it out there somehow, so you must be strong. Then you volunteered to be on the front lines..." She shrugs "I've been watching you since then."

My shoulders stiffen, and I wait for her to call me out. To reveal that she knows who I really am. Her eyes move across my face and the corner of her mouth turns up, but she doesn't say another word.

"How did you get here?" I ask, unable to stop myself. She's British, her accent thick, and ever since we got here, I've been wondering if she lived in the States before all this. Or if she got stuck here when everything went crazy.

"I was on holiday," she says, the expression on her face not changing. "My boyfriend and I came to the States to ski and got stuck when the virus hit. He died, but I didn't. As things changed and the world turned to rubbish, it hit me that I'd never go home again. Never know what happened to my family."

Her cool exterior cracks just a little, and she looks down. I want to ask if she had kids, but I can't seem to get the words out. Maybe it's better not knowing everyone else's tragedy.

"I'd like to help," I say instead. "I'm not sure if anyone is out there, but I think you're right. We should try to find out. See what the rest of the country is up to."

Corinne nods, and when she finally looks up, the smooth lines of her face are back where they belong. Composed and even and utterly in control. Just like her.

"Smashing," she says, but there's no enthusiasm in her voice. "I hope to have the radio here by tomorrow afternoon and you can start the next day. Day shift?" I nod in agreement. "I'll let Marge know you'll be moving to a less stressful job."

I almost laugh. Anyone who thinks that searching a broken world for survivors is less stressful than serving food is out of their mind, but the people here will probably see it that way. I'll be off my feet and nestled into a comfy chair. It will make everyone happy.

DECEMBER

CHAPTER FOUR

VIVIAN

It's cold as balls, and I'm starting to feel like the snow is never going to end. I have no idea if this is normal weather for Colorado, but I'm already tired of it. The drifts are up to my knees in a lot of places, and it doesn't show any sign of letting up. It's only December, though. Meaning we have the whole winter ahead of us.

"I'm sick of this," I mutter, kicking at the snowdrift in front of me.

Axl nods, but he isn't looking my way. It's too dark to really tell what he's focused on, but since we're walking the perimeter, I'd guess it's nothing and everything at once. Even though we haven't seen anyone or *anything* for close to two weeks, Axl is still jumpy. Part of it is the unknown, but the other part is that he doesn't want me out here. He wishes I would just stay inside where it's warm and safe. He'd rather have Angus at his side.

Too bad for him, we don't always get what we want.

"It's been quiet," I say instead of stating the obvious: he's brooding again.

"Can't last forever."

Axl shakes his head, still not looking my way, and I resist the urge to sigh. Maybe it's his time of the month.

Footsteps crunch against the snow behind us, and my spine stiffens.

"You hear that?" Axl whispers.

I turn my head and squint toward the trees at our backs as if that will help me see through the darkness. It doesn't, of course.

"Yeah," I whisper.

More footsteps head our way, and Axl raises his gun. He steps in front of me while simultaneously moving in the direction of the sound. The wind blows and more snow falls. Some from the clouds, but most from the trees above us. The flakes hit me in the face, but my heart is suddenly pounding too hard to notice the cold. Heat moves through me as my adrenaline kicks up a couple notches. The snow may have slowed the zombies down, but that doesn't mean it's stopped the people out there.

A branch breaks to our left, and Axl spins toward the sound, but just like before it's too dark to see anything. I hold my breath and grip my gun tighter, keeping it aimed at the ground while I listen. Waiting. Trying to figure out what's out there and where it's coming from.

Footsteps crunch again, this time so close I can tell for sure they're inside the fence. The sound is too big to be an animal, not that there have been many signs of wildlife in recent weeks. Animals seem to be as scarce as humans these days.

One more step has Axl moving forward, his gun up as he goes. He keeps his feet on the ground, shuffling them forward so they don't make a sound. It's a technique he's perfected over the last couple weeks.

"Axl?" a soft voice breaks through the silence, and all at

once the tension eases from my body.

It's Parvarti. I should have guessed. We've been out here for a couple hours now; it makes sense that she'd come to relieve us.

"Shit," Axl mutters, and I can just make him out in the darkness when he lowers his gun. He shakes his head.

Parvarti steps out of nowhere, materializing from the shadows like a ghost. Her small frame seems larger against the white backdrop of the snow, and the layers she's wearing make her look bulkier and less like a child. Not that she reminds me of a child much anymore.

"Sorry," she says even though her tone is so flat it could never pass for being apologetic. "I wasn't trying to sneak up on you. Just wanted to let you know that dinner was ready. I thought you might be hungry."

"You alone?" Axl asks, reaching back for my hand automatically.

Parvarti nods. "Al was almost done eating. He'll take the other side once he gets out here."

"Should stick together." Axl shakes his head because he knows he's talking to deaf ears.

Parvarti doesn't really care about her own safety any more now than she did when Trey first died. She still walks around like she's waiting for the world to fall on her head, and I'm losing patience with it. I had hoped being here would help her recover. That having a safe place would bring her back to us just a little. But it hasn't, and her indifference to life has become both terrifying and annoying. What's the point of going on if she doesn't want to put everything into surviving?

"Go eat while it's warm," she says instead of arguing.

Axl exhales, but it seems like he's run out of energy to argue. Just like Parvarti has. "Watch your back."

He heads through the trees, pulling me with him, and seconds later we step out of the bushes. The houses loom in front of us, barely more than an outline against the dark night. Lights flicker in a few windows, and when we pass the one that holds our animals, the quiet chatter of chickens is just audible over the wind.

Axl pulls me closer when I shiver.

"Guess you're a summer kinda person." He slips his arm around my shoulders, and I burrow into his side, trying to absorb some of his warmth.

"Yes." My teeth chatter when the wind blows harder. "I regretted settling in Kentucky the first winter I was there. I sh-should have gone further s-south."

His arm tightens around me. "Glad you didn't."

Not for the first time, I say a silent prayer of thanks for all the little things—good and bad—that happened in my life and led me to Axl.

"M-me too."

We reach Brady's house and hurry inside, stomping our feet against the layers of plastic he has down. Snow falls off, dropping into the little puddles of long-melted snow. I slip out of my boots, careful to steer clear of the wet spots when I set my sock-clad feet down. We've made it a point to respect Brady's wishes about the carpet, but even I'm beginning to find it a little tedious.

Axl and I head into the kitchen, where we're greeted by the sweet scent of cinnamon. The room is brightly lit, illuminating the large pot of spaghetti sauce perched on the stove. Next to it on the counter sits a dish of what looks like apple crisp. Brady must have finally decided to break open the can of pie filling he found. I've never been a fan of apple pie, but even my stomach jumps at the sweet scent of cooked apples.

Al stands when he sees us, planting a kiss on Lila's cheek before heading across the kitchen. "I'm on my way!"

Axl slaps the kid on the back on his way by. "Keep an eye on Parvarti."

The teen nods before hurrying out, and Brady slips out of his chair. "Let me get you something warm to drink."

"I'll get yours, go sit down," Axl whispers as his hand makes slow circles across my lower back.

52

I head over to join the others without arguing, taking Al's now-empty chair. Across from me, Sophia nods, her arms cradling a sleeping Ava. How the little girl can fit on her mother's lap with that growing belly is beyond me, but somehow they make it work. On the other side of Sophia, Max lets out a yawn that sounds like he's more than ready for bed.

To his right, Anne and Joshua sit as close together as always, but Winston is pulled away from the group some. Just like he's been since his daughter died. On the table in front of him sits a half-empty bottle of whiskey, and I try not to focus on it for too long. I've seen him with a bottle in his hand more often than not lately, and I can't help how uneasy it makes me feel. Especially when I know we could use it for something else. There are a lot of uses for booze these days that don't have a thing to do with chasing away your demons.

Brady and Axl come to the table, each one carrying a steaming cup of cider and a plate loaded down with spaghetti. My stomach growls again, this time louder. No one bats an eye.

"It's a tight fit," Brady says, setting a plate in front of me. "We should look into getting a second table."

We say it every day, but it never happens. It's crowded with all of us around this tiny table, but the ghosts of people long gone make it feel almost empty at times. They're always here. The ones we've lost to death, as well as the ones we've had to leave behind. We haven't forgotten them. Never will.

"We'll bring one over from another house," I say as I swirl my fork through the spaghetti, winding the strings of pasta around the tongs until it reminds me of a spool of thread.

"Yeah," Axl says, nodding.

We lapse into a silence so thick it's almost overpowering. After everything we've been through, I think the hardest part is not knowing what happened to Jon and Hadley. At least for me. I'm sure some of the others would have a different opinion.

The front door opens in the other room, and wind howls through the house. It's cut off only a second later when the door slams shut. I don't look up until Darla has staggered into the room, rubbing her hands in front of her to keep them warm.

"It's colder than a witch's tit in a brass bra!" she says, stopping in front of the apple crisp, practically drooling. "This is about the best thing I've seen in my whole life."

"You're welcome to have some," Brady says, heading over to her. "Take some back with you. I made two pans of it. Thought it would be a nice treat."

Brady digs in one of the island cabinets, pulling out a couple square Tupperware containers.

"Angus will be kissing your tiny ass after this," Darla says, taking the containers when Brady holds them out to her.

"How's he feeling?" I ask. Things with my mom have been better—I'm trying at least—but the tension will probably never be totally gone.

"Coughing his head off, poor baby." She shakes her head, and I roll my eyes. Angus is too old and too much of an asshole to be referred to as a baby. "I'm making him stay in bed just like the doc said, but he's fighting me every step of the way. Says he can't stand laying around when there's stuff to do. He's a stubborn one."

"I'll stop by in a bit and see him," Joshua says. "He should be through the worst of it, though. It takes a while to get over bronchitis."

"It sure is a bitch," Darla says.

She loads food into the containers like she's bringing it back to six people, not two. Not that any of us care. She and Angus are smart enough not to take the few resources we have for granted. If they don't eat it today, they'll eat it tomorrow. It won't go to waste.

When Darla's done, she waves over her shoulder before heading back the way she came. Once she's disappeared, we return to our crippled silence. I shovel another forkful of spaghetti into my mouth, chewing slowly while I look everyone over. It's late, but not that late, so I'm not sure why everyone is so quiet tonight. Still, there's something depressing about the mood tonight. Maybe it's just the winter blues.

Winston takes a swig from his bottle, and I stop mid-chew when his eyes meet mine. He doesn't put the bottle down, and the look he gives me is almost challenging. Like he's waiting for me to tell him to cut it out or give him a lecture. It's long overdue, but I'm not about to get into it with him right here in the middle of the kitchen. Plus, I think it would be better coming from Axl.

When I don't say anything, Winston looks away. He takes another drink before finally putting the bottle down, and at his side, Sophia lets out a deep sigh.

"Going to check on Angus, then turn in." Joshua sucks down the rest of his cider as he gets to his feet, acting like he's in a hurry to get away.

Maybe the tension isn't just about the winter. Maybe it's about Winston.

Anne follows Joshua without saying a word. Sometimes, I'm not sure if she'll ever recover from Jake's death.

Maybe there's something wrong with me for being able to move on so quickly.

Only a couple seconds later, Sophia gets to her feet as well. "We're going to head out too," she says. "Goodnight."

Axl and I whisper our goodbyes, but Brady gets to his feet. "Let me help you."

"Thank you." Sophia smiles gratefully as he walks with her into the other room, a sleepy Max trailing behind them.

Their absence leaves just Lila and Winston at the table with us, neither of whom seem too interested in conversation.

Axl watches them leave, silently sipping his cider while I finish off my spaghetti. The room is so quiet that it has me totally unnerved. I'll be happy when we can get back to the privacy of our room. Between Parvarti, Anne, and Winston, the company has been more than gloomy tonight. I'm not used to it. After what went down with Angus, things have been better. People have been in high spirits. Getting along. Looking toward the future with a sense of hope and promise we hadn't dared let ourselves feel before.

Brady comes back from helping Sophia and immediately starts washing dishes. As if scrubbing the sauce off the plates is more enjoyable than the thought of sitting back down.

Axl must feel the same way, because he gets to his feet. "You ready?"

I nod as I get to my feet, still chewing but more than ready to head out and be alone with Axl. The gloominess is getting to me.

"Yeah," I say after I've swallowed, carrying my plate over to the sink.

When I set it down, Brady smiles. "We're not a very lively bunch tonight. It's times like this when Angus's comic ability comes in handy."

"Sometimes I wonder if he's the glue keeping us together," I say, glancing back toward the table, where Winston is still staring at his bottle. Brady has a point. If Angus were here, he'd liven things up for sure.

"That would be something, wouldn't it?" Brady shakes his head and laughs.

"You need help with any of this?" I ask as Axl refills his cup of cider.

"No. If I'm still working on cleaning up when Parvarti gets back, she'll help me. She may be a silent companion, but she's a good one. Until then, I have Lila to keep me company. I know she won't head to bed until Al is back."

Axl snorts as he comes over, blowing into his steaming cup. "We all know what they'll be up to then."

"I wouldn't talk!" Lila calls. She pushes her chair away from the table and heads over, carrying both hers and Winston's plates. "I notice you two missing from the group just as much as Al and I."

Axl just grins at that, but I bust out laughing. "She has you there."

The legs of Winston's chair scrape against the floor, and

the laughter dies on my lips when he walks by. Not looking at us. Not saying a word. Since Jess was killed at the hot springs, he's gotten so distant that I forget he's around most of the time, and each week he seems to get worse instead of better. Sometimes when we joke around he even seems offended. Like the fact that we can still have fun is a personal insult to his daughter's memory.

"He's starting to worry me," I say as soon as he's disappeared into the other room.

"Poor Winston." Lila shakes her head. "Jess would hate seeing him like this."

Axl drains his cup so fast there's no way he didn't burn his tongue on the hot cider, but he doesn't even wince. "I'm gonna talk to him."

He sets the mug down, nodding to Brady when the other man takes it. Axl pauses just long enough to give me a quick kiss on the cheek before he heads after Winston.

"Sometimes I find myself wondering exactly what we're living for," I say, watching Axl disappear. "Remembering the past is painful, and there's very little hope when I think about the future. It's like we're swimming upstream. Even when I try to focus on the happy memories, I can't."

"'You forget what you want to remember, and you remember what you want to forget,'" Brady whispers.

I turn to face him, blinking, even though I know by this point that he's quoting something he once read or taught. He does that a lot.

"Cormac McCarthy," Brady says, going back to washing dishes. "I started rereading *The Road* — it seemed fitting given our current circumstances — and came upon the quote last night. For what felt like an hour I just stared at it. There's so much truth in that statement, don't you think?"

You forget what you want to remember, and you remember what you want to forget.

I turn the words over in my head a few times before I realize Brady's right. I want to be able to remember the amazing things we've been through. Finding someone to love in the middle of all this, creating a family and making it through situations so dire they seemed like a lost cause. But at night, when I'm lying in bed finding it impossible to sleep, I can only remember the horrible things. Emily's death and Hadley's disappearance, Trey sacrificing his life to save us after we'd been kidnapped and taken to the Monte Carlo. Why can't I think about how much we've overcome instead of everything that's been taken from us?

"I miss my parents," Lila says. "They weren't the best parents, but I can't stop thinking about them."

She leans her hip against the counter at Brady's side, and he focuses on her face as she frowns. The girl doesn't offer to help, but Brady doesn't seem to care. There's something about her that seems so much older than it did a when we first met. Physically, she looks the same—although a little thinner and not nearly as well-dressed. Her dark eyes are still striking against her olive skin, and her black hair shines just as much as it did that day she lay by the pool in the shelter. But she seems to have aged ten years since then.

"There's nothing unusual about missing the idea of something normal," Brady says.

Lila nods and shrugs at the same time. "I guess you're right. It's really the not knowing that's hard, though. And I'll never have the answers to my questions. They were in Europe when communication went down, and it almost feels like they disappeared into thin air. One day they were there, the next they were gone."

She blinks a few times like she's trying to hold in her tears. Without thinking, I reach over and pull her in for a hug. She returns it, sniffing a few times before she steps back and gives me a grateful smile.

"Just remember you're not alone," I say.

Lila lets out a laugh. "No chance of that happening. I can't even get in the shower without Al trying to join me."

Brady smiles, and I roll my eyes.

"Sounds like a man." I let out a deep breath, hoping to blow the tension from my body, then turn and head for the door. "I'm going to stop by and check on Angus before going to bed. I know Axl will want to."

"Goodnight, Vivian," Brady calls.

"Goodnight," I say, waving over my shoulder.

Lila mummers her goodbyes, and even though she's smiling, I can tell she's still lost in the past. Not that I can blame her. It's an easy place to get lost in.

I step out of the kitchen in time to hear Winston say, "There's nothing to talk about. I'm dealing with things in my own way and I'd appreciate it if people would stay out of my business."

"Everybody's worried," Axl replies.

I freeze, trying to give them some privacy. Hopefully Axl can reach Winston. They've had a good relationship since this whole thing started, working together to make decisions that saved a lot of lives. But lately Winston won't even join in on that, leaving more and more of the choices to the rest of us. Not even sharing his opinion. It's weird and slightly terrifying.

"Everyone just needs to worry about themselves," Winston says.

He steps into view, glancing my way as he shoves his feet into his boots. The expression in his eyes doesn't make him look angry though, just sad and worn out. I get how he feels. Life has turned into a struggle that has a lot more to do with the past than the zombies stumbling across the earth. It's hard just getting out of bed sometimes. Even when you have people you love who are there to help. And Winston lost the one person who was keeping him going. I can't help thinking I'd be feeling the same way if something happened to Axl.

When Winston has his shoes on, he jerks the door open and heads out, letting a burst of cold air inside in the process. The door slams when it closes.

"Any luck?" I ask Axl even though I heard how the conversation ended.

He slips his feet into his own boots, shaking his head. "Nope. He says he's fine. Dealin' the best he can."

"I'm sure that's true, " I say, pulling my boots on so I can join Axl at the door. "I just feel like he's not really part of the group anymore, and it's tough. We've lost so much already that the thought of losing Winston almost takes my breath away."

"We ain't gonna lose him," Axl says, his voice coming across harsher than he probably intended. I try not to let it bug me, but it does a little.

We step outside, and the cool air slaps me in the face, somehow snapping me out of the sadness that weighed me down just a second ago. Pulling me out of the depressing thoughts of the past and the worries about the future. Back to the now, which is what we need to focus on anyway. One day at a time. That's how we'll survive.

"Soon as Angus is better, we gotta go out. Get us some more coffee," Axl calls over the howling wind. "I can't take that apple bullshit no more."

I slip my hand into his and squeeze. "Just don't rush him, Axl. You know he's going to want to run out there the second he feels up to it, but he needs to take his time. This is serious. He could have died. Think about Jake."

Just mentioning the little boy we couldn't save has my insides tensing all over again. We tried to save him when he got sick, but we couldn't find the meds. We went to town after town searching, only to come up empty-handed. By the time we found some it was too late for him. That's how Jon and Hadley got separated from us, which makes it all so much worse. They went out looking for antibiotics for Jake, but they didn't come back. Then the boy died.

"Right," Axl says, nodding. "We gotta make sure Angus don't rush off before he's back to normal."

"I'm not sure Angus has ever been normal," I say, laughing.

Axl lets out a little half-laugh, half-snort as we cut our way through the snow and head toward the house Darla and Angus share with Joshua and Anne—and all the animals. The closer we get, the louder the squawking becomes. On really quiet days, I feel like we can hear them all the way across the street at our house. None of the people who live here seem to care, though, and I can't say that I really blame them. The sound helps keep me from panicking over our limited food supply.

When we step inside, we take off our boots even though the carpet is already ruined from people tracking snow in. The first floor is cloaked in darkness, but a light flickers in the hallway above. Darla's laughter rings through the air as we head up, followed only a few seconds later by Angus's hacking cough. He's been like this for weeks, and even though the cough hasn't subsided, it doesn't sound quite as painful as it did last week.

The door's open but we stop outside anyway, and Axl raps his knuckles against the doorframe.

"Come on!" Angus calls, waving us in. "Don't stand out in the hallway gawkin' like I'm on my deathbed. Ain't nothin' wrong with me that a little rest won't cure."

"I'm not sure about that," I say, stepping into the room.

"Now, now, Blondie, you an' me both know you can't deny how you really feel 'bout me no more. Not after all that sobbin' you did when you thought I was gonna die."

I roll my eyes, but it's half-hearted. I'll never forget the day Angus was bitten, and I don't think anyone else will either. Being trapped down in that cellar, thinking he was going to turn and that Axl or I was going to have to take care of him. It was one of the hardest things I've ever had to face, and that's saying a lot. It may have put some strain on my relationship with Axl—which we luckily managed to get through—but it also helped Angus's relationship with everyone else.

"You'll never let me forget that, will you?" I say, grinning down at Angus.

He returns my smile, and the glint in his gray eyes makes him look younger and softer than he has since we first met. "Nope. Made me feel real special."

Axl chuckles as he throws himself on the bed at Angus's feet. "How you feelin'?"

"Like shit, though that's got more to do with bein' stuck in this here bed than anythin' else. These walls ain't as comfortin' as they was back when we first found this place, that's for damn sure. I'm ready to get back on my feet. Go out huntin' or check out that town. We've been puttin' that off."

"Hope Springs?" I ask, really perking up for the first time today.

"Yup." Angus nods. "I been thinkin' 'bout it a lot, an' I say it's high time we check the place out. See if them folks are friends or not."

"We gotta be ready," Darla chimes in.

Obviously they've spent a lot of time talking about this.

"It ain't gonna happen," Axl says, shaking his head. "The timin' ain't good. Angus, you been sick, and you can't be out in the cold for hours just sittin' there stakin' the place out."

"They have a point, Axl," I argue, suddenly feeling like Judas. There's something very wrong about being on Angus and Darla's side in an argument.

Axl narrows his eyes on my face before shaking his head. "No. In the spring, maybe, but now ain't the time."

"And what if they decide to attack?" I snap. "Shouldn't we be ready?"

"They ain't gonna attack when there's three feet of snow on the ground. Not only would it slow them up, but it would make it a hell of a lot easier for us to defend ourselves from behind the fence." Axl shakes his head. "No. If they're smart, they'll wait 'til spring. And that's what we're gonna do. We'll stake the place out, but not 'til it's a little warmer and less of a risk. No point killin' ourselves for no reason."

Damn. He actually has a point.

"Fine," I mutter even though I'm dying to check out Hope Springs.

We've been going back and forth about this for months, but every time someone brings it up Axl successfully deflects every argument they have. I know he's doing it because he's afraid of repeating what happened at the Monte Carlo, but that doesn't mean I have to like it. I want to know if there are other good people out there or if we're alone. I want to be sure there's a reason to go on. To start a life. If every other group in the world is evil, I don't see the point in planning a real life. If this is all we'll ever have—scrounging for food and shivering through winter—then the most we can hope for is surviving. Not living.

CHAPTER FIVE

VIVIAN

"You pissed?" Axl asks from the other side of the room.

"No."

I pull my shirt over my head, shivering from the chill in the air. The kerosene heaters we got in Duncan help, but they don't keep the room as warm as I'm used to. The bedroom is too big or it's too cold outside, or maybe it's just that the heater is too small. Whatever it is, I can't change my clothes without my teeth chattering.

"You sound pissed."

I turn as Axl slides into bed wearing nothing but a pair of boxer briefs. Just looking at him makes me shiver even more.

"I'm not," I say, hurrying over to join him under the covers. "I get it. We don't know anything about these people and you want to make sure we're smart about this."

He eyes me as I slide closer to him, trying to steal the warmth from his body. Against mine, his skin feels like he just stepped out of a hot tub.

"How are you so warm?" I ask, pressing my cold feet against his.

"Shit. How are you so cold?" He wraps his arms around me, and I scoot closer.

"I'm always cold."

"I know."

"I can't wait for spring."

"Me too," he whispers as his lips move down to my cheek. "I know what'll warm you up now, though."

The shivers that have worked their way through my limbs change into tremors of pleasure when Axl's hands slide down my sides and his mouth covers mine. I kiss him back, and my body responds, but my mind is torn. Thoughts of our group and the long winter stretching out ahead of us make it impossible to focus on anything else. I try to push the worries away, but they refuse to stay hidden.

"Axl," I say, pulling back. "What are we going to do?"

He lifts his eyebrows, and the dim light from the kerosene heater emphasizes his grin.

"Not that," I say, laughing despite the tension in my body. "I mean about food. About Hope Springs. About surviving winter."

Axl lets out a sigh as he rolls onto his back, his gaze focused on the ceiling. Even though I can't help being worried, I feel bad. Sex has become less and less frequent as the stress of life collects on my shoulders. When we were on the move, I was able to ignore it a little. Pretend that all I needed to do was hold on until we found a safe place to live. Then things would be easier.

Now we have a safe place, but things haven't gotten easier. The dangers have changed—we're more concerned about starving or freezing to death than zombies at the moment—but they are ever present. What's worse is that I now have the added guilt of Hadley and Jon. We left them, and even though at the time we didn't have much of a choice, I can't help wondering if we could have done something different.

Could we have gone back to look for them? Not unless we wanted to draw attention our way. All we had was the Sam's Club truck, and rolling into town would have meant risking all our lives. The men who opened fire weren't messing around, and there wasn't a doubt in my mind that they'd try to kill us if we went back there.

Could we have stayed at the hot springs a little longer? I don't think so. The place was riddled with zombie bodies, making both the air and water polluted. Plus, Jake was sick. Staying where we were would have put the rest of us at risk too. We had no idea who or what might have been attracted by the gunshots from when we fought off the dead.

Could we have stayed in Millersville longer? No. That I know for sure. Zombies surrounded us, and getting out was the safest thing for everyone.

Could we have left better clues for them to follow? Maybe, but even if we had I doubt it would have mattered. There was so much snow coming down...

I sigh and roll over so I'm facing Axl. "I'm sorry."

"'Bout what?" he says, his eyes still on the ceiling.

"That we haven't been having a lot of sex lately."

The second the words are out of my mouth, I feel stupid. Because it's stupid. We're struggling to find food, and I'm apologizing about sex? But we've never had an issue finding time before. Even when we were on the road, we could sneak in a quickie here and there. Now though, we have a bed and a house and more time to ourselves than we could have ever imagined, but we're barely doing it. Maybe that's part of the problem, though. Before it felt like every moment together could be our last, but it doesn't really feel that way anymore. Now it seems like we've bought ourselves some time.

Axl turns his head my way, his gray eyes on my face. "Just bein' in a safe place with you is enough for me."

His arms wrap around me once again, and he pulls my body against his. I rest my cheek on his chest, listening to his heart thump. It's steady and strong and quite possibly the most beautiful sound I've ever heard.

"I love you," I say, giving in when my eyes grow heavy.

"Love you, which is why we ain't goin' to Hope Springs right now. We're gonna wait 'til it's safe an' we're gonna be smart 'bout it. 'Cause if I lost you, I wouldn't be much better off than Winston is right now."

I kiss his chest and wrap my arms around him tighter. "Then everyone would be in trouble. They depend on you for so much."

Axl doesn't respond, and as his hand moves slowly up and down my back, my body grows lighter and the world we're living in begins to drift away.

THE SUN IS STILL LOW WHEN I WAKE, THE RAYS barely strong enough to penetrate the thin curtains covering the bedroom window. I roll over to find Axl on the other side of the room, pulling on his pants. An impressive selection of weapons is spread out across the floor at his feet, all ready to be strapped on. Why he has so many is beyond me, though.

"What are you doing?" I ask through a yawn.

"Gonna go out. See if I can find a deer or somethin'. We gotta get some meat real soon here."

I sit up, suddenly wide awake. "Who's going with you?"

He shakes his head as he leans down and scoops a few guns up off the floor. "Parvarti and Al are sleepin', and Winston and Anne will be on watch."

"Angus can't go," I say, doing the math. When he shrugs, I slide out of bed. "You aren't going alone."

I hurry to pull on clothes, moving so quickly that my body barely has time to gather the usual collection of goose bumps. If Axl thinks he's going out there on his own, he's nuts. I've never gone hunting with him, but that doesn't mean I can't back him up. He's looking for animals, but who knows what he's going to come across.

"You gonna hunt?" Axl asks, freezing in the middle of strapping a couple knives to his belt.

"I'm going with you." He starts to argue, but I shake my head. "No one should be out there alone these days. Not even you. There's no way you'd let someone else go out by themselves."

Axl goes back to his weapons without arguing, but the frown on his face tells me he isn't happy. Doesn't matter to me. There are some things I refuse to compromise on, and this is one. Axl, no matter how all-powerful he seems to think he is, needs someone watching his back just as much as everyone else does. Even if it means we have an all-out war later, I'm going with him.

"You got enough weapons?" he snaps when I head toward the door.

"I do," I say as coolly as possibly. I'm not going to let him draw me into a fight no matter how much he wants it.

"It ain't just animals and zombies we gotta watch out for."

Seriously? Who does he think he's talking to. "I'm aware."

Axl stares at me for a second, his stormy eyes silently begging me to change my mind. When I don't offer to stay behind, though, he sighs and turns toward the door.

I follow, zipping my jacket as we head down. Thank God my coat and snow pants are white. I'll be able to blend in better.

Axl grabs his bow and a quiver full of arrows from the front room before heading out. Since I'm not good with the bow—despite numerous lessons—I stick with my gun. I'm just here for backup, anyway.

It's early, but the sun is already up and outside the snow is blindingly bright. I slip my hand into my jacket pocket and pull out my sunglasses as Axl and I head across the yard and down the street. My stomach growls, begging for breakfast, but I ignore it. If I bring it up, Axl will use it as an

69

excuse for me to stay behind. We won't be out long, and it's not like I haven't gone for days without eating before. I can handle it.

We're headed for the gate when Anne steps out of the woods, her gun in her hand but held loosely at her side. She heads our way when she sees us, but she doesn't smile. "Hunting?"

"Yeah," I say, smiling. Trying to get her to smile. "How's it been out here?"

"Quiet." She heads down the street at our side not looking at us. "I think you're wasting your time. I haven't seen anything other than birds in weeks."

"Same for us," I say, trying to sound optimistic. "But they have to be out there, right?"

Anne just shrugs.

"Let everybody know we headed out," Axl says, frowning when he once again glances my way.

"Will do." Anne turns her face toward us, squinting under the bright sun. "Good luck, I guess."

She guesses? What the hell is that supposed to mean?

"Gee, thanks," I mutter, moving faster.

I reach the gate first but don't look back while I wait for Axl. My face is warm, and I'm fighting the urge to scream. We have a place to live and a fence around us and for the most part things are looking up, but people are still fading away, and I'm furious. Not just at them either, but at life and God and this new world we're living in that smashes people's dreams to dust.

"You okay?" Axl asks when he reaches me.

"Peachy."

He glances my way before turning to undo the lock. I take a few deep breaths while he spins the dial, then the lock clicks open and he unravels the chain and my heart beats harder. Suddenly, I'm excited to be leaving for a few hours. I'm trying to so hard to stay positive, but it's almost impossible with everyone else so down. Well, not everyone. Al always has a smile on his face—even though he lost his arm—and Lila is pretty cheery. Brady's insanely optimistic most of the time, too. Even Angus and Darla aren't bad to be around, Lord help me for admitting it, but everyone else is so negative.

Axl pushes the gate open, and I walk through, pulling my knife in the process. I suck in a deep breath like I'm able to breathe for the first time in years, and it feels good. I feel lighter. Less trapped. Maybe the walls are too much for me. Maybe it isn't just the people.

Behind me Axl secures the gate, and when he's done, he starts walking again. Not saying anything. I move at his side, kicking up snow as we head out into the surrounding forest.

"They're all doin' their best," Axl says after a few minutes of silence.

"It's just a lot to take."

He nods, his eyes moving my way before going back to study our surroundings. "It is, but that don't mean you can't help 'em. They ain't lost. Not yet. And bein' there for them the way you was for me is the only thing you can do."

"What do you mean the way I was for you?" I ask, not stopping, but turning so I can see him.

"I mean you believed in me when all this shit went down. I knew I'd survive this thing, but I didn't think I could do much else. You kept me lookin' ahead. Thinkin' 'bout what I could do to get everybody else through this too. You just gotta do that with them, only you're gonna hafta show them that they can get themselves through this."

"I didn't know you felt that way. You were always so capable. It seemed like you knew that."

Axl shakes his head, and I turn to focus on the forest in front of us. Maybe he's right. It's going to be hard getting through to them, but I can't give up yet. Parvarti especially has to know that she's strong enough to pull through this. She's become so capable that Angus has nicknamed her Rambo. How much more proof does she need?

"I'll try not to let it bug me as much."

Axl stops after about fifteen minutes of walking, and already I'm shivering. When he sits in the snow, I don't move. Is this what we do? Just sit in the snow and hope an animal passes?

"We're stopping here?"

Axl looks up and frowns. "What did you expect?"

"I thought we'd walk around and look for animals."

"You do that and you're gonna scare them away. Gotta be quiet and listen."

"Shit."

I shiver but lower myself next to Axl anyway. Despite my thick gloves, my fingers already feel like ice, and the tip of my nose is frozen solid. Even though there's no way in hell I want Axl to be out here alone, I suddenly regret coming with him.

It's going to be a long day.

BY THE TIME WE GET BACK—EMPTY-HANDED—I FEEL like a snowman. It's close to dinnertime and my stomach is growling, and I'm pretty sure I'm never going to warm up. Too bad Axl and I will be on watch in a couple hours. I should have just enough time to thaw out before I have to shiver in the snow for hours yet again.

I really hate winter.

When we open the front door of Brady's house, we're greeted by laughter. After the sour mood I left in a few hours earlier, it's more than a welcome surprise. Even more so when I hear Angus's loud chuckle.

"Guess your brother's feeling better," I say, kicking off my boots. A little snow goes flying, landing on Brady's spotless carpet. I should feel bad, but I'm too cold and exhausted.

Axl eyes me when I walk by the spot without cleaning it up.

"I just can't," I say, making him chuckle. "I hope you have something hot." I have to raise my voice over the laughter when we walk into the kitchen. "Because we are half-frozen."

Brady smiles from the table where he sits with Angus, Darla, and Joshua.

72

"I made soup, so load up."

"Perfect," I say, heading toward the stove.

"Why you outta bed?" Axl asks, heading over to the table instead of the food.

"Figured a walk next door wouldn't hurt. Told you I was sick an' tired of layin' in that bed."

I fill two bowls with soup and head over, being careful not to spill any of the liquid. It's steaming, and even though I'm still freezing, scalding myself is not the answer.

"Just don't overdo it." Axl takes the bowl I offer him, and we settle around the table. "We need you better so you can start pullin' your weight 'round here."

"I'll be back on my feet next week," Angus says.

Joshua shakes his head. "On your feet is one thing. In the cold is another. You can help around the house, but you are not going hunting or on guard duty for another couple weeks. I don't think you understand how bad your bronchitis was."

Angus frowns and purses his lips like he's going to argue, but before he can, Darla puts her arm around him and leans closer. "You listen to the doctor. Understand?"

"Alright," he says, grinning at my mom.

Darla returns his smile, and a strange thing happens, or doesn't happen. I don't have the urge to spit or look away or pretend they aren't staring at each other like two fools in love. Angus told me how much he cared about Darla back in the cellar when we were still waiting for him to die, and it must have helped me more than I realized. Things have definitely gotten easier, and it suddenly hits me that I'm actually okay with their relationship. That all the irritation I used to feel has worn down, and now things feel almost normal. Like Darla and I have something big in common: we both made it to the end of the world so we could find the one person who would make us happy. It was a long and painful trip, for both of us, but it was all worth it in the end. Weird that I'd feel this way after everything that's happened.

When Darla looks up, her eyes meet mine. "What're you thinking?"

I shake my head and laugh. "Nothing. Not really. Just thinking about how strange life can be."

Darla raises her eyebrows and smiles, and I wait for her to ask if I've forgiven her finally. She doesn't, and I have a good feeling it's because she somehow knows what's going on inside my head and she doesn't want to push me. I can't say that I've totally forgiven her, not yet anyway, but I'm feeling better. Less angry and more hopeful. It's a relief.

"I take it you didn't get anything?" Joshua asks, drawing my attention away from my mom.

"Didn't see a damn thing," Axl says between slurps of soup. "Out there for hours and the whole time nothin' moved but the wind."

Some of the joy from a few minutes ago is sucked from the room, but it's unavoidable. We can't ignore the fact that we're having a tough time finding food. No matter how much we want to.

"So what do we do about this?" Brady asks, his tone as upbeat as it was when he talked about the apple crisp yesterday. "We should have a plan, even if it's only to go to Duncan when the weather clears."

"We got the animals if it comes down to it," Angus says, then turns his head so he can let out a cough.

"And there's Hope Springs." Joshua doesn't look up from his soup, almost as if he's afraid of how Axl will react.

"Spring," Axl says firmly, then turns to Brady. "Angus is right. We can butcher an animal if we gotta. We ain't gonna starve, and when spring comes we'll start plantin' some crops."

"We'll be fine." The words come out sounding way more optimistic than I feel, but everyone nods like they agree. I'm glad. It gives my words weight.

Brady gets up, clearing his throat. "If you'll excuse me for a minute, I need to use the men's room."

"Don't you mean little boy's room?" Angus calls, chuckling at his own joke.

Brady pauses and turns Angus's way. "Based on how

74

preoccupied you seem to be with size, I'm wondering if it's something you've had to defend yourself against in the past." He lifts his eyebrows and tilts his head toward Angus's crotch.

Axl chuckles, and I have to cover my mouth so I don't spray soup all over the place. Even Joshua lets out a little laugh. Angus, though, just scowls as Brady turns and walks away with a smile on his face.

When he's disappeared, Darla slaps Angus on the arm. "You need to stop being so mean to him!"

"I'm mean to everybody," Angus says, rubbing his arm. "That's how you know I like you. Plus, it ain't like he's not givin' it right back."

"You're a child," I tell Angus.

I lift my bowl and slurp up the rest of the soup until there's nothing left but a tiny drop. If I could stick my head inside the bowl and lick that out too, I would. Brady sure does know how to cook.

"I'm still hungry," I say, getting to my feet. "But now that I've thawed out I realize I also have to use the bathroom."

Axl gets up behind me. "I'll get more for both of us."

I hand him my bowl before heading into the other room, and when I step out of the kitchen, I freeze in my tracks. Brady is on the floor in the living room, scrubbing the little dot of snow I ignored earlier, and I suddenly feel really bad. He spends so much time cooking, and he opened his gates to us, probably saving our lives, and I couldn't even stop to wipe up a little snow. How selfish.

"I'm sorry," I say, going over to help even though it seems ridiculous. It's a stain the size of a quarter. "I was so exhausted when we came back that I let the spot go. I shouldn't have."

"No. I'm sorry." He exhales and looks up from his scrubbing. "It's silly and I know it, but Kristine was so picky about the carpet. It was the one thing we argued about. She didn't want shoes on in the house, and I was always forgetting. I didn't understand, but she would always bring up how important clean carpet is when you have a baby crawling around." Brady stops talking and looks away. "I know it's stupid to keep worrying about it now."

I let out a deep breath, knowing he just let a major part of his story slip out and he's not thrilled about it. As upbeat and welcoming as he's been, there's a part of Brady that's closed off. Pieces of his life he's kept tucked away. Whether it's because it hurts too much to share it with us or because he just hasn't come to terms with it, I'm not sure. But I know he's hurting a lot more than he lets on.

"It's not stupid," I say, kneeling down next to him. "We all deal with our pain in different ways, and this is how you're dealing. I know you lost a lot. No one blames you for wanting this."

"I think a part of me is still hoping it can all go back to normal." He looks over to where the tarp is laid out, covered in dirty puddles of long-melted snow. "I know it doesn't make sense, but I just keep wondering. What if someone is out there working on a cure? What if they can bring these people back? Kristine would want her carpet to look good."

"But..."

I try to remember what he told us when we first got here, but with so much happening so fast, it's all a little fuzzy. He said he cleaned out the houses and put all his neighbors down. He buried them; I know that for sure because we dug a grave for Jake in the same area. But Brady shot everyone who lived here, didn't he? I'm pretty sure he told us that.

Does that include his wife?

"You know that isn't possible," I say instead of asking a question I don't really want to know the answer to. Just thinking about it sends a shiver down my spine.

Brady looks back and gives me a sad smile. "I know. Sometimes, though, it's easier to live in a fantasy world."

"No one can blame you for that."

We lapse into silence, but I can't stop thinking about what he just said. I get the impression he isn't telling me the whole truth about Kristine. I believe she died—almost everyone did—and that Brady buried her just like he did with all his neighbors. But if I remember correctly, he originally told us he put his wife down *before* she turned. What if that isn't true, though? What if he buried her and then found out about the zombies? Would he have dug her up?

If not, would she have reanimated anyway? Underground...

The thought of his wife buried somewhere in this community, alive but under several feet of dirt, sends a shudder shooting through me. There's no way he did that for real. Is there?

CHAPTER SIX

AXL

Winston is startin' to worry me. Back when Jess died, I knew it was gonna be rough for him, but I didn't think he'd give up. Not after everything we fought for. But he's done just that. Let it get inside 'til it started eatin' him. Now he's drinkin'. It ain't just dangerous, it's wasteful. Usin' booze to ease his pain when we could be usin' it for other things. I've kept my mouth shut 'bout it long 'nough, but I can't do it no more.

I sneak outta the house nice and early, careful not to wake Vivian. The sun's just comin' up, givin' me 'nough light to follow the footprints in the snow, but I take my time. I need the walk to figure out what I'm gonna say. December's comin' to an end, meanin' we made it another month without losin' somebody. Next week Angus should be back on guard detail—long as the doc clears him—and I'm lookin' forward to it. Vivian's been with me every wakin' moment, which makes it hard to think sometimes. I'm always too focused on how she's feelin'. If she's cold or hungry or in danger, and it don't give me a lot of time to try and figure out what I'm gonna do 'bout Winston. Something's gotta be done though, and soon. We got too much ridin' on all this to let him screw it up.

The footprints head off into the woods, so that's the way I go. There are two sets movin' together, so I know it's Parv who's on duty. Winston is probably the only person she don't mind walkin' with, and it's mainly 'cause he don't make her talk. She's almost as bad as he is, but at least she pitches in. And she ain't drinkin'. Not yet anyways.

I catch sight of them standin' next to each other, starin' out through the fence. Parv is smokin', and when I get closer, I see that Winston's got a bottle in his hand. He shouldn't be drinkin' when he's on watch. Don't matter if Parv's here to back him up or not. It's too risky.

They turn when I get closer. Parv nods, but Winston just goes back to lookin' out the fence. He sighs like he knows what's comin', and I don't doubt it. He's probably been waitin' for me to say somethin' for a while now.

"Your shift already?" Parv asks.

"Just 'bout." My gaze moves to Winston, and his back stiffens. "Couldn't sleep, so I thought I'd come out an' see how the night went."

"As quiet as ever," Parv says, and I turn to find her watchin' me. She nods when our eyes meet. "I'm going to head up to the house since you're here."

"Sounds good."

Winston don't move, and Parv don't say goodbye before headin' off. I stand with my hands shoved in my pockets while her footsteps fade away, but even then I don't know what to say. The walk didn't do a thing to help me figure it all out.

"You may as well just get on with it," Winston says, keepin' his eyes focused on the world outside the fence.

"I'm worried 'bout you." It ain't what I wanted to say, but

80

that don't mean it ain't true. "You been drinkin' too much, and it's not just your life you're riskin'. What if somebody attacked and you was too drunk to help Parv out?"

"There's nobody out there." Winston shakes his head. "You and I both know no one is coming to attack us or save us or even help us. This is all there is. It's the end of the line and we're living on borrowed time, and I'm going to spend my last few days on Earth the way I want to." He turns to face me. "You can't do a thing to stop me."

"I wanna help."

I reach out, but Winston jerks away. "I don't need help. All I need is to be left alone."

"We been through so much. You can't just throw it all away!" My voice echoes through the woods, and Winston looks around like he's tryin' to see where it goes. I ain't sure if he's drunk or just outta his mind. It's hard to tell.

When he finally looks back, he holds my gaze for a few seconds while he takes a drink. When he's swallowed, he says, "I'm not throwing anything away. Don't you get it? There's nothing left to throw away."

He pushes past me, headin' after Parv while I just stand there. My gut is so heavy it hurts. Like it's full of rocks. I wanna call after him. Wanna tell him not to go, but I don't. I'm not sure there's anything else I can say.

JANUARY

CHAPTER SEVEN

GINNY

I shift in the leather chair, rubbing my abdomen when something flutters across my stomach. It's the baby moving. I know what it is, but I still have a difficult time wrapping my brain around it or the fact that I'm nearly to the halfway point. Jon, on the other hand, is beside himself. Every night he kneels on the floor next to my bed so he can talk to the baby for hours. Sometimes it goes on for so long that I find myself dozing off, but he never stops. I doubt he will. His enthusiasm has become more and more infectious as the days pass, and it's gotten to the point that I sometimes forget he might not be the father.

I keep one hand on my belly while I absentmindedly twist the radio dial with the other. It's been weeks, and I've spent hours upon hours in this chair, turning this dial and shifting through static to find someone or something. Nothing's happened though. Not for me or the three other people who switch off shifts. The world outside the walls of Hope Springs seems to have slipped into nothingness, getting lost in the swell off zombie bloodlust and human violence, becoming almost as extinct as the dinosaurs that used to rule this planet.

The constant hum of static fills the room, almost soothing at this point. So much so that I find my eyelids growing heavy and feel the pull of a nap. Curling up in a ball on the floor sounds amazing right now. If there was a couch in this office I might be more tempted, but I know the floor will be hard. I've become oddly accustomed to sleeping in a bed again.

I stifle a yawn as I twist the knobs, pausing at each new frequency for a few seconds. Waiting. Listening. Praying for a voice or some other sound that indicates the outside world hasn't really disappeared. But the eagerness I felt when I first started this job has begun to wane, and now I feel more like someone who has been shoved out of sight than someone who is playing an important role in the community.

The door opens, and I turn, leaving the static to its constant buzz.

Corinne smiles, her mouth stretching wide across her face and accentuating her high cheekbones. "Nothing?" she asks even though it's obvious from the crackle in the air.

"Just white noise." I shrug, and she mimics the gesture. It's our daily routine.

Corinne crosses the room until she's standing next to the desk, forcing me to stretch my neck so I can look up. She isn't staring at me, though. She's focused on the radio, and the smile on her face looks so forced that I could almost imagine it was drawn on. That's when it hits me: she doesn't really believe we'll find another group. This is all for show.

"How long are we going to keep doing this?" I ask, trying to ignore the sinking in my stomach at the thought that this place is the only real thing left in this world. The only real group of people. The only ones trying to start over. There's nothing left.

Corinne turns her gaze on me, and her face relaxes, changing her from a woman who shoulders the weight of an entire community to someone who's just trying to hang on. It's an expression I've never seen on her face. The loss and pain the world has endured is etched on everyone else here, whether it's their eyes or the way they walk or the slouch in their shoulders when they sit. It's there, the pain and struggle. But not Corinne. Since the day we arrived in Hope Springs, I've never seen her look anything but strong. She's been the pillar holding our community up.

"Corinne?" I whisper.

She lowers herself until she's sitting on the edge of the desk, her eyes focused on the carpet. "I try to hold it together, but I know I'll eventually hit a wall. One of these days, I'm going to need to put the hard truth of what we are facing out there, and I'm terrified what will happen then. There are good people here. People who will work toward the future whether or not the rest of the world is gone, but there are others who I truly believe are teetering on the brink of something very dangerous."

I sit up straighter, my mind going back to months ago when Vivian and I were huddled together in the Monte Carlo. I know exactly what Corinne is talking about.

"Lawlessness," I whisper.

Her eyes move up to hold mine. "Yes. I'm a hopeful person, but I'm also a realistic one, and I know what some men will turn into when they feel like they have nothing left to lose."

I swallow a lump that tries to rise in my throat, forcing it down to my stomach where it sits and grows. "I've seen it. Before we came here…" I squeeze my eyes shut but have to open them again when the face of that bald bastard flashes across the darkness. "I can't even describe to you what I went through."

"I guessed as much." I look up, and Corinne gives me a sympathetic look as her eyes sweep over me. "When you got here, it was obvious that you were hiding from something…"

The words hang between us until I have to clench the leather chair beneath me to keep my body from trembling. Corinne doesn't take her eyes off my face, and just like the day she first asked me to do this job, I have a feeling she knows more than she's letting on.

"You know?" The words pop out of me, so low and quiet that for a brief second I wonder if they were only in my head.

"Your secret is safe with me." Corinne gets to her feet, brushing her hands across her backside like she's sweeping dirt off her clothes even though she was only sitting on the desk. "The world is a different place, but some things never change, and I can understand your desire for anonymity."

"When did you figure it out?" I ask, unable to move even though my shift is up and Corinne is waiting for my chair.

"I could tell right away that you were hiding something, but I let it go. There was nothing threatening or dangerous about you, and I'm a firm believer in the importance of letting some things from the past go." She exhales slowly, almost like she is trying to blow away her own memories. "If we held onto everything, we'd never be able to move forward."

"Thank you," I say, once again fighting the urge to ask about her past and the people she left behind. She didn't ask me what I was running from, though.

Corinne nods, and I finally pull myself to my feet. I lift my arms above my head until my back pops, and the other woman slides into the chair. She stares at the radio like she's afraid to look at me. I'm thankful for the break in eye contact. After realizing she knows who I am, I'm having a hard time relaxing. The pounding of my heart has become constant and loud, and the urge to run is so strong I have to force my feet to stay still.

"Have a nice evening with your husband," Corinne says, reaching for the dial.

There's something about the tone in her voice that makes me freeze in my tracks. Makes me turn and study her. Really see her for the first time ever, and the pain and loneliness in every line of her body is so raw that it takes my breath away.

"Thank you," I say, putting a hand on her shoulder.

Her lips twitch, but she doesn't look away from the radio

as she flips to the next frequency. Static fills the room, ringing in my ears. My hand slides off her shoulder and I turn, heading for the door. I'm halfway there when the static fades and words break through the buzz, garbled and broken and almost unintelligible, but somehow still clear as day.

"CDC…Atlanta…Government…"

I spin around to find Corinne staring at the radio with her mouth hanging open. Frozen.

"The frequency!" I cry as I rush back, practically diving for the desk.

My hands reach the knob before Corinne's, and as I adjust it, the voice grows clearer.

"The month is January. We are alive and well in Atlanta. Walls have been constructed and we have a working government in place. The CDC is hard at work on a vaccine. All survivors welcome. The month is January. We are alive and well in Atlanta…"

Even before the message repeats itself I know it's a recording, and my first instinct is to believe that it's old. Something that was set up months ago when all this first started and has managed to survive even though everything else has disappeared, but then the recording starts again and the word January jumps out at me. It's recent, and the people who put it out thought far enough ahead to realize other survivors might suspect it's old. Meaning they're organized and planning ahead. And the CDC? A vaccine? It seems impossible, but amazing. The best news I could have ever hoped for.

"It's a recording," Corinne says, shaking her head.

"It is, but someone has to be there."

The hope I've felt slipping away over the last few weeks comes back, and suddenly all I can think about is Vivian and Axl even though I have no idea how they relate to Atlanta and this supposed walled city.

I grab the receiver, a piece of equipment I haven't bothered to mess with until now, and hold the button down as I raise it to my lips. "We're here!" I find myself shouting. "In Colorado. There are more survivors."

I release the button and wait, but the recording continues to repeat itself. Over and over again in a constant loop that makes my head pound.

"There's no one there," Corinne says, shaking her head.

"They have to be." I press the button again and say, "We are in Colorado and we have almost two hundred survivors."

I don't know what else to say, but I also know I can't give up. The recording is there for a reason, and even if I have to stay here all night, I won't stop. I cross to the other side of the desk and plop into the chair. There's no way I'm leaving. Not now.

"They can't man the radio twenty-four hours a day," I mutter, almost to myself. "That's all."

"That's a good point," Corinne says. "So we just keep trying. They'll check eventually."

"Exactly," I say, once again putting the receiver up to my mouth.

Time passes, but I don't give up. Every couple minutes I say something else, praying after each breath I let out that someone will answer. That a real, live person will come over the radio and ensure me that we are not in fact alone.

Corinne gets up every now and then and paces the room, but she doesn't leave and she doesn't take a turn with the radio. Almost like she knows I need to be the one to do this. Which I do, even though I'm not totally sure why. Every flutter that moves across my insides emphasizes exactly how much I need this to be real.

There are no windows in the office, but the clock on the wall ticks as the seconds go by, the time sliding away so fast it seems impossible. With each move of the minute hand the tension in me grows, becoming more intense as the hour hand makes its way around the clock. Time moves at an odd pace now that the world is gone. Sometimes it's so slow that it seems like just yesterday I sat in my trailer, sipping my sparkling water while someone else applied my makeup. At other moments, though, the time seems to fly by, making it seem like decades have passed rather than just months. Like

90

the fuzzy memories of the forgotten world are something passed down to me from the previous generation, rather than a life I actually lived not that long ago.

The monotone voice on the radio cuts out right in the middle of telling us that the CDC is working, and I freeze, tightening my grip on the receiver as Corinne and I stare at each other. Then I look down at the radio, holding my breath. But nothing happens. The transmission doesn't continue and no one live comes on. It's just a silence so thick I can almost touch it.

My hand shakes when I raise the receiver to my mouth, and when my thumb presses down on the button, it seems to fight back. "Is anyone there?" I ask, curling my toes to keep my legs from shaking. "This is Ginny Lewis up in Colorado. We're alive. We have survivors."

I release the button and Corinne sucks in a loud breath. Before she's even had a chance to let it out, the radio in front of us crackles.

"This is Major Hendrix at the CDC in Atlanta."

The muscles in my body turn to mush, and tears fill my eyes. Corinne exhales and lets out a half-laugh, half-sob.

"They're real," she gasps.

"I never doubted it," I lie. I push the button again and say, "I'm so glad to hear another person! We were starting to think we were alone."

"Not even close," Major Hendrix says, a small chuckle in his voice. "We have around four hundred survivors here, and we've been in contact with another group down in the Florida Keys. They're small, but growing. We have new people come in every day."

Four hundred people and more every day? It seems impossible, but they must be working to spread the word, just like Corinne and her team have been doing here since the beginning. Which means they're even more organized than I had hoped.

"The recording says you're working on a vaccine," I say.

"That's right. The doctors here have been working day and night, but so far no luck. We thought we had a breakthrough a few weeks back when we got in touch with the people down in the Keys. They had a girl with them who claimed to be have been bitten and didn't turn. But—"

"Someone is immune?" I ask, too excited to let the Major finish what he was saying.

Corinne's eyes get huge, and the smile that spreads across her face is the first real one I've seen since I met her.

"Was," Hendrix says, making Corinne's smile melt away. "She got overrun before we could bring her up here. If we had been able to get her, things might have been different. As it is, creating a workable vaccine won't be easy unless we can find someone else who is immune to this thing."

"Shit," I mutter with my hand off the button. For some reason, the idea of letting this man all the way down in Atlanta hear me cuss doesn't sit well.

"There has to be other people," Corinne says.

She's right.

I push the button again and say, "She's the only one you've come across who was immune?"

"Yup. But we may have made some bad choices before we found out." The major sighs. "We killed people who had been bitten pretty fast before we knew. Now we have to wonder how many of them might have been the key to fixing all this."

My hand drops to my lap and my mouth falls open as I think back to the shelter and James. When he was bitten, I was so sure that someone might be able to come through this thing, but as soon he turned, all my optimism disappeared. What if we did the same thing? Put someone out of their misery who just might have been the answer to all our problems? What if Nathan hadn't turned? We shot him so fast, didn't even hesitate because he wanted us to.

"You still there?" the major asks, breaking through my thoughts.

I nod even though he can't see me, then once again hold

down the button. "I'm here."

"You say you're in Colorado. Whereabouts?"

"Hope Springs," I say.

Elaborating would be nice, but to be honest, I'm not really sure what major cities are close to us. When we drove in we avoided anything that might be big and overrun, unwilling to risk it.

There's silence, then Major Hendrix is back. "Found you on the map. You got a lot of snow up that way?"

"We do," I say. "It's slowing the zombies down, freezing them. We've been able to clear the city out faster and with fewer casualties."

"That so." The Major makes a sound that I can't decipher, then says, "Hadn't even considered that might happen or I would have headed up that way myself. It's cold here, but apparently not cold enough to slow these bastards down a whole lot."

"You say you have a wall, though?" I ask, thinking about trying to accomplish everything we've done while also fighting the zombies.

We'd still just be starting instead of almost finished. Any day now the last few streets will be clear, then we'll get to work on the houses. That shouldn't take long. Then we'll have a real town and a life.

"We have a wall," Hendrix replies. "It's twenty feet high for about ten miles around the CDC. Took a lot of manpower, but we made it happen. Now things are safe."

"Ask about the government," Corinne whispers, drawing my attention her way.

She's been so silent this whole time that I had almost forgot she was here, but when I meet her gaze, I see the hope shimmering her in eyes. She was just listening.

"Your recording also mentioned a government?" I say.

"That's right. It's not exactly a democracy at this point, things are just too screwed up still, but it will be again one day. We're trying to figure out what works best under the circumstances, and unfortunately some people need quick and brutal justice to understand that we won't tolerate anarchy." He sounds slightly apologetic, and I almost tell him not to worry about it. We provided the men in the Monte Carlo with some quick and brutal justice, so I know what he means.

"Let me talk to him," Corinne says, holding out her hand.

I give her the receiver and sit back while she introduces herself to the major. She asks questions about their setup and laws, and I half-listen as a man all the way down in Atlanta tells her about the committee they've set up and the officials who have been appointed. Corinne takes notes while my head spins, going around in circles while I think about the walled city and another group down in Key West and the CDC working to fix all this. No matter what I try to focus on though, it always comes back to one thought: somewhere in this world a person is walking around with the solution to all of our current problems pumping through their veins, and they might not even know it.

Corinne talks for a bit longer before setting up a time to talk to Hendrix again tomorrow. When she's finally ended the call, the silence that follows is thick and full of possibility.

"This is the answer I've been looking for in so many ways," she says after a few minutes.

"What do you mean?" I ask, my head still spinning from all the new information.

"There are other people and they're working on a vaccine, which means there's hope. But they've also managed to configure a government. It's something we need, but I've been met with resistance every time I mention it."

"Why?" I can't think of a single reason anyone honest wouldn't want a working government.

"I'm not American," Corinne says with a shrug. "Something Dax likes to point out every time we bring it up."

"Dax?"

I don't know the big man well, but he never seemed like someone who would be such a pain in the ass. He smiles a lot. Is always willing to pitch in. He's brought so many survivors back that he's like a celebrity around here.

Corinne nods slowly, studying me like she isn't sure what to say. "He's given me some problems."

I blink, waiting for her to elaborate, but she doesn't. "What kind of problems?"

"I can trust you to keep this between us?"

"Of course. I mean, I'll tell Jon, but that's it."

"Dax doesn't take orders well. I put him in charge of search parties so he felt like he had some power, but once winter set in, he became restless again. I'm afraid he's going to try to take control if we don't do something soon."

Shit. The last thing I want is a struggle for power. We have enough to worry about, and something like that is only going to bring everything crashing down on us.

"You're going to form the same kind of government they have in Atlanta?" I ask.

"It makes sense," Corinne says, looking down over the notes she made when she was talking to Major Hendrix. "Having a president right now wouldn't work. People are too spread out, most probably still trying to find a community like this. A committee being set up in the working areas makes a lot more sense. It would keep tabs on the person in charge and any decisions being made. We also need a judicial officer."

"Like a sheriff?" It makes sense. Corinne can't be expected to handle everything, and even if a committee is elected, someone needs to be the one to *enforce* the decisions made.

"Do you think it will work?" Corinne asks, looking up from her notes.

"I think it's a good idea, but as far as what everyone else is going to think, I'm not sure."

She gets to her feet and lets out a deep breath. "We'll discuss it over the next week. For now, I need to go so we can let everyone else know that we've gotten in touch with the CDC. You and I are the only two people who know right now." Her shoulders relax, and she smiles. "We could use some good news."

95

"It has been a while," I say, getting up as well.

Things have been better since winter hit, but it's still been rough with a baby dying and no new survivors coming in. This news will give everyone the boost we desperately need.

CHAPTER EIGHT
JON

The lobby is buzzing when Jim and I step inside after our shift. I'm covered in zombie gunk, exhausted, freezing, and sore, and all I really want to do right now is see Ginny and grab a bite to eat before turning in for the night. We're later than usual, but we're so close to getting the city cleared out that none of us really care about the extra hours we're putting in. We need to get these bastards while they're frozen. Hopefully the kitchen saved some hot food for me. Marge remembers sometimes, but it doesn't happen a lot. It's the only reason I miss Ginny working there.

"What do you think that's all about?" Jim asks, nodding toward the group of people gathered in the lobby.

I shake my head and let out a deep breath. "Good news, I hope. After the last few months, I've gotten used to not hearing about people dying every day."

Jim snorts. "No kidding."

The top of Corinne's head is just visible in the middle of what looks like a mob. Dozens of people surround her, all talking at once, their voices so loud it seems like they're competing to be heard over the others. After a second, another head comes into view, this one much lower than Corinne's. It's gone in a flash, buried in the sea of bodies, but I'd know that spiky brown hair anywhere. Ginny.

"Maybe more survivors came in today," I say, knowing how worked up Ginny gets every time it happens.

Just the thought of her in the middle of that mob has my own optimism clawing its way to the surface. What if Axl and the others arrived today? Is that what this is all about?

Jim heads their way, calling over his shoulder, "Only one way to find out."

I follow him, and with each step, Axl's knife seems to grow heavier at my waist. It's been a lifesaver to me more than a few times since we got separated, so the idea of giving it back hurts, but I always swore I would. That one day we'd see our old group again and this knife would return to its rightful owner. It was my way of holding onto the belief that happy endings do exist, something difficult even in the face of my love for Ginny.

There's so much talking that even when we're standing right behind the crowd it's impossible to decipher what's going on. I catch a few words, none of which make sense, and shake my head as I try to figure out exactly what has these people so worked up.

A scrawny man who seems to be having trouble standing still looks my way, and when our eyes meet, he smiles so big I have to do a double take. People smile around here—we have a pretty decent setup and we're safe—but no one smiles like *that*. The guy looks like he just won first prize in a raffle or something.

"What's going on?" I ask when he doesn't look away.

His eyes get big and round, and he shuffles his feet excitedly. "You haven't heard?"

"If he'd heard he wouldn't have asked," Jim says, pulling

a cigarette out of his pocket.

"You can't smoke that in here." I nudge him with my elbow so he knows I'm serious. Ginny and our baby are way too close to that cigarette.

Jim rolls his eyes, but he doesn't light up.

The little man is still smiling when he steps closer to me. "They found survivors!"

"Told you," I say, elbowing Jim again.

My partner snorts. "What's the big deal? No one threw a party the day I came in."

The little man blinks, then shakes his head, his smile never fading. "No. Not like that. On the radio. Down in Atlanta."

Jim's mouth drops open, and even though I feel like I'm frozen in place, I'm pretty sure mine does too. "What?"

"That's right. They have the city walled in and the CDC is working." The scrawny guy dips his head closer, somehow reminding me of a chicken. "There's another group in Florida too, and they had someone with them who was immune!"

"Immune?" Jim says the word like he's never heard it, and I'm right there with him.

Immune? No way. That can't be right. We've been fighting these dead bastards for months and no one has ever been immune. Although... Now that I think back, we didn't have a lot of tolerance once we knew a person could turn. Al got his arm chopped off, but everyone else who had been bitten got a bullet to the brain. The end. Maybe the kid is immune? Maybe Joshua cutting his arm off had nothing to do with him surviving.

"Shit," I mutter, shaking my head.

"I know!" The little guy is back to shuffling his feet, and the roar of voices around us has grown so loud that I find it hard to think.

I'm still shaking my head when I push my way through the crowd. Ginny's eyes meet mine when I find the center, and I grab her arm, pulling her back and away from the mob. It's partly because I want to talk to her and find out what's going on, but also because this group suddenly reminds me too much of fans who got so excited when their football team won the big game that they decided to riot. No way I want her in the middle of that.

"What are you doing?" Ginny calls over the voices.

I don't answer until we're out of the sweaty throng of people and on the other side of the lobby. Even then it feels like every word that pops into my head is the wrong thing to say.

"Did someone tell you?" Ginny asks

"They said you found someone on the radio," I say, feeling like a fool for believing it even though everyone here seems to take it for the gospel truth.

"In Atlanta," Ginny replies. "The CDC to be exact."

"Shit," I mutter, shoving my hand through my hair. "So it's real."

"I spoke to them myself," Ginny says. "It's been nothing but silence for weeks, and then tonight there was this recording. It was a man and he was repeating the same thing over and over. *The month is January. We are alive and well in Atlanta. Walls have been constructed and we have a working government in place. The CDC is hard at work on a vaccine. All survivors welcome.'*

Ginny's words echo through my brain. The CDC is trying to create a vaccine. There's a government. Somewhere out there, people are doing the same thing we are: rebuilding. Surviving. Trying to start again. Ginny slips her hand into mine and smiles. Somehow I do the same. It doesn't feel forced or fake or awkward the way I thought it would, either.

It's the best news we've heard in months.

"What else did they say?" I ask.

"It took a while to get someone on the other end," Ginny says. "I think they have the recording playing around the clock in a continuous loop and only stop in every so often to see if people are responding. But I finally got ahold of someone. A major. He said they've built a wall and cleaned out the city just like we're trying to do. They set up a government that's slightly different than the old one, but they have people in charge. They screen everyone going in and out of the city, and they have doctors at the CDC working to create a vaccine." Ginny takes a deep breath, and then says, "That's not all. They're also in contact with a group down in the Florida Keys. They had a girl down there who was bitten, only she didn't turn."

"She was immune?" I ask, still trying to wrap my brain around it all.

"Yes. They were hoping she was the key to creating a workable vaccine and were getting a team together to go down and extract her. A group of zombies got her before they could, though."

"Shit," I mutter.

"But if one person is immune, it stands to reason that there are others out there," Ginny says. "At least that's what they think."

"We need to work harder at finding survivors." I let out a deep breath. "We've slacked off because the weather was making it tough and we were trying to clear the streets, but we need to go out again. Redouble our efforts."

Ginny nods and squeezes my hand, and for a second we just stand there staring at each other while everyone else in the lobby chatters excitedly. I'm thrilled to find out there are other people, even more excited to find out people can be immune to this thing after all. But none of those things really changes the life I have mapped out for Ginny and me.

CHAPTER NINE

JON

The snow on the ground is so thick today that I feel like I'm walking through the ocean. It drags against my legs as I move, seeming to push me back. Like the drifts are trying to prevent me from getting to the bus. Like they don't want me to do my job.

"Don't you want these damn zombies out of here?" I mutter, moving faster. Pushing harder against the snow that's past my knees in some places.

"You talking to yourself?" Jim calls from where he's leaning against the bus. Smoking, not waiting for me.

"Just trying to give myself a pep talk," I lie.

"No reason for that." He pushes himself off the bus as he drops the cigarette to the ground. It sizzles when it hits the snow. "We're fighting snowmen at this point. All we need to do is destroy the brain and drag the bodies to the truck to be hauled away. It's a cakewalk compared to what we dealt with during the fall. And we're almost done. I can't believe we finished as fast as we did."

"Doesn't mean it isn't freezing," I mutter, pulling my hat down lower so it covers the tips of my ears.

"You still bitching about that?" Jim snorts. "You should be thanking God that you're alive to freeze your balls off instead of a frozen pile of rot just waiting to be burned."

"Excuse me if I find it difficult to be thankful in the midst of getting frostbite."

Jim lets out a deep laugh and slaps me on the back as he heads toward the bus. "Come on. Let's get the last little bit of town cleared out, then you and that lady of yours can move into a house."

I follow him on board, half my focus on what we're about to do while the other half of my brain is still mulling over the knowledge that we could have more than just a house to look forward to. If all goes well, one day the CDC will ship us a box of shots and this damn virus will be wiped out.

I follow Jim down the aisle, dropping into the seat at his side. We have two more blocks to clear, and the city will be secure. Doesn't seem like much until I focus on the fact that we're headed toward the hospital. It was left for last on purpose. We all knew it was going to be a pain in the ass. Even with the dead frozen it's going to suck, because until we get inside, we have no way of knowing how many are still up and moving around. For all we know, the hospital could be swarming with them.

"Last hard day," Jim says, pulling on his gloves. "We clear the hospital first, then all we have to do is drag bodies to the truck. Piece of cake."

"Right," I mutter with a snort.

The bus turns a corner, and the hospital is suddenly looming in front of us, it's white exterior grimy against the pure blanket of snow covering the parking lot. The sight of it takes me back to another hospital and another day, back to Vegas where I was crowded into a van with three other men I hated. Three men who were there for reasons that made me so sick I had a hard time not spitting in their faces every time they opened their mouths. The fat asshole who couldn't stop talking about how excited he was to get laid—as if the girl in question had any choice in the matter. Then there was the Hispanic guy who drove the van. He was quieter, but the gleam in his eyes when the fat guy spoke was unmistakable. It was that tattooed prick who really got under my skin, though. He didn't just want to rape, he wanted to torture. The things that came out of his mouth would make a serial killer shiver. And there I was, just sitting there, stalking the hospital with them. Waiting for some innocent and unsuspecting woman to fall into our trap. That's how I met Ginny. Back when she was Hadley Lucas and every man in the Monte Carlo got a hard on just thinking about having a go at her.

What kind of a person does that make me?

"What the hell are you doing?" Jim grunts, making me turn.

It hits me then that the bus has stopped and everyone is filing out, but I'm still sitting. Lost in my thoughts.

"You distracted?" Jim growls before I've had a chance to reply to his first question.

"No," I say firmly as I pull myself to my feet.

The blood pumping through my veins is hotter than lava thanks to my own anger and self-loathing. That's what I focus on as I head out of the bus. The guys who were with me, and the asshole I was back when we took Ginny and Vivian from that hospital. The fact that it was pointless because Megan, my sister and the only reason I was there in the first place, was already too broken to be saved.

Jim is right behind me when we step down, and in front of us, the other clearers have already positioned themselves outside the door. The ones in front are poised, their guns raised and aimed at the doors as two other guys get ready to pull them open. I draw my knife and tighten my grip on it, while behind me, Jim readies his flashlight. We've discussed the plan for clearing the hospital over and over again the last couple days, and the preparation has made me less nervous, but it's impossible not to have a few butterflies. Not when you're facing something like this.

"Stay focused," Jim says.

I nod and squeeze Axl's knife tighter, the image of him firing at me as our van pulled away burned into my brain, right along with the terrified expression on Vivian's face when she was first brought to my room.

"Now!" someone in front yells, and the doors are pulled open.

Jim and I are at the back of the group, but that doesn't matter. Everyone knows where they're supposed to be, and the second we step through the doors, I head that way almost as if I'm on autopilot. Behind me, my partner has his flashlight up and aimed straight ahead, allowing me to keep my hands free as I walk. My gaze moves across the dark and shadowy hallway until I find the sign I'm looking for. Most of our group is headed to the emergency room because it will have the most zoms, but not Jim and me. We are on our way up to the ICU, which could be just as dangerous.

"Stairs," I say as I pause outside the door leading to the stairwell.

Behind me Jim grunts, and I shove the door open and step back, waiting for movement. Nothing happens, and the lack of stench tells me the way is clear, so I go. Moving up the stairs. Keeping close to Jim and trying to stay out of the beam of the flashlight. Every now and then my head dips in front of the beam and the stairwell in front of us goes dark, but all I have to do is adjust my movement and the way is lit up again.

Our heavy breathing and the pounding of our footsteps echo through the darkness as we move, making it impossible for my heartbeat to reach a normal rhythm. But I don't stop until we make it to the third floor.

"Take a second," Jim says when I reach for the knob. "Take a few breaths and give yourself a second to calm down."

"Not sure that's possible," I say.

Jim doesn't answer, and the silence that falls over us is

broken only by the occasional thump from the distance.

"You focused?" Jim says after a few seconds. "You leave whatever had you distracted back on the bus?"

"Yeah," I say even though it's a lie.

The distraction is here in every breath I take. In every shadowy corner stands someone from my past, glaring at me for letting them down or screwing them over. Megan with her face covered in bruises and tears streaming down her cheeks. That tattooed asshole from the van who won't stop looking at the knife in my hand, the same one that Axl sank into his forehead. Girls I turned my back on when the men around me were using them for sport. And most of all, Hadley Lucas, who is forever trapped in the Monte Carlo. They're all here, blaming me for what happened.

"Let's go then," Jim says, his voice sounding far away and dreamlike.

I turn the knob and yank the door open. Running inside. Jim is behind me with the flashlight, illuminating the way when the first zombie charges, still fast and ripe despite his months in this place.

A scream rips its way out of me when I swing my knife toward him, the blade slashing through his face and into his brain so easily it shocks even me. He falls and I pull the knife free just as a second bastard charges. In the beam of the flashlight his face is so distorted that I find myself frozen, blinking to clear the image as he growls and rushes my way. No way the snake tattoo curled around his neck is real.

The tattoo disappears and I'm brought back to the present and what my goal here is: kill the bastards. I drive my knife into his head and he falls, and this time when the zombie charging me takes the form of the fat bastard from the van, I don't hesitate. He falls, and more come my way, each one a ghost from my past. Brad, that truck-driving asshole who betrayed us; Mitchell, the prick who couldn't accept the fact that he wasn't rich anymore; other men from the Monte Carlo I saw so briefly I can't believe my brain is even able to remember what they looked like. They run and I stab and they drop and it goes on and on until I feel like my lungs are going to explode. Then the last one drops, and silence falls over us as Jim pans his flashlight around, waiting. But nothing comes.

He turns on me, putting the light right in my face and making me squint. "What the hell was that?"

"I was killing zombies," I say, turning away from him and heading down the hall. "The area isn't clear yet."

Jim jogs after me, not saying a word, but every time I glance his way the fire in his eyes makes me cringe. We move through the halls of the ICU, searching the dark corners for other bodies. A barely moving creature with both legs missing below the knees tries to pull itself toward us, but I stop him with one jab to the brain. Other than that, the ward seems to be empty.

When we've checked everything, Jim grabs my arm and forces me to turn. "You have thirty seconds to tell me what kind of demons you're fighting."

"And if I don't tell you?" I ask, suddenly angry that Jim seems to think he's the only one who gets a say in how all this goes down.

"I'll be looking for another partner. We may be done with the hard part for now, but come spring all these assholes will probably be back, and I'm not going to have someone at my side who can't keep his head on straight." He glares, and even in the darkness of the hospital, his eyes seem to flash. "Is this about your girl? About who she is?"

My shoulders stiffen against my will, and even though I try to relax, I know it's too late. Jim saw it.

"I don't know what you're talking about," I say, shaking my head.

"Don't give me that bullshit. I had her pegged the first time I saw her. Hadley Lucas. Shit. You know how much free time I had to just sit on my ass and watch movies when I was in prison? Too much." Jim lowers the flashlight, giving my dilated pupils a rest. "I don't blame her for trying to hide, but what I don't get is why the hell she acts like she's about to be

108

jumped every time she looks over her shoulder."

"We all went through bad shit when this first started," I say, looking down. "You know that."

"Yeah well, that doesn't tell me why you look at her like a puppy who got caught chewing on his master's favorite shoes."

"Bad shit," I mutter.

Jim doesn't say anything, and when I finally lift my head, I find him staring at me. Still waiting.

"Something happened when we pulled into the hospital parking lot," he finally says.

"It was my fault, okay?" I snap, then shake my head. "That's all you need to know. Ginny went through some really bad shit and it was my fault. It wasn't just her either. My sister, she's dead because of me. I tried to save her, but it was too late, and the things I had to be a part of to try and get her back…" I shake my head. "Bad shit."

"You said that," Jim replies, letting out a deep breath. "Bad shit is my middle name, so I get what you're feeling. But you need to remember one thing: none of that stuff is you."

"Is that how you live with yourself?" I spit at him, wanting to take the focus off my crimes while bringing his to light. "I can't help wondering exactly what kind of bad shit sent you to prison."

"You don't want to know what I was before all this, golden boy."

"Was? So you're telling me you're a changed man?"

Jim snorts and turns away. "Aren't we all?"

He has a point, but I can't help being pissed that he still won't tell me. He seems to think that he needs to know all my deepest, darkest secrets. What makes him any better?

"I shared," I say, grabbing his arms. "Now it's your turn."

Jim shakes me off, barely flinching, then pulls out a cigarette. He shrugs as he pops it between his lips. "You hardly shared."

"Then you *hardly* share. I need to know whose back I'm watching. Are you a dangerous man?"

Jim lights his cigarette, watching me the whole time. He takes a long drag, holding the polluted air in for a second before blowing it out of the corner of his mouth. Never once taking his gaze off me. "You of all people should know that every man is dangerous given the right circumstances."

"That's not what I mean and you know it," I hiss, stepping closer.

"I had a shitty childhood. Parents were addicts, and most of the time I was left to fend for myself. So I did. Did it so much that it got to the point where the things going on around me didn't matter. It didn't matter who I hurt when I swiped someone's purse, or later when I held up a liquor store. It also didn't matter when I had to shoot someone to get away. It was all part of survival for me." Jim inhales another mouthful of smoke, and it comes out when he says, "So yeah. I was a dangerous man. Still am, only now the only assholes who have to worry about it are the dead who get in my way."

I step back so I'm out of his cloud of smoke. "That's all I wanted to know. I just had to make sure it wasn't something else."

"Rapist?" Jim says, his eyes narrowing on my face.

I flinch, and there's no way he misses it, but he doesn't look smug or even satisfied.

"Thanks for telling me," I say, turning away from him. "Now let's get these bodies out of here."

THE BUS PULLS TO A STOP, AND I HAVE TO DRAG myself out of my seat. My arms ache from dragging bodies all day, and there isn't a millimeter of dry or warm skin on my body.

"Can't wait to get a hot shower," I mutter as I pull myself to the front of the bus with all the other men on the clearing crew.

"Hot tub would be nice right about now," Jim says even though we've barely spoken since our confrontation in the ICU.

The groan I let out sounds almost orgasmic, but my partner doesn't bat an eye. He probably feels the same way. After all the work we've put in the last few weeks, we deserve it. But no matter how sore or tired or freezing I am, I have to admit it's a good feeling. Because we've finally finished. We finally cleared the last street and loaded the last body that isn't covered in snow. The fence is up and being reinforced. Next week we'll be working on cleaning out houses and moving people in. We've done it.

I'm practically skipping when I step off the bus, so excited to talk to Ginny that it takes me a few seconds to realize she's standing in front of me. She's shivering, the snow up to her knees, probably soaking wet too since she's only wearing jeans. But the expression on her face tells me she doesn't care. Especially when my eyes meet hers and they light up, the green stark and vivid against her pale skin and flushed cheeks.

I hurry toward her, slipping a little when my feet hit a patch of ice hidden by the snow. Ginny giggles as she reaches out to steady me, and I smile in return. All the anger from earlier forgotten. All the guilt and pain of the past gone in the presence of her smiling face.

"We're done!" I say, practically yelling.

Ginny's smile doesn't fade, but the look she shoots me says she doesn't quite believe it's true. "You're finished?"

"Cleared the hospital today and dragged out all the bodies. Tomorrow they're going to work on reinforcing the fence while my crew does another sweep of the streets to make sure we got all the bastards. And Corinne will get another group on cleaning out the houses. We're going to have a home soon."

Ginny's lips curl into an even bigger smile, and she runs her hands over her stomach. "A home. I can't believe such a thing could exist in this world."

I pull her in for a hug, allowing her body heat to wash away the shivering in my bones. "It can and we're going to have it. Me and you and our baby. We're going to have it all."

She nods, and even when she lets out a little sniffle, I don't let her go. Instead I hold her tighter, trying to reassure her. When I look up, my gaze meets Jim's. Everyone else seems to have hurried to get inside, but Jim stands not too far from us. Just smoking and watching, the expression on his face giving away nothing about what's actually going through his head.

CHAPTER TEN

JON

I was starting to think this day would never come," Ginny says, her back to me as she scans the dorm room one final time.

"You have everything?" I ask from the doorway, anxious to get out of here and start a new chapter of our life. It's only up from here on out. I can feel it in every inch of my body.

Ginny nods but doesn't turn. I know she isn't sad to say goodbye, but I can't help wondering if she's a little scared to move forward. I'll be with her, a fact I don't go a day without reminding her of, but the future still scares her. Mainly because we have no idea what's going to happen, and no matter how much I want to, I can't protect her from everything. With each passing day, the baby grows bigger and our past slips farther and farther away. Part of that is good: saying goodbye to Hadley Lucas. But another part scares the hell out of her because it might mean admitting Vivian and Axl and the others are gone for good.

"I'm ready," Ginny says even though her voice shakes with uncertainty.

"Let's go, then."

She turns my way, and I grin, every inch of my body vibrating with excitement like a little boy on Christmas morning. It causes the worry lines etched across Ginny's forehead to ease just a little.

She comes to join me, and together we head down the hall to the stairs. Just like us, other people are heading out to their assigned homes. Starting a new life that is full of possibility and shockingly full of hope.

I grab Ginny's hand the second we step outside, giving it a squeeze and shooting her a smile at the same time. The snow is still thick, but the sidewalks have been cleared enough to make our walk easy. I shiver when the wind blows, but I'm so full of happiness that I don't really feel the chill in the air at all.

"The house has three bedrooms," I say, winking. "One for us and one for the baby."

"And a third for guests?" Ginny says with a snort.

"No." I watch her out of the corner of my eye. "The third will be for our second child."

Ginny narrows her eyes on me, but I don't crack a smile. "We haven't even gotten through this pregnancy and you already have me knocked up a second time?"

"Just wishful thinking."

There's more to it than just the simple hope for a second child. Wishful thinking encompasses the birth of this baby and its survival and the love that I know Ginny sometimes doubts she will be able to give it. It also includes us. That we stay happy and safe enough to create a second life. That's where my desire to have more comes from. If we had a baby after this, it would mean so many amazing things about the future.

We reach our new street, and once again I give Ginny's

114

hand a squeeze. Three houses go by before I stop in front of a little brown one made of brick. I picked it out specifically for Ginny and me. It has a porch with a swing and a couple empty flowerpots that will be perfect when spring comes. Ginny could drop a few seeds in and see what happens. Maybe. It seems like something a normal person living a normal life would do, which is who she wants to be.

"What do you think?" I ask, holding my breath as my wife, the love of this new life I'm starting, looks the place over.

"It's..." Ginny takes a deep breath, but no more words come out.

I turn to face her, the smile melting from my lips. Maybe it's too simple. I picked it because it was small and quaint and I knew that's what she wanted, but maybe she's not sure anymore. Maybe she's comparing this house to the place she lived in before all this, back when she was the famous Hadley Lucas and life was filled with everything fine and expensive.

"You don't like it?" I ask when she still doesn't say anything.

"No," Ginny says, taking my hand. Her eyes fill with tears, which she tries and fails to blink away. One slides down her cheek, and even though I want to brush it away, I keep my hand where it is. Waiting. "That's not what I meant. It's just so overwhelmingly optimistic, and even though I want to be excited, it scares the shit out of me."

"Hey," I say, pulling her to me. Hugging her against my body as we stand on the sidewalk in front of our new house, surrounded by snow. "It's okay. You don't need to be scared anymore, and any time you start to feel that way, I want you to look at the ring on your finger and remember that I've made an oath to always be with you. To keep you safe no matter what it costs me."

Ginny nods, her cheek rubbing against my chest. Wiping away the tears. I know there are a million doubts in her mind, but I can only hope and pray that none of them have anything to do with me. I will die to keep her safe, and I want her to know that.

"You want to go inside?" I ask, pulling back. "See our new home?"

Ginny wipes away the tears still shimmering on her cheeks. "I do."

"Let's go, then," I say, taking her hand and pulling her up the stairs with me.

We step into the small living room, and Ginny freezes, letting out a deep sigh of contentment. I scan the room as she looks around. It's neat—cleaned by the crew assigned to the homes—and shabby even compared to my old way of life, but perfect in my eyes. The couches are worn and comfortable-looking, and the dining room table that sits halfway between the living room and kitchen has enough room for six people. Six. I can't imagine ever having that many people in my home. Everything looks comfortable and warm and inviting. It's a relief to find the pictures of the former inhabitants have been removed, making it seem more like it belongs to Ginny and me than to the past.

"It's so perfect," Ginny says, shaking her head. "Exactly what we need. Nothing more and nothing less."

"I knew you'd like it," I say, squeezing her hand as I pull her farther into the house.

I take her down the hall, past the bathroom—which isn't useless, thanks to the electricity now running through the whole city—and a small bedroom, painted pink. The next one is decorated in blues and greens with little white clouds on the walls. Ginny smiles when I look her way, and I can't hold back my own grin. There is something so amazing about the thought of Ginny bringing my children into this world.

The door at the end of the hall is open, and Ginny pokes her head in, her eyes moving over the queen bed that sits dead center. It takes up most of the room, but to me it's exactly what it needs to be. A symbol that we are starting something new and real and better than anything we could have ever hoped for in this world.

116

"Thank you," Ginny says, turning to face me.

I wrap my arms around her and cover her lips with mine. The tenderness in her kiss is unmistakable, but it doesn't overshadow her desire. My mouth moves faster over hers, my tongue sweeping into her mouth as we stumble toward the bed—our bed. I pull my shirt over my head and Ginny follows my lead, then my lips crash back against hers. We fall to the bed, still dressed below the waist, but it doesn't take long for me to decide I need to fix that. I pull the zipper on Ginny's jeans down as I kiss my way over her chest to her stomach, pulling her pants over her legs in the process. She kicks the pants away as I take care of my own jeans, and then I'm back on her and we're both naked and every move of Ginny's lips tells me that she can't get enough of me. That she loves me and needs me and can't picture a life without me. Together we are perfect. More than anything I could have ever hoped for in the wake of the virus. Ginny is my future, and being here now, as our bodies move together, I know that everything will be exactly as it should be as long as she's by my side.

"I love you, Ginny," I say, my lips brushing her earlobe.

"I need you," she gasps, making me groan and move faster. "Always."

FEBRUARY

CHAPTER ELEVEN
AXL

I rub my hands together and blow into 'em, but it don't do a thing. I've never felt cold like this in my life. We had winters back in Tennessee, but they weren't nothin' like this. Snow fallin' on us a foot at a time like it's tryin' to kill us. It might even succeed if we ain't careful.

"We been here for three hours and we ain't seen a damn thing," Angus mutters, shakin' his head.

He spits, and I watch the little brown spot melt its way through the snow like it's acid burnin' through a piece of metal.

"I got a bad feelin' about this whole thing," I say, still starin' down at the spot. "We can't get us a kill pretty soon and we ain't gonna have a choice. We're gonna hafta butcher some of them animals. That's gonna make spring rough, too."

Angus shifts on his side of the deer stand and the whole thing shakes, but I don't blink. It's secure. I set the thing up myself just to be sure it was done right. Not that Angus don't know how, I just trust the thing better when I'm the one that's done it.

"We still got them MREs," he says.

"Yup, but they ain't gonna last long. We got fourteen people and 'bout three hundred of them packages left?"

"Sounds 'bout right."

Angus spits again while I do the math in my head real fast. The numbers seem all wrong, so I do it again, but it comes out the same. Shit.

"Fourteen people eatin' two meals a day, that's twenty-eight a day. We got three hundred, so that means with us eatin' two meals a day, it's only gonna last us 'bout a week and a half."

Angus turns so he's facin' me. "You're shittin' me."

"Nope."

He narrows his eyes on me like he don't believe it. "You don't got a calculator. How'd you figure that out?"

"I ain't a dumbass, Angus, I can do math in my head."

"Shit." Angus stares at the ground with his lips puckered. "Maybe you shoulda gone to college. Maybe I was wrong."

"Shut up," I snap. "That's got nothin' to do with all this. College don't mean shit, and all that other stuff is in the past, anyhow. We gotta worry 'bout this right here. 'Bout what we're gonna eat and how we're gonna keep all them people alive."

Angus nods, but he don't stop puckerin' his lips. He's been different since I got shot leavin' the shelter, and the bite changed him even more. He's still a hard ass sometimes, but he's tryin'. I know it ain't just for my sake neither. It's like he suddenly has some kind of hope for the future or something.

"We're gonna have to go further out to hunt," he says. "Take 'nother trip to that town or one farther away."

"The huntin' we can do, but with all this snow it's gonna be hard to go out lookin' for supplies. We ain't got no plows, and this shit is deep. If we do it, we're gonna hafta take them snowmobiles, which'll leave us exposed. I know we ain't seen no zombies lately, but who knows what the towns are like. We're sittin' here assumin' all them bastards froze, but we don't know nothin' for sure."

"Shit," Angus mutters again.

"Yeah."

We go back to sittin' in silence. The trees 'round us move when the wind blows, and snow falls from the branches. The sun is behind the clouds, but I can tell it's gettin' late. We gotta be thinkin' 'bout headin' back soon or we'll be stuck out in the dark. We got no flashlights since all the batteries died two days ago, and we got no hope of findin' more unless we make a run.

"Should head back," Angus says like he's read my mind.

He scoots across the stand so he can climb down, and I follow, thinkin' the whole mess through. Feelin' responsible for where we are.

"We shoulda gone south." Maybe if I hadn't been shot, maybe if I'd been thinkin' different, I woulda made the right call. It's hard to say.

"No use bringin' all that up." Angus grunts and jumps the last two feet to the ground. "We're here now. It ain't like we can pack everybody up and move 'em. Not with all this damn snow on the ground."

He's right, dammit.

I climb down with my lips puckered just like Angus. It's an old habit that I've never really liked, but there are more important things to worry about now. Who cares if I look like I just sucked on a lemon? Nobody in our group. Hell, we're all gonna be prayin' for a lemon to suck on in a few weeks.

Angus an' me hike through the snow, headin' back the way we came. We ain't seen a sign of the dead since early December, and even then it was only a frozen pile of decayin' flesh. The bastard could hardly open his mouth, forget tryin' to attack. If we make it through the winter, we may be in luck. I don't see how these things will be able to come back from all this. Course, I don't know a whole lot 'bout it neither.

"How long's it been since we lost Hollywood?" Angus asks out of nowhere.

"November." I shake my head, wishin' like hell Hadley and Jon hadn't gotten lost. "Goin' on three months now."

Angus swears. "You think they're alive?"

"Hard to say." I exhale and look 'round. Even though Vivian's back at the house, I have a hard time forcin' the words out. She ain't lost hope, but I can't see how the two of 'em coulda made it on their own. Not with Hadley bein' knocked up too. "Doubt it."

"Blondie's takin' it real hard."

"Yup."

"You never told her?"

Damn. Wish I hadn't told Angus. Wish it had never happened. "Shouldn't have told you. It didn't mean nothin'."

"Like hell, I'm your brother. You had to tell me."

"Whatever. Don't go runnin' your mouth to nobody. Vivian don't know, and she don't need to. I don't got a clue why Hadley kissed me, but as far as I'm concerned, it never happened."

"Whatever you say." Angus spits, then grins. "Still, not many people can say an actress made a move on 'em. That's gotta be something."

I roll my eyes. Leave it to Angus. "She ain't an actress no more. I don't know what it was 'bout, but it wasn't 'bout me."

It's a damn lie, though. I know what it was 'bout, at least partly. I saw Hadley hidin' in the bushes that day and went to see if everything was okay. There she was, holdin' a pregnancy test, lookin' like I caught her robbin' a bank. She was scared shitless, and kissin' me had somethin' to do with that. I just know it. People do crazy things when they're scared.

Angus exhales and watches the steam rise in front of him. "We can always butcher them animals if it comes down to it. I know we wanted to wait 'til we had some bigger numbers, but if it comes to that or starvin', we got no choice."

"Yeah." I nod. "We still got a lot of them canned goods

124

we took from Sam's Club too."

"Will that and the MREs get us through the rest of the winter?" Angus narrows his eyes on me like he thinks I'm gonna lie.

"Doubt it. Not all the way."

"Then we gotta go," Angus says. "Gotta head to that town and see if we can find us some more food. Gotta do what we can to make sure everybody is good."

I nod, thinkin' it through. I hate to even think 'bout doin' it when the weather's been so shitty, but Angus is right. It's gotta be done.

"Let's do it, then."

First thing I see when the fence comes into view is Vivian standin' at the gate. It ain't her turn to take watch, but I knew she'd be there. Freezin' her ass off, refusin' to go inside 'til I was back. Least she's armed.

She sees us and moves to unlock the gate, holdin' it open for us to walk through. I give her arm a squeeze on my way by.

"Nothing?" she asks as she pushes the gate shut behind us.

"Didn't see a damn thing."

"Livin', dead, or walkin' dead," Angus chimes in.

We take off toward the houses, and Vivian sighs. "We're in trouble if we don't get some supplies."

I nod and Angus spits, but none of us says a damn thing. Ain't much we can say 'bout it. We all know it's true, and the stress of it all is startin' to take its toll. Things was good right after Angus got bit. People was gettin' along. The future looked so fuckin' bright I thought it would blind us all. But it's goin' downhill fast.

The house comes into view, and a few seconds later, the front door opens. Brady steps out and looks 'round, and when he spots us, he pushes his way through the snow. It'll take him a minute to get to us since the snow is all the way up to his thighs. He don't look like he's got nothin' good to say, so I ain't exactly in a hurry.

"What's goin' on now?" I call when he's still more than six feet away from us.

"I think one of the cows is sick."

"Shit," I mutter. "Is it from not eatin'? If it is, I say we just kill him now. That way we at least get some meat out of it."

Brady shrugs. "Hard to say, but if I had to guess, I'd say he's starving. We could be taking a risk by eating him though. If he's sick with something else and it makes all of us sick, we'll be in real trouble. It could kill us all."

"Not sure we're gonna last much longer either way." I press my lips together and stare at the snow like it's gonna tell me what to do. "We gotta try somethin'."

"I agree."

I look up and meet Brady's gaze. He's worried, just like me. We've been tryin' to keep everybody fed, but no matter how many times we work on ways to ration the food, it ain't enough.

"I'll get on it," I say with a sigh, headin' for the house.

"Axl," Brady calls after me.

I turn and find the three of them standin' in the same place as before. Starin' at me.

"Parvarti's on it already. You don't have to do everything yourself, you know. We're all in this together." Brady lifts his arms, and for some reason it reminds me of a one of them statues of the Virgin Mary people used to put on their dashboards. Wish he could work a few miracles for us. We need it.

Angus spits, and Vivian comes over to stand next to me. She puts her hand on my arm, and I know she's thinkin' the same thing. She's been tellin' me for weeks that I gotta let others help. It ain't easy. Every time I walk through the front door, I feel like everybody turns to look at me. Like they're askin' me what I'm gonna to do keep 'em warm and fed.

"I got a responsibility to them people," I say, pointin' to the house. Just thinkin' 'bout walkin' in there makes my stomach harden. It feels like somethin's eatin' away at me from the inside out. "I gotta keep them alive."

"No one's blaming you for our circumstances. You did your best, you still are, but you can't control everything." Brady shakes his head.

Angus spits again, then kicks snow over it. "We're gonna be just fine. We been through worse shit than this. Dead bastards are freezin', and it won't be long before the animals realize it's safe to come out. We'll hunt, find us some meat, and we'll make it through the winter. We're just all gonna hafta come together."

Brady and Vivian look at Angus like he's crazy, and I know it ain't 'cause they don't agree. It's cause them words don't sound right comin' outta his mouth. Angus don't work with people. Especially not these people.

"You're brother's right," Brady says, shakin' his head like he can't believe he's sayin' it. Makes two of us.

"We could also check Hope Springs out," Vivian says.

Course she'd bring that up. Even though we decided spring was the best bet, she can't stop thinkin' 'bout it. She's been wantin' us to go there since we heard 'bout it, only I can't shake the feelin' that somethin' ain't right 'bout that place.

"We'll kill the cow, but we can't eat it," I mutter, still starin' at the snow.

"Shit," Angus says. "Seems like a damn waste. Can't we risk it?"

"No." I shake my head and look up, meetin' my brother's gaze. "Tomorrow Angus and me'll go out on the snowmobiles. Head to Duncan and see if we can find us some more supplies."

"And Hope Springs?" Brady asks.

I look up and hold his gaze. "We wait 'til spring like we already decided. It's the best thing to do."

Brady nods and Angus grunts, then they turn and head toward the house. Vivian shivers at my side, and it hits me how cold it is out here. I was so focused on what was goin' on that I forgot I been freezin' my ass off for the last few hours.

I put my arm 'round Vivian and pull her with me as I follow the others. "Let's get inside and get warm."

"I don't understand why you won't give in about this." She moves closer to me, turnin' her head so her warm breath hits my face when she talks. "You'll risk a trip to Duncan, but you won't even take the time to stake out Hope Springs. We don't have a single reason to think the people there are anything other than a group of survivors trying to make a go of it. Just like us."

"Would you have passed the Monte Carlo and thought the same thing?" I ask.

She exhales, and it takes her a few seconds to say, "I don't know. Probably."

"Then you should understand why I'm bein' careful. We ain't goin' through that again. We've survived too much, and I won't risk it."

"Okay," she says, sighin' again. "Just promise me that if things don't get better soon you'll consider it."

"If it comes down to starvin' or takin' a chance on that town, we'll take a chance. But we'll plan ahead." We reach the house, but before we follow Angus and Brady inside, I stop and turn to face Vivian. "But it ain't gonna come down to that. Angus and me'll find some supplies. We'll get us a kill, too. I'm gonna take care of everybody. I swear."

"I know you will," she says.

Vivian kisses me lightly, then pulls me into the warm house after the others.

CHAPTER TWELVE

AXL

"You sure you know how to get there?" Brady asks.

"Yup," I say, not lookin' up from makin' sure the trailer is secured to the snowmobile. "Duncan ain't far, and it should be cake to get there. Assumin' the zombies really are frozen and we don't run into anybody who wants trouble."

"Don't even suggest that," Vivian says.

I look up to find her standin' next to Darla, both women huggin' themselves against the cold.

I wish Vivian would go inside. Never in my life have I wanted to keep somebody safe the way I do her, and she makes it almost impossible. She's too determined to be in the thick of things all the time. We had us a helluva fight last night when she said she was comin'. I wasn't sure if I'd be able to get her to back down, but I finally did. She's stubborn as hell.

"It'll be fine," Darla says.

Angus drops a bag onto the trailer and nods. "That's right. You got nothin' to worry 'bout. I'll bring him back."

"If I can trust anyone with his life, Angus, it's you," Vivian replies. "Unfortunately, you aren't God."

Brady snorts and glances up at Vivian. "Unfortunately? Can you imagine a world where Angus had god-like powers?"

"Right," she says, laughin'. "Women would be walking around naked and dip would grow on trees."

I chuckle as I stand. I love my brother, but that sure would be a messed-up world.

"Like Dopey here could do a better job," Angus mutters.

"Ignore them." Darla steps between them so she can hug Angus. "You just focus on what you gotta do. And you be sure to bring yourself back safe too."

"We'll be good." I finish tyin' everything off and move toward Vivian. "We gotta get a move on if we wanna be back before dark."

"Be careful," Vivian says.

She throws her arms 'round me, and even though I'm anxious to get movin', I hug her back. I ain't worried about goin', not with how slow things have been lately, but that don't mean I'm gonna rush off. This here is what I'm fightin' for.

"We'll be back before the sun sets," I say, my lips brushin' her hair.

"You better."

I let her hug me for a few seconds longer before pullin' away and turn to find Angus already on his snowmobile. The few bags we have with emergency supplies and extra weapons sit on the trailer, tied down so they don't fall, but otherwise the thing is empty. Hopefully it will be full when we get back.

I swing my leg over the snowmobile and start the engine, givin' Vivian one last look before I pull my goggles on. Angus waves to Darla once before takin' off, and I follow. Headin' over the snow-covered streets toward the gate, where Al and Lila wait to let us out. We slow when we get closer, but we don't hafta stop. Once the gate is open, Angus speeds up, headin' out of our little town. I give the teens a wave as I speed by, followin' my brother through the gate.

We head toward Duncan, passin' nothin' but nature covered in snow for miles and miles. Everywhere I look, the stuff is untouched. Not a single footprint from an animal or man or zombie. It's unreal.

After 'bout fifteen minutes, Angus slows in front of me. I follow his lead, pullin' over next to him when he comes to a stop.

He rips his goggles off, pointin' to my left. "Look at that!"

I pull my own goggles off, but it takes a second for my eyes to adjust to the bright sun reflectin' off the snow. Even when they do, I can't see nothin' but a branch covered in white. When it hits me what I'm really lookin' at, I let out a low whistle. What I thought was a stick pokin' outta the snow is actually an arm, and behind that is a head. The longer I look, the more the bodies come into view. They're spread out 'cross a ten-foot stretch of land. Frozen solid.

"Damn," I say, shakin' my head. "How many you think there are?"

"Hard to say. Dozens?"

Angus spits, then hops off the snowmobile and heads over. I almost tell him to be careful, but there ain't much of a point. Them zombies ain't goin' nowhere, and they sure as hell ain't 'bout to get up and bite us. Even if they did, Angus is immune.

I climb off my own snowmobile and follow, too curious 'bout the whole thing to hang back.

"Seems like a good time to take care of 'em," Angus says, pullin' out his knife. "If we can find the heads."

He actually has a point.

He leans down and brushes the snow away 'til a skull comes in view, then slams his knife into the head. Almost no black leaks out—must be too frozen—but little moans break through the ice and a couple limbs twitch like they're tryin' to move. They don't make it far, and they're slower than hell. These things are more harmless than sheep right now.

"Sounds like a plan," I say, followin' Angus's lead.

"Careful now. One of these bastards sinks his teeth into my hand and all I'm gonna need is a Band-Aid. They get you, and it'll be a bullet to the brain."

"Don't know that for sure," I say, jabbin' my knife into the head closest to me. "Maybe I'm immune too. We're brothers."

"Maybe, but I ain't 'bout to risk it. You let me take the chances while you play it safe."

I ain't gonna argue, even if I know there's no way in hell I'll ever be able to just stand on the sidelines when trouble hits.

Angus and I move 'cross the bodies, stabbin' one zombie after the other. I stop countin' after ten and just focus on finishin' this up so we can move on. I told Vivian we'd be back before the sun went down, and I plan on keepin' my word. Only a part of it has to do with my promise, though. The other part is the fact that there's no way in hell I wanna get caught out here in the dark.

It only takes us a few more minutes, and when we're sure we got 'em all, we head back to the snowmobiles and move on. We don't see any other zombies before we hit Duncan, but with all this snow, we could be drivin' right over 'em. We'll have to come out again when it gets warmer, after some of the snow has melted but not before the bodies have had a chance to thaw. Assumin' they do. We still don't know what's gonna happen come spring.

We reach Duncan and follow the same course we took last time, headin' through a neighborhood and cuttin' over to where all the stores are. Sam's Club will be our first stop even though we ain't sure there's gonna be anything there. Who knows how much them folks from Hope Springs left behind. Nothin', if they was smart.

Just like every other inch of land we crossed since leavin' home, the streets of Duncan are clear. We pass a few piles of snow that could be a body or two but don't stop to find out. Much as I like the idea of takin' 'em out when they're down, I don't wanna waste the time right now. We gotta be sure we have time to go to a few places since I'm not holdin' my breath that Sam's Club will have much more than a few missed cans — and most likely it'll be shit we don't wanna eat.

We park right in front of the door, which is wide open, and the second his engine's off, Angus pulls out his knife. I do the same as I scan the area, but it's still clear and as silent as a tomb. Never heard silence like this, not even when we was out on the road for weeks at a time. Back then we was still able to find some animals, but now the birds have mostly flown south for the winter and all the four-legged creatures seem to be hidin' — or dead. It's like the virus wiped them all out too.

"Well, let's go on in and see what's left," Angus says, headin' for the door.

I wade through the snow after him, which has drifted a good five feet into the store. It's dark all the way in the back, but the sun shines in through the open door and windows 'nough to light up the front a little, which is good, since we're outta batteries. Gonna hafta see if we can find some more.

"This way," Angus calls, headin' into the darkness.

I follow, scannin' the boxes we pass to see if there's anything we might wanna come back for after the snow melts. Trampolines and fake Christmas trees and a display of holiday decorations — not much I'd wanna haul outta here. We pass the jewelry counter, but it's already been ransacked. I move closer, and my feet crunch across the broken glass spread over the floor. Ain't a single ring or necklace left in the case. Weird that somebody would bother takin' all that.

"What you suppose somebody wanted with that shit?" Angus asks.

"Who knows? Can't think of anything we'd need it for, that's for sure."

"Just dumb, I guess."

Angus turns away from the counter, and I follow, but I can't stop wonderin' 'bout the jewelry. Don't make sense that the person who took it all is just dumb. I can't imagine many people that dumb still bein' alive after all these months—you gotta have smarts to make it through this shit—so by my thinkin', the morons were probably the ones killed off first. Which makes me think whoever took this stuff had a purpose. What, though, I don't know.

I take inventory of the stuff that's been cleaned out as we move back through the store. Movies and video games got left behind, along with the toys, but all the clothes, blankets, and pillows, and even a lot of the books, are gone. All the shampoo and soap and lotion and other hygiene products are missin' too. The aisle that used to have vitamins and protein bars has been cleared out, but the candy is still sittin' there, and the further back we go, the more empty shelves we pass. All the canned goods, all the prepackaged snacks. Cereal, flour, cookin' oil, and condiments, all gone. Ain't nothin' left of the food except the stuff that went moldy months ago and whatever was in the freezer. The stink of rotten meat is enough to make anybody's stomach turn, but even with my stomach spasmin' the way it is, I can't stop thinkin' 'bout the store. It's been picked clean.

"Nothin' left," Angus says. "Unless we wanna take back a few boxes of candy bars."

"I was hopin' they missed the protein bars. At least that woulda given us somethin'."

"Took some weird shit, though."

Angus heads back to the front of the store with me right behind him, goin' for the liquor. I'd be pissed if I didn't already know what he was thinkin'—booze is good for a few things other than drinkin', and Winston has 'bout wiped us out. If we found more, though, we could use it to start a fire or clean injuries when we run outta rubbin' alcohol. Be a good thing to have, but I got a feelin' anything that woulda been useful is gonna be long gone.

134

"Well, shit," Angus says when he comes to a stop in front of me.

I look over his shoulder and sigh even though I ain't surprised. There's plenty of beer and wine coolers left, but anything with high alcohol content has been taken.

Angus exhales and spins 'round, scannin' the store like he's trying to figure out where more stuff might be stashed. I head back toward the front, though. No point in hangin' 'round when there's nothin' left.

"What's that?" Angus says behind me.

I turn to find him headin' toward the registers. Even though I think he's wastin' time, I follow. Better to stick together.

When I get closer, I see what he's lookin' at. The belt leadin' up to the register is piled with a bunch of stuff like somebody's waitin' to check out. Good stuff too. Nuts and jerky, boxes of protein bars, peanut butter, and cans of fruit. There are even a few packages of batteries—somethin' we really need—and six bottles of vodka. It's a good haul and I won't walk away from it, but I ain't sure why it's sittin' here. No way whoever cleaned this store out just missed it.

"What's this?" Angus picks up a piece of paper and holds it out in front of him, squintin' at the words.

I go to his side and read the thing twice, but even after the second time, I don't got a clue what to say.

Hello and Greetings from Hope Springs!

As you can see, we've cleared the store of anything useful, but these supplies are meant as a gesture of peace and an invitation to join our community. If you haven't heard of us, please know that we are not far from here and we are friendly. More than that, we are dedicated to keeping survivors safe while starting over. We hope you will come join us, but either way please take these supplies so you can move forward.

Sincerely,

The Hope Springs Community

"I'll be damned," Angus says, shakin' his head. "They left

this shit so whoever came next wouldn't totally starve."

"Sure sounds like it."

I look back and forth between the note in Angus's hand and the supplies lined up next to us, and I can't help wonderin' if maybe I was wrong. Maybe we should check the place out after all.

"You think it's a trap?" Angus asks.

"What?" I tear my eyes away from the food so I can meet his gaze.

"This here note. Sure would be a good way to lure people in."

"Shit," I mutter. "I hadn't even thought 'bout that, but you got a good point. How do we know we can trust 'em?"

"Not sure, but I do know I wanna get all this loaded up and head out. We could swing by one more store. See if they left more stuff. If they did it here, I'd bet they did it down a ways at the Wal-Mart too."

Angus heads off to get a cart, and I jog after him. Another good point.

After we've loaded the supplies onto the trailer, we head down to Wal-Mart, where we find much of the same. Everything of any real use stripped from the store—includin' all the campin' and huntin' gear—and a pile of supplies up by the front. Just like Sam's Club, they've left a lot of high-protein foods that will help get us through the worst of things, and they've even included some first aid and survival gear this time. Sleepin' bags and a fishin' rod with some tackle. Whoever did this is either as merciful as Mother Teresa or as diabolical as the devil himself. It's hard to say which it is, though.

By the time we get everything loaded onto the trailers, it's gettin' late. Even though I promised Vivian we'd be back by dark, I can't help feelin' like we need to check out a few more places. The stuff we got is good, but it ain't gonna last us all winter.

"We could try a few houses," I say, rubbin' my hands together to keep 'em warm while Angus ties everything up.

136

"Probably should." He blows out a deep breath, watchin' when the steam rises over him. "Apartment might be better."

"How's that?"

"'Cause there were a bunch of people livin' close together. It'll give us more places to check without havin' to haul our asses through the snow."

"Makes sense," I say, lookin' 'round.

I spot a place 'cross the way that looks like it was pretty nice before all this. We go someplace shitty and there ain't gonna be no food. People who didn't have a lot of money didn't have extra food layin' 'round. I know 'cause that's what I grew up with.

"How 'bout that one," I say, pointin' toward the building.

Angus nods when he spots the place. "Yeah. That one looks like it'd be good. Let's go on over there. If we take too long, we can always sleep there for the night, too."

"I promised Vivian I'd be back before dark." I shake my head and climb onto the snowmobile.

"Don't you know promises are made to be broken?" he says as he pulls his goggles on.

Angus chuckles and starts his engine, flyin' away before I can tell him to shut the hell up. He's grinnin', though, and I find myself smilin' too as I head after him. I'm so used to Angus bein' a pain in the ass that I'm ready to argue with everything he says. Only the stuff he's been sayin' lately don't need no arguin'. He actually seems happy, which for Angus is damn strange.

We head 'cross the parkin' lot and over the street, turnin' when we reach the apartment buildin'. Angus heads 'round the side, pullin' to a stop soon as the snowmobile ain't in clear view of the road, and I park beside him. Back here, people passin' by shouldn't be able to see us. If there are any people out here, that is.

"Let's start on the first floor and see what we can find," Angus calls, headin' for the open door with a duffle bag slung over his shoulder.

I grab mine and hurry after him. "Sounds good."

It's cold inside the buildin', but not enough to mask the stuffiness in the air. I pull my knife and find myself thinkin' 'bout the one Angus gave me back when we was kids. I ain't seen it since we was at the hot springs, and I'm startin' to think it got lost. Probably happened when the horde attacked. It sucks 'cause I liked that knife.

Angus draws his own knife as he leads the way, lettin' out a low whistle. A scrapin' sound echoes through the hall, and I hold my breath, waitin' to see if zombies or anything else is gonna come runnin'. Nothin' does, so we keep movin'. It sounded more like small animals than a zombie, which is good. A few rats would give us some food if we don't find nothin' else.

The first apartment we come to is locked. Angus digs a crowbar outta his bag and uses it to pry the door open. The crack of splinterin' wood echoes through the hall, but still nothin' comes runnin'. Either they're frozen or the place is empty. I'd guess the second one.

"Kitchen," Angus says, steppin' to the right when we walk in.

I follow, and we make fast work of goin' through cabinets, findin' some canned chili and SpaghettiO's and a couple boxes of mac and cheese. Almost everything else we come 'cross has gone bad long ago, includin' a couple boxes of cereal and a bag of rice that've been chewed through by some kind of rodent—mice, if I had to guess. I even manage to find a bottle of vodka in the freezer, although the stink is so bad when I open the door that I gag and almost lose my lunch.

"Let's check out the rest of the place real quick," I say, headin' to the back, breathin' through my mouth to ease the nausea. I'll be glad when the world stops smellin' so bad.

It don't take long to search the rest of the place. There's only one bathroom and two bedrooms, along with a few closets. We find batteries and some first aid stuff—basic, but still stuff we need. We also take some cold medicine, Tylenol, shampoo, and soap. They're all things we're gonna need for the rest of our lives but might run out of. Angus even swipes a box of condoms from the bedside table before we head out.

After that, we work our way down the hall, checkin' every apartment on the right side before movin' to the left. There seems to be a pattern, though. Any apartment we gotta pry open has a few things we need, but the other ones are picked clean.

We get a decent load of stuff on the first floor, then take it out to the snowmobiles before headin' up to the second floor. It goes pretty much the same, and we come out with a big collection of canned food and three cases of water we found in apartments we had to pry open.

"Guess whoever looted this place didn't wanna bother breakin' down doors," Angus says as we head out. His arms are loaded down with the water, and he's gruntin' more with each step.

"Seems like it." I shake my head and reposition the bag I'm carryin' on my arm. "But why the hell not?"

"Beats me, but I'm sure glad they was too lazy to get it done."

Once we've loaded all the supplies from the second floor onto the trailer, we head back inside so we can check out the third and final floor.

"Gettin' dark," I say over my shoulder as we walk up.

"Yup. Hafta move fast or we ain't gonna be able to see a damn thing."

We reach the third floor, and I push the door open but stop in my tracks when the smell of shit hits me in the face.

"Son of a bitch," Angus mutters, coverin' his nose. "What the hell you think happened up here?"

"Septic problem?" I say, tryin' not to breathe outta my nose. It don't work, so I dig out my scarf and wrap it 'round my face to cover my nose. Even with it on, the stink is so bad it makes my eyes water. "But I think if that were the problem it would smell on the other floors too."

Behind me, Angus gags and bends over. I turn away when he upchucks on the floor, and my own stomach

139

jumps, forcin' me to swallow. Zombies I'm used to by now, even if they don't smell good, but this is something we ain't had to deal with yet.

When Angus is done heavin', he wipes his mouth. "We gonna check it out anyways?"

I shake my head, all ready to tell him I don't think it's worth, it when outta nowhere a gunshot booms through the hall.

Angus swears, and we both hit the ground, causin' him to swear even more. He scoots over and wipes his hand on the floor, and I realize that he landed in his own puke. It's the least of our worries though, especially when a second gunshot breaks out and dust rains down on us.

"Let's get the hell outta here," I say, inchin' back toward the door, wantin' nothin' more than to get downstairs before this asshole blows our heads off.

"Get out of here or I'll blow your head off!" somebody yells, echoin' my thoughts. "I don't want any cannibals near me!"

"Cannibals?" Angus whispers.

I shake my head and move closer to the stairs. "I don't know what the hell he's talkin' 'bout, but I know I'm okay never findin' out. Let's hightail it outta here."

Angus nods, but as we move, the guy fires again. Drywall explodes above us for a second time, and my heart goes crazy. Then Angus is on his feet, pullin' me up after him, and I'm runnin' into the stairwell. Movin' downstairs faster than I thought possible with Angus right behind me as another gunshot goes off behind us.

CHAPTER THIRTEEN

AXL

We don't stop runnin' 'til we're outside, and even then I barely pause to pull my goggles on. Whoever that asshole was, I wouldn't put it past him to try an' take us out from an upstairs window. Bastard was outta his mind.

We hop on the snowmobiles and speed off, but Angus don't head the way I thought he was gonna. I follow, keepin' real close to him and swearin' every couple seconds. We already had one close call today, and I ain't interested in hangin' 'round to see what other trouble we can get into.

Only one street over, Angus pulls between two houses. I follow, slowin' to a stop right behind him in the backyard of a house. When I kill the engine, Angus's laugh bounces off the houses 'round us and echoes through the emptiness.

"That was the damndest thing I ever did see!" he calls. "And you know what I keep thinkin'?"

"That you're glad you didn't get your balls shot off," I mutter, swipin' the goggles off my face so I can get a better look at him.

"That too. But I keep wonderin' if that son of a bitch didn't know 'bout the zombies. If he thought they was just people goin' 'round eatin' each other."

Some of my anger fades as I think it all through, but it don't make sense. It can't.

"No," I say, shakin' my head. "That'd mean he's been up on that third floor this whole time, and that don't make no sense. He had to have come out at some point. Right?"

"Hard to say. People do some crazy shit." Angus shrugs as he slides off his snowmobile.

I don't move. "What the hell are you doin'?"

"Wanna check a few other places out."

I look 'round like I'm expectin' zombies to close in on us, but the place is clear. Don't mean it's gonna stay that way, and I ain't lookin' to get into any more trouble.

"We gotta go, Angus. It's gettin' dark."

He digs through the supplies on the trailer, ignorin' me 'til he finds a flashlight and new batteries. "We're here. Might as well take a good look 'round."

I exhale, and steam rises up in front of me. Angus is right, but that don't mean I like it. I promised Vivian we'd be back by dark, and I know she's gonna be worried sick if we don't make it. Still, we're here and we don't know when we're gonna make it back. We need supplies. Bad.

Angus takes two steps toward the house before turnin' to look at me. "You comin'?"

"Fine." I sigh, but push myself off the snowmobile anyways. I got a bad feelin' 'bout this, but Angus has got a point.

We head through the snow, and my eyes are workin' overtime every step of the way. My heart's poundin' like crazy and I can't help feelin' like we're 'bout to get jumped. The area's clear, though. We make it 'round the house without a problem, and find the door wide open. It don't give

142

me much hope that there's gonna be anything useful inside, but Angus don't hesitate before goin' in. When the hell did he turn into such an optimist?

It's so dark inside the house that I can't see a damn thing. Thankfully, the people of Hope Springs left us a flashlight and batteries. Angus flips the thing on, lightin' up the room, and a shiver runs down my spine. The carpet's covered in brown streaks, and they're leadin' down the hall like somebody barely alive dragged themselves back that way. Or got dragged there by somebody else. I've seen enough dried blood over the last few months to know what it is, but I still ain't used to it. Hope I never am.

"It goes this way," Angus says, followin' the trail.

"Where the hell you goin'?" I hiss, not movin'.

"I wanna know what we're dealin' with, then we can look 'round."

Why's he always gotta sound so reasonable these days?

I pull my knife and follow Angus, feeling like the walls are closin' in on me as we follow the trail down the hall. It goes all the way to the end and stops at a closed door. Angus tries the knob and my body tenses, but it's locked. Of course, that don't stop Angus. He backs up, then rams his shoulder against the door. The wood splinters and the thing bursts open, and Angus stumbles in. The beam of his flashlight bounces 'round the room when he drops it, makin' it tough to focus on anything. He bends down to pick it up just as a low moan breaks out, but I don't even have time to tense up before the thing is lit up by the flashlight. Once I see the poor bastard, I can't feel nothin' but pity.

"Must've hurt like hell when he dragged himself down here," Angus says, shakin' his head.

He moves the light 'round, lightin' up the zombie in front of us. His legs are nothin' but bones with a little meat stuck to 'em in places, and his arms ain't much better. Even his stomach and chest have been chewed on. The damage is so bad that he can't even drag himself toward us. Hell, he can barely lift his head. All he can really do is chomp his mouth.

"Finish him off so we can look 'round," I mutter, shakin' my head.

Angus nods, and two seconds later his blade is stickin' in the dead guy's skull. The thing goes limp.

"Let's check this place out," I say, headin' toward the kitchen with Angus right behind me.

I've only set one foot in the livin' room when the sound of voices makes me freeze. Angus flips his light off and ducks down behind a chair, and I dive after him. The front door is wide open, givin' us a view of the front yard and street. I hold my breath when a few seconds later a light comes into view.

"Being out this late is stupid," someone outside says. "We should head back."

"Not yet. We need to check out a few more places."

Three figures come into view, stoppin' in the middle of the street. From where we are, I can't make a single thing out other than their shapes, but one of them is a big guy.

I duck when he turns our way, his flashlight shinin' into the livin' room Angus and me are hidin' in. The beam shines into the room, makin' long shadows, but leaves the corners dark. I freeze and hold my breath, cursin' Angus. We shoulda gotten the hell outta here when we had a chance. Now we're trapped and outnumbered by at least one. Could be more, though. Who knows how many friends these men have?

"We check this place out?" a man asks.

"I think we stopped at this house last time," another guy answers.

"I don't think so," says a third dude.

The light gets brighter as footsteps crunch through the snow. I slip my knife back into my belt and instead pull my gun. Next to me, Angus does the same.

"What you wanna do?" I whisper.

Angus shakes his head. "Stay put."

I nod as the footsteps get closer, and I find myself prayin'. Askin' God to send these men on their way. To hide us and our snowmobiles and our supplies. It's somethin' I ain't never done before, except maybe back when Vivian was missin', but I ain't gonna feel bad 'bout it now. It ain't just 'bout me. It's 'bout all our people. They're dependin' on Angus and me. We get caught or killed right now, and they're gonna starve for sure.

The footsteps stop so close that I can hear the dude breathin'. The flashlight moves 'round, lightin' up more of the room. I hold my breath, and Angus must too, 'cause I don't hear him breathin'. Not too far from us, the man's feet scuffle against the ground.

"Yeah," he says, his voice so loud it makes my heart thump faster. "We checked this one out. I remember all this blood."

He's there a second longer, his flashlight movin' 'round a few more times before the light is suddenly gone. I start to breathe easier, but then the light is back and he's movin' again. Only he ain't goin' away. He's comin' in.

"Thought we did this one," another guy calls.

"I was wrong," the guy who is now inside the house says. He stops when someone else steps into the room. "We came in, but we didn't search the place. Remember? We saw something moving across the street and went to look."

"Oh yeah." The second guy chuckles. "Found those people."

"Yup."

A shudder shoots through me, but I ain't sure why. They didn't say nothin' 'bout what they did with them people, only that they found 'em. Anything coulda happened.

"Where you think this blood goes?" the first guy says.

"Shit if I know," guy two says, and all I can think is: right past us.

The guy takes another step, and I know he's 'bout to round the chair. Then he'll be standin' right in front of us, and I wouldn't be surprised if we caught him off guard enough to make him shoot. If he has a gun. I don't know for sure since I couldn't see him, but I ain't 'bout to take any chances.

I stand, poppin' up right in front of the guy with the flashlight. He swears and steps back, and the guy standin' by the door rips out a weapon. Only it's too dark on that side of the room for me to see *what* it is.

"It's alright," I say, holdin' my hands up. My gun is still in my right hand, but I don't let it go. It ain't aimed at them, but I want them to know that I got it and that I ain't above usin' it.

"Where the hell did you come from?" the second guy says.

"Was searchin' the place when you came up." I keep my voice calm and level and as unthreatenin' as possible. "Wasn't sure if you was trustworthy, so I figured hidin' would be the best thing to do."

I choose my words carefully so I don't let on that Angus is behind me. They can't see him yet, and I don't want them knowin' he's here just in case things go bad. We gotta make sure at least one of us gets back home.

The first guy shakes his head and points the flashlight down, givin' me a chance to get a better look at him. Just like I thought, he's huge. Big and broad. He's probably got a good forty pounds on me. Don't mean I can't take him, but it does mean it's gonna be a helluva lot harder.

"You don't have to worry," he says, his voice boomin' through the empty house. "Although I'm not going to lie, I feel like shooting you in the leg for scaring the shit out of me."

The second guy laughs, but it's jumpy and puts me even more on edge than before. The third guy ain't 'round, and not knowin' where he is has me uneasy as hell.

"Where's your other friend?" I ask, tryin' to look past the first guy. It's dark outside and I can't see shit.

"He probably went on to the next house," guy one says. "We're just looking for supplies, same as you."

"We have a house on the other side of town. Some expensive place that had a big fence around it before all this started," the second guy blurts out, earnin' him a glare from the big guy.

146

"Relax," I say, tryin' to ease the big guy's mind. "I got a place. I don't wanna keep you from livin' your life, just like I'm sure you don't wanna keep me from livin' mine."

"No," the first guy says. "We aren't looking to expand, and we don't want any trouble."

"Good."

I pause and look back and forth between the two, tryin' to figure out what they're thinkin'. They don't got their weapons aimed at me now, which is good, but something 'bout them still makes me nervous. Sooner we get outta here, the better.

I nod toward the door, my hands still up. "You mind if I head out then?"

"Not at all." The first guy looks at guy two, who steps away from the door.

It leaves my way clear, but I can't say I'm exactly comfortable with how they're actin'. They're too accommodatin'. They ain't interested in askin' questions 'bout me or how many people I got livin' with me, which ain't any less suspicious than somebody askin' too many questions would be. Normal people are gonna wanna know how you've survived and what you've seen. They ain't gonna let you walk away without askin' something.

I look back and forth between the two men, tryin' to decide what to do. Angus and me can't leave our shit behind, but headin' home ain't exactly the best idea right now. They could follow us, and with the way they're actin', I wouldn't put it past them.

I glance down, and Angus's eyes meet mine. He nods and a second later gets to his feet, earnin' us another bout of swearin' from the men in the room. I lower my hands, still keepin' my gun down but not puttin' it away. They gotta be reminded that I'm armed.

"You have anyone else back there?" the first guy barks, his eyes so narrowed they look like black holes in his face.

"That's it," I say slowly, my own eyes dartin' back and forth between the two men in front of me.

"Had to be careful," Angus says. "You can understand."

"Shit." The big guy shakes his head and motions for the door. "Get out of here before you give me a heart attack."

Angus and me move at the same time, and I keep my eyes on the first guy the whole way to the door. Even though guy number two seems more jumpy, it's the other one that has me on edge. He's the one in charge. Nobody's gonna do a thing unless he gives the go ahead.

We make it to the door without gettin' attacked and Angus hurries out into the snow, but I've only set one foot outside when the first guy says, "Where have you been hiding out anyway? It seems like we would have bumped into you before now."

"Almost made it," Angus mutters just loud enough for me to hear.

I turn just as movement in the yard catches my eye and the third guy comes into view. Angus don't move, so I can only assume he's got me covered. When I turn back to face the livin' room, the other two guys have moved so they're standin' side by side in the center of the room.

"We found us a place not too far from here," I say. It ain't gonna be enough information and I know it, but I gotta try.

The first guy's eyebrows shoot up. "Just the two of you?"

"Just us," I lie.

He nods, but the look on his face tells me he knows I'm full of shit.

"Lonely life these days," he says, narrowin' his eyes on me even more. "Every group we've come across has been full of men. I keep thinking we'll find some women one of these days, but so far nothing."

"Makes you a bit paranoid," guy number two says. "Know what I mean? Somebody's got to have a woman or two tucked away. Just keeping them to themselves."

"Doesn't really seem fair with the way things are," the big guy says, drawin' my attention his way. "People should spread the wealth."

I nod, but it takes a few seconds to get any words out. My

throat is too tight. "I don't know nothin' 'bout all that. We been too focused on stayin' alive to worry 'bout women."

"Fags," the second guy says.

"I don't think so." The big guy's eyes narrow on me even more, then move behind me to Angus. I look back long enough to find my brother lookin' over his shoulder. When I glance back, the big guy's glarin' at me again. "I think they're brothers, and I don't think they're alone."

"You can think whatever you wanna think," Angus growls from behind me. "We got nothin' to hide."

I take a step away from the men in front of me, raisin' my gun as I move. "But we are gonna get outta here."

The men don't answer, and they don't try to stop us. Angus moves too, headin' back the way we came, and I follow. I walk sideways as we round the house, keepin' one eye on the front of the house so they can't sneak up on us. They don't follow, but I can't shake the feelin' that they're gonna try and figure out where we're headed. If they do, it's gonna be bad.

"What you wanna do?" Angus asks when we reach the snowmobiles.

I throw a leg over mine as I pull on my goggles. "Head out. See if they follow us."

"If they do?"

"Shit," I mutter. "I don't know. Find a place to hide out 'til daylight?"

Angus nods as he climbs on his own snowmobile but says, "There ain't much between here and home."

"No shit," I hiss.

Damn. I wish we'd gone home after we came 'cross that first crazy dude.

Angus don't say a word as he starts his engine. He takes off, and I follow. When we round the corner, all three men are standin' in the front yard. I almost duck when we fly by, half-expectin' them to open fire. Thankfully they don't, but that don't mean they ain't gonna try to follow us.

We head out of town and back the way we came, weavin' our way through the snow and trees. The wind feels like an icy slap against my face, but I don't give a shit. I need it. What the hell was I thinkin', lettin' Angus talk me into goin' against the plan like that? It was dumb, especially when I know how reckless he's been lately. He seems to think he's immortal now that the dead can't kill him, but he keeps forgettin' 'bout what a man can do.

Angus turns a different way than I was expectin', and I follow him without hesitatin'. We don't wanna lead these assholes straight home, that's for damn sure. After a bit, he slows and motions for me to move forward. I do, pullin' to his side just as he stops. He doesn't turn the engine off when he points to the left, and in the distance, I can see the outline of a house.

I nod, knowin' he's thinkin' of settlin' in there for the night. If them assholes do follow us, hopefully the wind has blown snow over our tracks from this mornin' and they head this way. It's a risk, but one I know we gotta take.

The closer we get, the clearer the house becomes. It's two stories, with a big front porch and a detached garage off to the side. The perfect place to stash the snowmobiles for the night, assumin' we can get in.

Angus must be thinkin' the same thing, 'cause he heads that way, pullin' to a stop in front of the little building. I stay where I am, lookin' over my shoulder to make sure nothin' sneaks up on us. It's quiet other than the snowmobiles, though. Good. Hopefully it stays that way.

In less than a minute, Angus has got the garage door open and is back on his snowmobile. He pulls in beside an old, beat-up Ford pickup and I follow, parkin' next to my brother. We grab a few things off the trailers and have the garage door shut a few seconds later, then we're headin' on up to the house. I'm lookin' over my shoulder every step of the way, but the night is blacker than the pits of hell and totally silent.

The front door is closed but opens when I try the knob. Angus flips on the one flashlight we got and waves me in

150

after him when he steps inside. I shut the door, throw the deadbolt, and pull my knife so fast it feels like one quick movement. I'm jumpy as hell, but the house feels empty. It's stuffy and cold, and every time I inhale, dust fills my nose. No hint of death in the air. Nobody's been inside this place for a long time.

Don't mean we don't gotta be careful.

"Here goes," I say just before lettin' out a loud whistle.

Angus and me don't move an inch as we wait, but nothin' comes runnin'.

It's good enough for me, but I turn to face Angus. "You think we oughta check it out?"

"Naw." He lowers his flashlight. "It's clear."

I turn and head deeper into the house. "Good. Then let's see if there's a fireplace."

We're in luck. Not only is there a wood-burnin' fireplace, but there's a huge pile of wood and a stack of newspaper by it. It only takes two seconds to find some matches in the kitchen, too. When I come back into the livin' room, I find Angus standin' at the window. He don't move to help while I get wood piled up and start a fire, but I ain't complainin'. We gotta have somebody on lookout.

"You think they're gonna come after us?" I ask, focusin' on the paper burnin' in front of me.

"I'd bet my life on it."

"Now or in the mornin'?"

"Hard to say. Be tough to follow our tracks now. Guess it depends on what kinda supplies they got and how motivated they are." I glance over to find him lookin' my way. "Who knows how long it's been since they had a woman."

"Shit," I mutter as a shiver moves through me that don't got a thing to do with the cold.

Angus nods and looks back toward the window. "Hopefully the other tracks are covered real good."

I don't echo his hope.

The fire catches a little more with each passin' second, so I sit back. The wood is nice and dry, thanks to the months of sittin' in the house. We got real lucky, but I can't feel too good right now 'cause I got no clue what's gonna happen. If these assholes are gonna come after us, and if they do, which tracks they'll decide to follow.

"You gonna yell at me?" Angus asks after the fire's good and high. "Tell me I'm an asshole and that I shoulda listened to you?"

I'm pissed, but I ain't 'bout to get into a fight over it. It ain't worth it when we got other things to worry 'bout.

"Nope. Pretty sure you know you shoulda listened to me. And it ain't like Vivian's the only one at risk right now. Darla's there too. That means you're just as pissed as I am right now."

"Pissed don't even come close to coverin' it." Angus shakes his head. "Scared to death is more like it. I ain't never really cared 'bout a woman like this before. I know Darla can be a pain in the ass, but I love her. Can't believe it myself most of the time, but it's true."

I shake my head. It's gonna be a while before I can get used to Angus bein' so open 'bout things. Before he got bit, he did everything he could to make sure people thought he didn't have feelings, so hearin' him talk 'bout them like this blows my mind.

"The end of the world will play tricks on you," I say after a few seconds. It's all I can manage to get out.

"Hell, this ain't the end of the world," Angus says, turning to face me. "This is the start of a whole new one."

I snort. Angus is right, only I ain't sure exactly what this new world has got in store for us. Nothin' good, if all the stuff we've gone through so far means anything.

Angus turns back to face the window, and we don't say a thing after that. He stares outside while I keep my eyes on the fire. The flames get bigger and brighter 'til the whole room is lit up, then I go 'round lookin' for more candles to light. The more rooms we got lit up, the more these bastards are gonna think this is where we've been livin' if they do show up.

I find a couple candles on the dinin' room table and a few

others here and there, then set them up in another room as close to the front window as I can get without riskin' a fire. Angus don't ask what I'm doin', so he must have a good idea, and he don't look away from that window for more than two seconds. It's gonna be a long night.

"You wanna take turns?" I ask, headin' over to look out the window with him.

The fire is bright, but not bright 'nough to make it impossible to see outside. Not the way electric lights always did. We still have a pretty good view of the front yard and the driveway, all the way down to the little bit of street visible through the trees. If they show up, they ain't gonna be able to surprise us.

"I ain't gonna be able to sleep," Angus whispers.

I look toward my brother out of the corner of my eye, not sure what to say. He's been different since he got bit, but he still likes to pretend he's a hard ass. And he ain't never told me he loved Darla before. I had my suspicions, he said he cared 'bout her back when he got bit, but I was pretty sure he'd have to be on his deathbed to say the words out loud. I ain't exactly sure how to act around this Angus.

"They're gonna be fine," I say, slappin' him on the arm. It's the only thing I can think to say to him.

"They might've slacked off since we ain't 'round."

"No. If anything, they'll be more alert when we don't come back tonight. They ain't gonna let somebody sneak up on 'em."

Angus nods. "Yeah. I think you're right."

"I am," I say, then turn and head into the kitchen. "Might as well check out their supplies while we're here."

Angus don't answer, but there's no reason for him to. He woulda thought of the same thing if he weren't so worried 'bout Darla.

I'm just as worried—so much so that my stomach feels like somebody has filled it with cement—but I gotta keep my mind on something else or I'm likely to go crazy. So I go through the kitchen cabinets, puttin' stuff aside that we need before headin' through the rest of the house. I find a shit ton of useful stuff, but none of it is big enough to help chase away the nervous energy shootin' through me, so I head back to where Angus is still standin' by the window.

Eventually we pull chairs over so we can sit, but we don't move other than to throw a log on the fire every now and then. The night moves on and the fire crackles, and outside the wind howls enough to make the house creak around us, but nothing else happens.

Finally my eyes grow heavy, forcin' me to stand so I don't fall asleep. Angus is so still that I ain't even sure he's blinked this whole time. I stretch my legs and pace, tryin' to keep my body awake. Every time a wave of exhaustion sweeps over me, my stomach clenches. I gotta stay awake. Gotta know if these assholes follow us.

Behind me, the chair creaks and Angus whispers, "Look."

I stop pacin' and hurry to the window just as a truck pulls into the driveway. It don't drive any closer to the house, though. It just sits there with its headlights pointed up the drive like they're stakin' us out.

"What're they doin'?" I mutter, lowerin' myself back into the chair at Angus's side.

"Don't know for sure, but I'd guess they're watchin'."

I scoot to the edge of my seat, waitin' for the truck to come closer. Angus and me sit in silence for a couple minutes with nothin' happenin'. When they finally do start drivin', it ain't forward.

"They're leavin'!" Angus says, gettin' to his feet as the truck backs away.

It pulls onto the road, pauses, then drives away. Nothin' else.

"Shit." Angus drops back into the chair. "Now what?"

"We stay," I say even though I ain't totally sure if it's the right call and just thinkin' 'bout sittin' here all night has my stomach as hard as a rock. "They might try an' come back. Take us by surprise after we go to sleep. I say we blow out the candles and let them think we've turned in for the night."

"Sounds like a plan."

Angus gets up and heads into the other room while I stay where I am. I don't got any other ideas, but a part of me worries that I'm makin' the wrong choice. That doin' this is gonna mean somethin' bad for Vivian or somebody else back home.

But goin' back is too risky. Right?

"You don't think we should head back tonight?" I call.

"No. It's dark and they took our bait. I'd bet my left nut they're gonna head back this way."

The lights go out in the other room, and I turn as Angus heads back in. I'm wide awake now, too jumpy to even consider goin' to sleep, and I know Angus ain't gonna calm down any time soon. Not with as worried as he is.

"Wanna play cards?" Angus asks, holdin' up a deck.

I snort. "We got nothin' else goin' on."

I'M DEAD ON MY FEET BY THE TIME DAWN COMES. We've been playin' cards in the front room for hours—far enough over that our small flashlight can't be seen from the road but close enough that we'll see it if the truck pulls down the drive again. The sky has just started to lighten, and by now the game we've been playin' has started to lose all meanin'.

"They ain't comin'," Angus says, throwin' the cards down.

"You ready to go?" I am, but I ain't sure how I'm gonna stay awake long enough to get back. I feel like I'm 'bout to fall over.

"Yeah. Let's get the hell outta here."

We throw some snow on the fire before we head out, takin' the supplies I found with us. I can only hope the air is cold enough to keep me awake on the fifteen-minute drive home. The sun has started comin' up, but it's still dark, and I'm fuckin' exhausted. I'm ready to strip down so I can sleep for a few hours. I don't sleep much, but even I gotta have more rest than this.

We get the snowmobiles outta the garage, and Angus heads off. I follow, the trailer bouncin' 'cross the snow behind me. We ain't too far from home when a deer jumps out in front of us. It's a doe. Angus whoops when he sees it and whips out his gun, not even slowin'. Thankfully, we've had more than enough practice shootin' at movin' targets—although the deer is a helluva lot faster than the zombies ever were.

The animal jumps over piles of snow as it dashes across the field. Angus fires, and the sound of the gunshot echoes through the silence, even louder than the engines. The deer keeps runnin', so Angus fires again, and this time the thing jumps in the air. It runs a few more steps on wobbly legs before collapsin' on the ground, and Angus lets out another whoop of joy that can be heard even over the snowmobiles.

I follow him over to the deer, comin' to a stop just as he hops off his snowmobile. The deer is layin' on the ground, not breathin', and under her the snow has turned dark red.

"Look at that!" Angus calls. "We got us some food!"

"'Bout time. I was really startin' to think the zombies had killed all the animals."

Angus grins up at me from where he's kneelin' on the ground, and it hits me hard. I ain't ever seen my brother look this happy. Not even before the virus hit, which is just crazy.

"Don't you worry, little brother. I told you a long time ago that I was gonna take care of you, and I ain't changed my mind yet. We're gonna get through this. Together."

I laugh even though I'm beat and I know everybody back home is probably worried sick. This deer is gonna hold us up a little bit, but it'll be worth it, because it'll mean food.

"Let's get this thing field dressed and on the trailer so we can head back," I say, pullin' out my knife.

"Good thing we brought that tarp," Angus replies, still grinnin'.

I return the smile, feelin' lighter than I have since we left home yesterday mornin'. Looks like our luck is finally changin'.

CHAPTER FOURTEEN
VIVIAN

I wrap the blanket tighter around my body, wishing for the hundredth time that I'd decided to drag the kerosene heater downstairs last night. At the time it seemed pointless. I was sure Axl would be back any minute, because he'd promised me he would be home before dark. Even after the sun set I didn't think he'd be gone the whole night, though. All I had to do was lay on the couch for a little bit, then Axl would be home and we could go up to bed. Together.

That isn't what happened, though. Instead the night stretched on and on, and even though I was totally exhausted, I found it impossible to sleep. Now it's nearing dawn and Axl still isn't home, and I'm more awake than ever. And freezing.

A soft rap on the door makes me sit up, but I'm so twisted in the blanket that I almost can't get off the couch. My legs get more tangled, and I stumble forward, nearly falling on my face before I somehow manage to break free. My heart is pounding like crazy as I hurry across the room. It isn't Axl. That I know for sure—he'd never knock on his own door— but it could be someone who has news.

I rip the door open so hard it nearly knocks me over. Darla is standing on the porch, and she jumps back like I scared the shit out of her. It's still dark, but in the distance, there's a little bit of light peeking over the horizon.

"I wake you up?" Darla asks, looking past me into the house.

"No. I haven't slept a wink."

My mom nods as she wrings her hands. "Me neither. I'm worried sick about them boys. You think they're okay?"

"They're fine," I snap, then shake my head. "I'm sorry. I'm just worried."

"I know."

We stand there for a second in silence, just staring at each other. At first I don't know what to say. Why's she here and what does she want from me? Then she looks past me into the house again, and it hits me. She wants to come inside. Probably doesn't want to be alone, and I can't blame her. Right now, even Darla's company is better than being alone for another second. I'm about to drive myself crazy.

"You want to come in?" I ask, stepping aside.

Darla nods and walks in, but she doesn't sit. She just keeps wringing her hands.

I shut the door, but not before a burst of cold air has forced the temperature inside the house to plummet another ten degrees. More shivers work their way through me, and I pick my blanket up off the floor so I can wrap it around my shoulders before lighting a candle. No sense sitting in the dark now that Darla's here.

The light flickers across the room, highlighting the dark circles ringing my mom's eyes. The skin on her face has begun to sag thanks to the weight she's lost, and her dark roots are so long now that I've considered getting a box of dye for her next time I go out on a run—assuming Axl lets me go again.

If he ever makes it back here.

"I'm about to go insane," I say, throwing myself on the couch. "They have to be okay."

"I know how you feel." My mom sits too, and I look up to find her watching me closely. "You sure it's okay that I'm here?"

"Yeah," I say before I really have a chance to think it through.

The weird thing is, it's true. I'm glad she's here. Sharing my worry with her may help me relax a little. May make the time go faster. Maybe I should have gone over to see Darla last night. Why did I sit alone for hours when I could have shared my worry with someone else?

Oh yeah, because I don't like Darla.

Only, I'm not sure that's true anymore.

"I'm sure they just got held up," I say, almost laughing at my own stupidity. "They'll be back any minute."

"That's right," she says, nodding. But she's still wringing her hands. "Don't mean I'm not worried."

I swallow. "I know. Me too."

"I know I've made a lot of mistakes in my life, but Angus ain't one of them." Darla's brown eyes meet mine, and she smiles, but it's tense and also a little hesitant. "You are."

My already fragile emotions are shaken even more by the expression in her eyes. She's apologized—in her own way—a couple times. Tried to make things right. I've pushed her off so many different times it's become a knee-jerk reaction. But this is different. She's admitting she should have done things differently, which is one thing she's never done. And she seems sincere.

"It's fine," I say, focusing on the floor and not my mom.

"No." Darla's voice is so firm that I'm forced to meet her gaze again, and when I do, I find it impossible to look away. "I want you to know I mean it."

My eyes fill with tears, but I brush them away and get to my feet. I need to deal with Darla one of these days, but this isn't the right time. There are too many other emotions going through my head to focus on my mom right now.

161

Later, after Axl and Angus are back and I know they're okay, that's when I'll deal with this.

"I get it." I sniff and turn to face the door, suddenly desperate to get out of the small room. "We should head over to Brady's. Help get breakfast ready so the guys have a hot meal when they get back."

"That'd be real nice," Darla says, the disappointment in her voice thick.

I grab my jacket and boots, focusing on the zipper so I don't have to look at my mom. She may still feel like shit about the whole situation, but there's a part of me that's lighter because I know this part of my life is coming to an end. I'm getting close to being able to not just forgive her, but to say the words out loud. It's a huge step for me, and I actually find myself looking forward to leaving the anger behind.

But later. After Axl is back.

When Darla and I head outside the sky is still pretty dark, but in the distance the sun is trying to break free, the top of it just visible over the horizon. The snow sparkles under the orange glow of the morning sun as my mom and I make our way across the yard, heading toward Brady's house. I shove my hands into my pockets and exhale, watching as a puff of steam floats into the air.

"I can't wait for spring," I say, glancing toward Darla to shoot her a smile. It's meant to be a peace offering, and when she returns it, I think she must know that. I'm not ready to say the words, but I want her to at least know I'm not a horrible person. I look back toward Brady's house, but on impulse say, "I'm trying. I'm close. I'm just not there yet."

"You let me know when you are," she says, and even though I don't look her way, the relief in her voice is obvious.

We've just reached the road when a horn blares, cutting through the silent neighborhood. My heart jumps and Darla squeals, and we both freeze. It happens a second time, echoing through the air and bouncing off the houses around us. Making it almost impossible to figure out where it's coming from.

"What was that?" I ask, looking around as if I'll be able to see through the houses and the darkness to find the source of the sound.

Darla shakes her head, and just like me she looks around. "Car horn?"

"The guys didn't take a car."

"Maybe they had to pick one up?" Darla turns so she's facing me. "Maybe that was what held them up?"

It makes so much sense that I find myself laughing. "They're back. Thank God!"

Darla and I hurry down the street together, heading for the gate. Al and Lila pop out of the trees to our right, and just like us, they seem to be chasing the sound of the horn. When they see us, the teens hurry our way with their guns out and their eyes wide and full of fear.

"What was that sound?" Lila yells.

"It has to be Axl and Angus!" I say, waving toward the gate. "Who else could it be?"

The second the words leave my mouth, my stomach drops. It might not be them. Running down there without thinking ahead could be dangerous. If it isn't Axl and Angus, it could be anyone, and who knows what they want from us.

"Be ready just in case," I say, pulling my gun.

Darla's eyes get huge when she looks my way, but Lila and Al nod. Together we jog down the street, but stop when we round the bend and the gate comes into view. A truck sits on the other side of the fence with its lights on and the engine running. The doors are closed and no one gets out, and the glass is too tinted to allow us to see inside. If this were Axl and Angus, they'd get out so we knew it. They wouldn't play games like this.

I flip the safety off on my gun. "I don't know about this."

"I was thinking the same thing," Al says.

The truck's horn blares a third time, and the engine revs. My fingers tighten on my gun.

"Lila, go back and warn the others," I say without looking away from the truck.

She takes off, causing whoever's in the truck to honk yet again. If zombies were a concern right now, I'd worry that all the noise was going to draw a horde our way. Thankfully we don't need to worry about that, but whoever's in that truck is a little more questionable.

"Stay alert," I say as I start moving again.

Darla and Al are only one step behind me, and we're still ten feet from the fence when the passenger door finally opens and a man steps out. I stop moving, and behind me, the others do too.

On the other side of the gate, the man jumps down, smiling as he waves. "Hey there! Are we glad to see you!"

Al steps in front of me. "Nice to see more people," he says, moving forward but stopping when he's still six feet from the fence. "It's been a while since we saw other survivors."

"No kidding! We weren't sure if we would ever see another group." The man's smile is big and wide and more unnerving than he probably realizes.

Al glances toward the other side of the truck, then back at the man. "Who do you have with you?"

"My wife." The new guy smiles as his eyes move over Darla, then me. "She's a little unsure of new people."

Al glances back, and when our eyes meet, I can tell he doesn't believe a word this guy is saying. The teen gives the new arrival a tense smile when he turns back to face him. "That's something we can understand. It's hard to trust people these days."

The man frowns, but it's brief. When he smiles again, my fingers tense around my gun. "There's a lot of bad stuff happening out there. We've been looking for somewhere safe, and it seems like you've got yourself a nice setup. You think you can find it in your heart let us in so we can rest? We wouldn't be much trouble, and it seems like you have plenty of room."

Before Al can answer, a crack echoes through the air, faint but unmistakable, and everybody freezes. We've all heard enough gunshots at this point to know what it is, but where it's coming from and who fired it is the real concern. It could be Axl and Angus, or it could be someone working with this guy. For all we know, they're firing at our friends right now.

Al shoots me a look as the man on the other side of the fence glances around, trying to look terrified. Nothing about it comes off as real, though. It's way too practiced. I shake my head just a little, and Al nods. I watch as he subtly flips the safety off on his own gun.

"What was that?" the new arrival says.

"A gunshot," Al replies, his voice even and calm.

The man's eyes get huge. "Let us in!"

"We can't do that," I say, and I don't miss it when the guy's gaze moves toward me. And I definitely don't miss the expression in them.

This guy is a shitty actor.

A second gunshot echoes through the air, and suddenly the guy has a gun out and pointed our way. All pretense of fear disappears, and instead he's sneering like a gangster in a movie. "Open the gate or I'll shoot the kid."

Al raises his own gun just as Darla and I do.

"I don't think so," the teen says.

The driver's door opens, and a big guy gets out, pulling a gun as well. "Open the gate."

"You'll have to kill us," I say, my voice coming out a hell of a lot calmer than I feel.

Footsteps crunch through the snow at our backs, and I almost let out a sigh of relief. Parvarti or Winston or someone must be on their way to help.

I look over my shoulder just as a man runs up. He throws his shoulder into Al, who stumbles forward, putting his stump out to stop his fall. I spin to face the man, and his fist slams into my stomach, sending me flying. I crash to the snowy ground, gasping as all the air leaves my lungs. Somewhere near me, Darla lets out a cry of pain, and even though I don't see what happens, I'm not the least bit surprised when she hits the ground next to me.

"Stay down," the guy standing over me says, pointing his gun at my head.

"One more ran toward the houses!" one of the men on the other side of the fence yells. "A teenage girl."

The man above me leans down and flashes me a smile—like we're buddies or something. "Teenagers. Am I right?" He winks, then straightens back up. "I took care of her before she made it."

"Stop fooling around and get this gate open!" the other man yells.

"Be right there." The guy above me scoops my gun up off the ground, shooting me a smile that makes me want to slap his face. "Don't go anywhere," he tells me, then turns and jogs toward the fence.

He's only taken two steps before I'm scrambling across the snow to where Al and Darla are sprawled out. "You okay?" I hiss, still struggling to fill my lungs with air.

Al nods, but the teen is holding his stump like he may have done some major damage. Just what the kid needs: to break what little bit of his arm he has left. "Yeah. The guy got my gun."

"Shit," I mutter, looking toward Darla.

"Didn't bring mine," she says, her face all scrunched up. "Dumbass mistake. That's what it was."

"Someone else must have heard the horns," I say, glancing back toward the houses. I don't see a damn thing, though. Where the hell are they? I look back to find the men struggling to cut the lock, and ice shoots through my already frozen body when I think about what will happen if they get through the gate. "We can't let them in here."

I'm on my feet a second before the lock drops into the snow, running forward. In front of me, metal clinks against metal as the men unravel the chain, but I don't slow. My feet slide as I pull out my knife, but I manage to hold onto my footing. The chain drops, and the guy who first stepped out of the truck looks up. His eyes get huge when he sees me.

"Look out!" he calls.

The man who knocked me down spins to face me, but he's too late. I let out a scream as my blade sinks into his stomach, the flesh soft and mushy. Warm blood runs over my hand, and the guy grunts. His hands cover mine, and he wraps his fingers around my wrists. Pulling my hands away from his body with his eyes focused on the red spot spreading across his shirt.

"You bitch," he snarls.

"Shit!" another man yells, just as the third calls, "Get this damn gate open!"

Behind me Darla screams something just as the man in front of me releases my wrists. His hands go to my neck and he squeezes, compressing my esophagus until it feels like he's going crush it. My throat burns, and my mouth opens and closes as I gasp for air I can't find. There's shouting and footsteps, and in the distance a low hum I can't place. Maybe it's in my head though, because everything is fuzzy as I claw at the hands trying to crush the life out of me.

"Vivian!" someone screams.

My mind flashes to the past. To a blonde woman who used to tuck me in at night. To a smile that was almost a carbon copy of my own. I remember, almost like it happened yesterday, a soft voice singing as the woman brushed the hair out of my face. Her hands soft despite the cuts, and her expression gentle even though she was covered in bruises.

"Mom," I manage to croak as tears pool in my eyes and the edges of my vision turn to black. *Help me…*

Suddenly the hands are gone, and I drop to the ground. My mind slowly begins to focus. All around me there's screaming, and the hum I was sure I'd imagined is back and growing louder by the second. A gunshot echoes through my head as I work to fill my lungs. I roll to my side, the snow cold but oddly comforting as I blink and work to focus. The sun is so bright now that it's reflects off the white surrounding me, making it impossible to see. Through the bright light, I can just make out a struggle. A flash of blonde hair catches my attention, but is gone a second later when a gunshot cuts through the noise, followed by a cry of agony. The scream is still echoing in my ears when Axl and Angus's voices join the chaos, then another gunshot.

My head spins when I force myself up, but it only takes a second to focus. The snow around me has turned red and the yelling hasn't stopped, but the only thing I can concentrate is Darla. Two feet away from me. Gasping as she grabs her stomach and blood seeps through her fingers.

My arms shake and my head spins as I pull myself across the snow to her side. "Hold on," I say, pressing my hands over hers. Knowing there's nothing I can do. "Hold on."

"Vivian!" Axl yells, and I look up to find him and Angus barreling toward us on the snowmobiles.

Darla gasps again, and my eyes fill with tears.

"Help!" I scream.

The brothers are headed my way, and behind me, someone shouts. I glance over my shoulder, and through the bright sun I can just make out a few figures as they run across the snow. Our friends are finally on their way, only it may be too late.

"Vivian," Darla whispers, reaching up to touch my face.

"You're going to be okay," I say, my body shaking as I take her hand in mine. "I promise."

It isn't true, and we both know it. A gunshot to the stomach is a death sentence. Joshua can't fix her. Even if he had a hospital at his disposal he couldn't. Not now. Not in this world.

"Darla!" Angus calls.

Feet crunch against the snow as people close in on us from both sides. Angus and Axl, who have parked their snowmobiles outside the fence, and others from behind me. Joshua drops to the ground at my side a couple seconds before Angus reaches us. He slips across the snow, practically falling beside Darla. His eyes are so big they're twice their normal size.

"No," he mutters, shaking his head as he reaches for Darla's hand. "No!"

"Let me take a look at her," Joshua says.

Angus shoves the doctor's hands away, letting out a growl when Joshua pushes back.

Axl comes from out of nowhere and grabs his brother's arm, pulling him away. "Let the doctor do his thing."

Angus nods, but he doesn't take his eyes off Darla. She grabs his hand with the one I'm not holding. Joshua moves her shirt aside, and her face scrunches up as her fingers clamp down on mine. It grinds my bones together, but I barely feel it.

The doctor looks up, and his gaze meets mine. He shakes his head. "There's nothing I can do."

Angus blinks twice, then his face crumples. "No!"

My mom slips her hand out of his and presses it against his cheek. The smile she gives him is distorted and strained. "You'll be alright. Don't you worry."

"I'm sorry," Angus says. "I shoulda come back. Shoulda been here."

Darla gasps and squeezes her eyes shut. Blood seeps from the hole in her stomach, but Joshua doesn't try to stop it. Maybe it's better this way. She's in pain. The sooner it's over, the better.

When her eyes open, they're focused on me, and suddenly I remember the images that went through my head as the man choked me. It was her. My mom. All these years I've been so focused on my anger that I couldn't remember the good moments. The times when she cared for me even though she was bruised and hurt. The times she sang me to sleep.

"I'm sorry," Darla whispers.

My eyes fill with tears, distorting her face. I blink and they drop to my cheeks, running down my face. I don't wipe them away.

"No," I say, giving her hand a squeeze. "I'm sorry. I could have handled this better. I could have listened. Could have given you the forgiveness you wanted. I wasted so much time."

169

Darla squeezes my hand, but it's so soft, I almost don't notice. On the other side of her, Angus fights to maintain control. The hand that's not holding hers is clenched into a fist, and his body shakes with barely concealed sobs.

"I...loved...you," she says, her voice as soft as a breeze.

More tears fall from my eyes as a whoosh of air leaves Darla's mouth. Steam rises up in front of us and is carried off by the wind, and I wait for more to come. For my mom to fill her lungs one more time. To be the fighter she's always been. Only this time, it doesn't happen.

The sound Angus lets out is so loud it seems to shake the trees. Above us, birds fly from branches, squawking as they soar into the sky. Angus shakes his head and pulls Darla into his arms, his big body covering hers, hugging her to him. He sobs. Harder than I've ever thought possible. His whole body shaking with the force of it as his cries echo through the sky.

I drop Darla's hand and sit back, my own crying quieter and more controlled, but just as painful. So many wasted moments over the last few months. It was stupid and childish, and I should have known better. Hadn't I lost enough?

Axl comes to my side, and I lean my head against his shoulder. My eyes survey the damaged, moving past the open gate and the truck parked there, both doors still hanging open. The snowmobiles sit at its side, the engines still running. Three bodies other than Darla's lie in the red snow, and all around me stand my friends. As shaken by the loss as I am, I'm not nearly as destroyed as Angus.

CHAPTER FIFTEEN

VIVIAN

No one says a word, and I'm pretty sure we're all in shock from what just happened. I know I am. Darla's dead. I'm not even a hundred percent sure how it all went down. A truck showed up — how they found us, I don't have a clue — and they attacked. One man was already on the inside. He'd knocked out Lila, which was why she didn't get help right away. When all hell broke loose, I lost track of everything, but somehow Darla got shot.

"We gotta bury her," Angus says, getting to his feet, holding Darla in his arms.

He walks off, trudging toward the houses through the snow, and no one stops him.

I get up too, but my legs are so wobbly I almost fall back down. Axl steadies me as he stands, his eyes moving over the ruin left in the wake of the attack.

"What happened?" he asks.

"I-I'm not sure." I rub my hands together, suddenly very aware of how cold they are.

"These guys just showed up," Al says. He still has his stump cradled to his chest, and Joshua heads over to check it out. The teen brushes him off. "I'm fine." He lets out a deep breath and shakes his head. "It all happened so fast. They were trying to open the gate and Vivian attacked. She stabbed the guy, and he started to choke her. I stepped in to help, but by then the guys had the gate open and one jumped me before I could do anything. Darla grabbed a gun and shot the third guy, then she went to help Vivian. It was too fast to really know what happened, but I think she tried to shoot the guy, and he managed to turn the gun on her."

"She saved me?" I ask, blinking. Unable to fully process what Al's saying.

The kid nods. "Yeah."

It suddenly feels like that man is choking me again. The world goes out of focus, and the impact of what just happened hits me head-on, making it tough to breathe. Darla died trying to save me. It seems so ridiculous after everything we've been through, but it must be true.

Axl says something about getting things done, and around me people move. The truck and snowmobiles are driven in, and the gate is shut. Somehow another lock appears — where it came from, I don't know — and the bodies are dragged somewhere to be dealt with later. Axl looks my way, frowning, and even though I know it's ridiculous, I can't help thinking that he's judging me.

I turn away, hugging myself as I walk back toward the houses. My body shakes, but I'm not sure if it's from the cold or what just happened. In the distance, I can see Darla's body laid out next to Brady's house and the garage door open, but Angus is nowhere in sight. I keep moving, holding myself tighter.

I pick up the pace when Angus reappears, holding a shovel. "The ground's too frozen," I call.

"Gotta bury her." He shakes his head, his eyes focused on

172

the shovel. "Gotta."

I stop four feet away from him, shivering. My teeth chattering. The wind sweeps across the street, bringing a dusting of snow with it and blowing my hair across my face. It tickles my nose, but I don't push it away. Angus doesn't move either, and I think it's because he knows I'm right. We can't bury Darla until the ground thaws out.

"We can wrap her in a tarp," I say. "Keep her dry until it warms up a little. It's cold enough that she won't—" I stop, biting back the word. *Rot.* It's too harsh and too close to reality. We've seen what a rotting corpse looks like too many times. Angus doesn't need that picture in his head. "She'll be okay until then."

Angus purses his lips, and his gaze moves to Darla. He nods once, then turns back to Brady's garage. Behind me, voices are carried on the wind, along with the crunch of footsteps in the snow. I don't look back, though.

The others walk by, silent as they head for the house. Al's good arm is around Lila, who has a nasty cut on the side of her head and blood matted in her hair. Brady follows with Joshua and Anne. Winston trails after them with Parvarti. Sophia and the kids must have stayed inside where it was safe.

Axl stops at my side and puts his hand on my back. "You okay?"

"Yeah," I say, but shake my head.

Angus comes back with a tarp, and without being asked, Axl moves to help him. The three of us work together to spread out the tarp, struggling against the breeze. Axl and I hold it down while Angus gets Darla, lifting her so gently you'd think she was a porcelain doll. He lays her down, and Axl moves to cover her, but his brother stops him.

"Give me a minute."

Axl steps back. "You wanna be alone?"

"No," Angus whispers. "Just need some time."

Axl moves so he's standing at my side, slipping his arm around my waist while Angus kneels next to Darla.

He brushes the hair off her forehead and whispers something I can't quite make out, but I don't need to hear what he says for it to affect me. Just the look on his face as he stares down at her has my heart cracking in a way it hasn't since Emily died. All the people we've lost since then, and none of it has hurt me as much as the grief-stricken expression on Angus's face does right now.

After a few seconds, Angus stands. Axl wraps the tarp around Darla, then lifts her body and carries her into the garage.

AXL STOPS TALKING AND SITS BACK, HIS EYES moving around the table where everyone but Angus is crowded. He's just finished telling us everything that happened since they left. From the men they ran into while in Duncan and how the brothers tried to lead them away, to the crazy guy who opened fire and the note they found. They got a deer and some supplies, which is good news, but it doesn't change the fact that Darla is dead and we don't know who these men really were. Do they have friends? Can we expect more visitors? Do they have something to do with the note left in Sam's Club, and what does it mean?

"What do you make of it?" Brady asks when he looks up from reading the note for himself.

"Isn't it obvious?" Sophia shakes her head like we're all nuts for questioning things. "They're friendly."

"Not totally sure 'bout that," Axl says.

"They didn't attack us when we saw them in Duncan last fall," I point out. Of course, after what we just went through, I'm thinking I might be on Axl's side this time.

"They could have just said to hell with anyone else who comes along and taken everything in Sam's Club, but they left supplies," Joshua says.

Sophia nods excitedly. "And an invitation to join them!"

"It ain't that simple," Axl says calmly.

"Why not?" Anne asks from the other side of the table.

174

Like Sophia, she seems optimistic, even a little excited about the prospect of going to Hope Springs.

Until today, I was with them.

"We don't know their motivation, that's why." Axl leans forward, frowning. I know he wishes his brother where here to back him up—obviously they already discussed this whole thing last night when they were hiding—but after what just happened, it's probably going to be a few days before Angus can think of anything other than Darla. "They could be doin' this for a number of reasons, and runnin' off without thinkin' it through could get us killed."

"Why in the world would they leave supplies if they weren't friendly?" Sophia exhales and shakes her head. "I'm sorry, I just can't understand why you would think this is a dangerous situation."

"Maybe they're cannibals." Everyone turns to look at Al, whose cheeks turn red. "Just saying. I read an awful lot of zombie books—"

"Reading zombie books isn't the same as real life," Lila says, rolling her eyes.

"Isn't it?" Al arches his brows in a challenging way, and all the air gets sucked from the room.

The kid's got a point.

"Okay," Brady says, nodding slowly like he's thinking the whole thing through. "Why don't you tell us some of the stuff you read in your books."

"Are you kidding?" Anne asks. "You can't be taking this seriously."

"Just think about it this way," Brady says calmly. "Those books may have been fiction, but they came from someone's head, meaning someone had those thoughts. Maybe it was a person who would never act on them, but how many people who read those stories would have acted on them given the right situation? There's no law. No one telling them what they can and can't do. So why would they stop? Especially if it was—in their opinion—the difference between life and death."

"Shit," Joshua mutters, and I can't disagree with him.

I look around, but no one seems ready to argue with Al. If anything, they look like they want to hear more. Except Winston, that is, who once again sits in the corner saying nothing, barely a part of the group. At least he isn't drinking—yet.

When no one argues, Brady turns to toward Al. "Go ahead. Tell us what you know."

The kid clears his throat. "Umm…Okay. So, I read a lot of stuff and what happened in Vegas wasn't that far-fetched." He looks at his hands, and I can't help thinking he's avoiding looking directly at me. "But there were other things too. People who turned cannibal when food became scarce, luring survivors to their towns with the promise of safety. Other groups who would kill anyone they came across, just so they could hoard their supplies."

"Why would they do that?" Anne asks. "Wouldn't people want to work together so they could rebuild?"

Al shrugs. "Honestly, in the stories it was more about power."

"Power for its own sake," Brady mumbles. "It's what a lot of men live for. They don't know why they want it, and the moment it's attained they find themselves wishing for more."

"Yeah, well, I don't know anything about that," Al says. "What I do know is that there's no way I'd ever just stroll into that town without doing some very good recon. Especially after what just happened."

"Which ain't exactly possible with all this snow. We'd have to sit out there for a long time to get a good idea of what they're up to, and in the meantime, we'd be freezin' our asses off." Axl crosses his arms, frowning. "And after today, we gotta be even more careful."

"Did the men who attacked us say anything that would make you think they were from Hope Springs?" I ask.

"Not exactly, but I ain't 'bout to dismiss the idea."

He has a point. It's not like we've seen proof that anyone else is around.

"So we don't go?" Sophia asks. "We just ignore the fact that there's a town full of people only twenty miles from us?"

"I think Axl is right," Brady says. "Given what we know right now—which is essentially nothing—we'd be smart to wait until spring."

"I agree." Joshua pushes his chair out and gets to his feet. "We've lost too much to risk it. Spring will be smarter."

"Spring." Sophia sighs and runs her hand across her stomach.

She's getting bigger every day, and it's a constant reminder that we have to keep everyone safe and fed. We may have lost people, but we'll be gaining another one soon. Who knows what will happen after that? Lila and Al are always sneaking away, and they're not the only ones. Accidents happen. Joshua and Anne have been spending a lot of time together too. Who knows what'll come of that.

Then there's Axl and me…

People stand to leave, but I don't move. Axl gives Al a nod, and the kid breaks out into a smile—the hero worship thing is getting out of hand. He may have matured over the last few months, but I get the feeling Axl will always be his hero.

When everybody has headed out, I move over to sit next to Axl.

"You pissed?" he asks.

"No. A little disappointed. I was hoping we could check it out, see if Jon and Hadley made it there, but you're right. We need to play it safe. Especially after what just happened."

"Spring," Axl says. "I promise we'll check it out."

I nod, but I can't get any words out. The discussion was necessary, but the timing was bad. Darla's dead and I'm still processing it, which means I'm not sure if I'm reacting the way I normally would. Hope Springs should be a priority, right? Seems like it, but I also don't know if we can trust anyone anymore. Our track record with other people hasn't been great.

"Should check on Angus," Axl says, shaking his head. "He's pretty tore up 'bout this."

"You think he'll pull through?"

Axl nods, his eyes focused on the table. "Yeah. Angus is a strong son of a bitch." He looks up, his gaze holding mine. "He loved her. Just got through tellin' me all 'bout it last night. Never heard Angus talk like that."

I take Axl's hand and give it a squeeze, and when his eyes shimmer with tears, I know he's not just hurting for his brother and what he lost. He's probably thinking of me, too. Of how he'd feel right now if it had been me instead of Darla.

"Angus will be okay," I say. "He's found a purpose in this world, and I don't think even this can take that away from him."

"I hope you're right."

So do I.

MARCH

CHAPTER SIXTEEN

JON

March moves in and the winter weather begins to clear, giving us a very welcome relief from freezing temperatures. It hasn't warmed up completely yet, but the lack of more snow falling has given us two things: the opportunity to branch out and look for more survivors, and the chance to find out if the zombies will in fact thaw out.

The first I look forward to with an enthusiasm I couldn't have imagined, but my emotions surrounding the second one are mixed. I never—not even for a second—thought the zombies would be killed off by the cold, so I don't really share the disappointment that seems roll through Hope Springs when the damn things start wandering up to the fence again. Instead, an odd sense of normality settles over me. Almost like now that my suspicions have been confirmed, it will be easier for me to move forward from here on out.

With the streets clear and finding survivors our new main objective, Jim and I have been moved to Dax's crew. Since finding out the CDC is working toward a vaccine, everyone in Hope Springs has been itching to search the area. The hope that we might be able to find someone who is immune to this thing has brought a new wave of optimism to our community.

"Everybody ready?" Dax calls.

I look up from where I'm leaning against the wall at Jim's side. He and I may have a complicated relationship, but I still trust him with my life. Plus, he's one of the few people on the crew that I actually know. Most of these guys have been working with Dax from the beginning, and they aren't exactly thrilled to have us new guys around. They act like we've been sitting on our asses in a cushy office instead of clearing the streets of Hope Springs.

Jim drops his cigarette and crushes it with the toe of his boot. "Not sure about this whole thing," he says, smoke coming out of his mouth with the words.

"Why's that?" I ask as we head over to the truck together.

"I know you heard about the whole mess with the committee." Jim lowers his voice and looks around like he's afraid someone may be listening.

"Yeah. Ginny told me all about it. Dax and Corinne had it out, but the committee backed her up. I'm not convinced it means a whole lot. Maybe Dax just thinks he'd do a better job. I mean, he kind of had a point." Jim's eyebrows shoot up, and I shrug. "Corinne isn't an American and the government she set up isn't a democracy."

"She didn't come up with the system. Atlanta did."

"But she put it in place here without batting an eye." I zip my jacket and shake my head. It's warmer, but still cold, and the leather will save my ass if the zombies are thawed out enough for a fight. "Don't get me wrong, I don't think it's a bad system and I don't think Corinne's doing a bad job. But Dax standing up to her doesn't necessarily make him a bad guy."

"Let's hope not," Jim says with a snort.

Meaning he doesn't believe that. I glance toward him out of the corner of my eye as we stop behind the rest of the group. Does Jim know something about Dax that I don't? The guy's always seemed okay to me—even if he and Corinne have had a couple run-ins. He didn't bring Ginny and me in, but the people he did save love him. It's kind of creepy how much everyone looks up to the guy, but that isn't his fault. Is it?

"Let's load up!" Dax calls even though everybody is already climbing into the back of the truck.

I head that way, walking at Jim's side but watching our leader. Dax towers over everyone else, and if he weren't smiling so much, he'd probably be intimidating. But he is. He's always in a good mood, always smiling. Always ready to chat and tell a joke.

My eyes meet his, and Dax's grin somehow grows wider. "Jon! How's that wife of yours doing?"

Jim glances my way but doesn't stop when I do. I ignore the uneasy way my stomach rolls at the expression on my partner's face.

"She's good," I say, focusing on Dax.

The big man nods, smiling yet again. "Great news! Why don't you ride in the truck with me so I can hear all about it? We're all looking forward to her proving that we can beat this thing."

"Sure," I say, but only take one step toward the truck before turning around to face Dax. "Just don't say anything like that to her, okay? She's feeling a lot of pressure from everyone. It's tough getting her to relax when people won't stop bringing it up to her."

Dax's smile fades, but only for a second. It comes back full force when he nods and slaps me on the back. "Sure thing! No problem."

Once again, my stomach twists as I turn away from our leader and head to the passenger side of the truck. Damn Jim. He's gotten in my head about this whole thing, which is just dumb. There's no reason for me to be uneasy about

Dax. He's just being friendly. Doing exactly what everyone else in town is doing: trying to stay optimistic despite all the babies we've lost. They aren't *trying* to put pressure on Ginny.

Just like the buses we use for clearing, steel plates have been welded over the windows of the truck, and the back is just as reinforced. I can't help feeling like an extra in a *Mad Max* sequel that never got made when I pull myself inside. Especially with my leather gear and the heavy weight of my weapon belt pressing on my waist.

It has to be wrong to feel like such a badass during the zombie apocalypse.

Dax climbs into the driver's seat and grins my way as he starts the engine. "Ready?"

"Surprisingly, yes. This is the first time I've left the walls of Hope Springs since Ginny and I arrived last November." I have to admit it feels good. Like I'm a normal human being instead of a survivor cowering behind the safety of some fence. "Where are we heading?" I ask as I lean forward so I can get a better look out the front window.

"Duncan," Dax says, his blue eyes flashing. "Other than Hope Springs, it's the biggest city for about forty miles. We cleaned the stores out pretty good but left some supplies for anyone who might stop in, along with an invitation to join us in Hope Springs. No one showed up saying they'd found the stash, so I'm thinking it will still be there."

"Someone could have found the supplies," I say with a shrug. "Maybe they just don't trust anyone."

"How's that?" Dax asks, glancing my way. The sun shining through the window reflects off his blond hair as he gives me a strange look. "We left supplies to show our goodwill. Why would anyone interpret that differently?"

"Because now that everything has gone to shit, there are all kinds of assholes just dying to exploit other people. Trust me, we were on the road for a while, and you wouldn't believe the shit I saw."

Dax purses his lips and nods as his eyes narrow on the road. "Good point." He glances my way. "So you saw some bad shit out there?"

"Lots of it," I mutter, my good mood slipping away.

"Like what?"

Something about his tone causes my stomach to clench yet again, but when I look his way, there doesn't seem to be anything in his eyes other than mild interest. That has to be all it is. He's been in Hope Springs almost this entire time, and he's just curious what the rest of the world is like now.

Doesn't mean I want to rehash it all.

"You have an imagination," I say, waving him off. "I don't need to go into all that. Humans can be ruthless, and the end of the world brings out the worst in some people."

"Yeah." Dax nods slowly. "So you're talking cannibals and stuff?"

I turn in my seat so I can get a better look at him. Is he for real?

"I didn't see any of that," I say, studying him. Trying to get a better read on the guy. Thinking about Corinne and Jim and how they both seem to see Dax in a different light than everyone else. "But I guess it's possible."

Dax isn't deterred. "So the things you saw... Rape? Using people for sport? That kind of thing?"

"I don't want to talk about it," I snap, not even caring when Dax's eyes cloud over.

I turn so I'm once again focused on the road in front of us and the snowy world flying by rather than the images of the things I witnessed at the Monte Carlo. The things I let slide by because I was so intent on saving my sister that I couldn't risk stepping in. It makes me sick to my stomach whenever I think about it, and I'm pretty sure the ghosts of those women will always haunt me.

Dax doesn't say anything else, but when I risk looking his way, his expression is thoughtful. Something about it gives me the creeps. For some reason, it seems like more than just morbid curiosity.

We haven't said a word in more than five minutes by the

time we roll into Duncan, and I can't stop squirming. The sooner I get out of this truck, the better.

The sun is high in the sky, and it sparkles across the melting snow, illuminating areas where zombies are still buried in the drifts, many of them struggling to get free. In the distance, a few zoms are visible as they stumble through the slush. No doubt unsteady on their freshly thawed limbs. There are a lot of them, but I know once the snow is gone for good, there will be even more.

"Can't believe they pulled through," Dax says, shaking his head as he turns into a residential area.

"Did you think it would kill them?" I ask, avoiding looking his way. He's never struck me as a creepy guy before, and I can't help thinking that I might be overacting to his questions. Not that it feels that way right now.

"I had hoped it would, I guess." Dax snorts. "I guess that's really all we have anymore, though."

"At least we have that," I mutter.

I see Dax nod out of the corner of my eye but keep my gaze ahead.

We turn the corner, and a plaza comes into view. There's a Sam's Club and Wal-Mart, as well as a few other stores lining the strip mall. All through the parking lot, tracks cut through the snow. It's hard to tell how recently the area was disturbed, though. They're a combination of tire prints and what look like snowmobile tracks, as well as dozens of footprints. They seem too neat to be zoms, but anything is possible. The reality we're living in now is proof of that.

Dax pulls the truck to a stop in front of Sam's Club, throwing it into park. Neither one of us moves to open the door as the other truck stops behind us. Instead, we take a few seconds to go over our weapons and prepare ourselves. The zoms may still be thawing out, but that doesn't mean they aren't going to be dangerous. A select few people may be immune, but there's no way I'm going to take a chance. What are the odds I'm one of the lucky ones?

"What's the plan?" I ask, craning my neck so I can scan

the parking lot. There's no movement either around us or inside the building as far as I can see, but I'm still going to do a little bit of recon before I head out.

"We go in and see if our supplies are still intact. Then we'll head across the parking lot to the residential area, keeping an eye out for any signs of life."

"That's it?" I ask, unable to hide my annoyance. "Did you look over a map or plan out where we're going or anything like that?"

Dax shakes his head. "No point. If someone's around, we'll find them easy enough."

He throws the door open and hops out, immediately shouting off orders like there's no need to worry about being quiet. I can't stop the irritation that started in my stomach from working its way through me. Angus and Axl never would have run off with such a dumbass, little thought-out plan. We always had a map, always did our homework. We were ready for anything. Dax has gotten sloppy or cocky, and I'm worried it's going to come back and bite one of us in the ass. Literally.

I glance around when I hop out. A closer look tells me that the tracks through the snow were most definitely made by snowmobiles. It's tough to figure out exactly how long they've been here, but it doesn't look really recent. Of course, with the rapidly melting snow, it couldn't have been that long ago either.

"Someone was here," Dax says when I round the truck.

Behind him, the other men are looking around, studying the area just like I did before I got out. Dax alone seems to think there isn't much danger. It makes me wonder about him a little more. Is he unconcerned because he has some kind of a God complex or because he knows that if someone succumbs to a zombie bite, it won't be him?

Dax sniffs and looks toward the open Sam's Club door. "Let's go."

We follow as a group, none of us relaxing despite Dax's laid-back attitude. Jim appears as if out of nowhere, falling into step at my side, his knife out and ready while his other hand rests on the gun at his waist.

"You get the impression this wasn't planned very well?" he says quietly, almost out of the side of his mouth.

I nod.

"Don't get it. We planned every little detail when we cleared, so I just figured Dax would do the same. It's the only way to be sure we all get out of this in one piece."

"Doesn't seem to be the intelligent thing to do," I say.

Jim snorts.

Dax stays in the lead, heading through the store with the rest of us trailing after him. He doesn't stop until he reaches the last register, and the frown that turns down his lips when he stares at the empty belt gives me the impression that he's pissed.

"They took it but they didn't come to Hope Springs." He shakes his head.

"I told you," I say, making him look up. "Trust. There are a lot of people these days who just don't trust anyone."

"Yeah," he mutters. "Came across a group like that back in the fall. They were loading up on supplies right here, and we tried to talk them into coming with us, but they said they had a safe place. I would have pushed it, but the one guy seemed like kind of a hothead."

I perk up the second he says *hothead*. I can't help thinking of Angus.

"Did you get their names?" I ask hesitantly.

Dax lets out a laugh that sounds oddly pissed-off. "They weren't the most open group I've ever come across."

"And they didn't tell you anything about themselves?"

Jim looks at me like I'm nuts, and around me, the other men shuffle their feet, clearly nervous and ready to move on.

I can't let it go, though. "What did they look like?"

"Survivors. There were three men, two white and one black, and three women. One was blonde and had huge—" Dax clears his throat and glances away as he rubs the back of his neck. "Never mind about that. There were two blonde

188

women, and the third had darker skin. I didn't get a good look at her and she didn't have an accent, but she may have been Hispanic."

"Was there anything about these people that stood out?" I ask, getting excited. "Anything unusual?"

Something inside me squeezes tight, and all I can think about is the description he almost let slip. I can read between the lines, and I know exactly what he was going to say: *huge tits*. If anyone matches that description, it's Vivian.

"The two white guys did most of the talking, and they were borderline hostile. It was clear they didn't trust me, but they didn't really seem like they were in charge. They made the decision not to come with us as a group." Dax presses his lips together as he thinks it through, but a second later shrugs. "That's it, really. I didn't ask names or anything. Sorry."

Damn. I was really hoping he'd give me something solid I could take back to Ginny.

Dax waves toward the doors, and his voice echoes through the building when he calls, "Let's head across the street to the residential area. There are some apartments that would be a prime place for a group to hide out."

I follow everyone to the door, ignoring the weird looks Jim keeps shooting my way as I think the whole thing through. "It can't be them," I mumble, shaking my head.

After only a few steps, Dax snaps his fingers and spins around to face me. "Oh yeah! They did say one thing that was totally crazy, though."

"What was that?" I ask, coming to a stop.

"They asked if I'd seen Hadley Lucas. You know, the actress? I got a good laugh out of that one." Dax chuckles as he starts walking again. "Can you imagine her stumbling through our gates?"

"That is crazy," I say to Dax, who's laughing too hard to notice the expression on Jim's face.

It *was* Vivian and Axl! They were alive and right here just a few months ago, and Dax talked to them. Even asked them to come to Hope Springs. How the hell have Ginny and I been in Hope Springs for all these months yet never heard about this?

I force my legs to move again, following the others to the front of the store, with Jim watching me the whole way. The sun is blinding when we step outside, and in the distance, a few more zombies are visible. None too close, though.

We move across the parking lot as a group, the melting snow squishing under boots and filling the silence that I've almost gotten used to. I keep my eyes moving, constantly scanning the distance so I can keep tabs on the zoms, but of course my brain is on other things. Based on Dax's description, I can only assume the group he came across last fall included Vivian, Axl, Angus, Darla, Parvarti and Winston. Which means at least those six people made it out of the hot springs safely. Who died there is still a mystery, and I'm not dumb enough to think the winter didn't claim another victim or two. A lot has happened since Dax saw them here last November. Weather and a lack of food could have done them in, and who knows if they've run into hostile groups. Anything could have gone down.

"So you gonna tell me what's going on?" Jim asks. He takes a drag from his cigarette, sucking the chemicals into his lungs before blowing it back out, his eyes on me the entire time. "Were they friends of yours?"

"The group we were with before all this," I say, my eyes moving to Dax.

He's at the front of the pack, so I doubt he'd be able to overhear our conversation, but I still need to make sure. Ginny doesn't want people knowing who she is, and I still haven't even told her Jim knows.

"You get separated?"

"Yeah," I say, letting out a deep breath. "We went on a run and got ambushed by some men. Ginny and I were in a different store than the others, and by the time we came out of hiding, they were gone. They left a note that said they'd headed back to our camp. I can't blame them. We didn't know what was happening, and hanging around was too risky." My eyes dart to his and then away. "We ran into some assholes back in Vegas, and that whole experience was still fresh in our minds. It probably had something to do with how things went down."

"Better safe than sorry," Jim says.

"True," I mutter, thinking about the last time I felt really safe. Even now, within the walls of Hope Springs, I can't shake the feeling that everything could come falling down around us. All it will take is a huge horde or a group of men who decide they deserve our town more than we do. "Anyway, by the time Ginny and I made it back to our camp, they'd been overrun. They left us a note and we followed their trail as far as we could, but the snow made it impossible after a while. By then my main goal was getting Ginny to safety."

"So you came to Hope Springs," Jim says with a snort.

I turn to look at him, but his gaze is focused on the group in front of us and I can't read his expression. "What does that mean?"

"Nothing. Just that I'm not sure anything can be completely safe anymore. People are assholes, and a zombie apocalypse is only going to make that more obvious."

"This coming from a guy who was sitting in prison before all this shit went down."

He turns his gaze on me, studying my face for a few seconds without blinking. "Exactly why you should listen to me. I know bad people. Spent years living with them before this. Some people would even say I was one."

"Does this have to do with Dax? Exactly what do you think he's going to do?"

Jim looks ahead, his eyes focused on the front of the group. "Not sure, really. Corinne is a strong woman and the committee is a good start, but keeping everyone in line is a bigger job than even she knows. I'm just afraid one of these days people are going to get tired of taking orders."

"Corinne doesn't give orders," I mutter even though I can't deny that Jim has a point.

He shrugs and goes back to smoking, and we continue our walk across the parking lot in silence. Around us other men talk in quiet voices, and in the distance a few stumbling zoms are visible, but otherwise the day is quiet.

We cross the street and head toward a couple apartment buildings, pausing only when a zom gets too close and someone has to take it out. Jim and I are at the back of the group, too far away to be affected by anything approaching us from the front. That doesn't stop me from constantly looking over my shoulder, though. Behind us, zombies drag themselves across the melting snow, their progress slow but steady. It will take them a while to catch up, but eventually we're going to have to take care of it. This is an instance when I think we should have spent more time teaching people how to use a bow. If Parvarti were here, those bastards would be down by now.

"Okay!" Dax calls as he turns to face the group. His words echo across the parking lot, and a chorus of weak but intimidating moans follows. Our *leader* doesn't bat an eye. "We're going to split up. We'll send one group into the building to my left, and a second into the one across the parking lot. They're three stories, so I want the bigger groups divided into a couple smaller groups. Each one takes a floor, keeping your eyes open for supplies and survivors. Got it?"

People nod and murmur their approval, and once again I'm struck by our total lack of preparation. We should have more of a plan before going into an unknown building. The zombies are slow and we're wearing leather, so even if they surprise us, we should be able to get the upper hand without much effort. But men? They could have guns, and a leather jacket isn't going to stop a bullet.

"This is stupid," Jim mutters, dropping his cigarette. He steps forward and interrupts Dax. "Don't you think we should have more of a plan?"

The big man's eyes snap Jim's way, narrowing until they're so small he looks like he's trying to shoot lasers out of them. "What was that?"

192

"We need a plan. When we were clearing, we always made sure to have the whole thing planned out before going in. It saved lives."

Dax takes a step toward Jim, his forehead creased and his gaze harder than steel. "I'm in charge for a reason. You may have been behind the fences for the past few months, but I've been out here doing runs. Even when we had two feet of snow on the ground, I came out. Risking my life. I know what's out here and I know how to handle it, and I'd suggest you do things my way if you want to live. Understand?"

Most of the men around us shoot dirty looks Jim's way, but my partner doesn't back down. Not even when Dax moves closer and straightens his shoulders, giving emphasis to his big frame. The guy is huge—like a football player on steroids—and he towers a good five inches over Jim. I don't know a lot of these guys—only Mark, Gretchen's boyfriend, really—but judging from their expressions, I'd guess they're on Dax's side.

My partner snorts. He doesn't step back, but he does shrug. "Whatever you say, boss." His tone is so thick with sarcasm that the word comes out sounding like an insult.

Dax exhales as he turns around, his hands clenched into fists. "Split up," he barks and moves toward the first apartment building.

Most of the men head in the opposite direction, probably trying to avoid being with Dax when he's in such a foul mood, which forces Jim and me to head into the same building as our fearless leader. Great. That should make for a pleasant experience.

Five of us head inside, and Dax doesn't waste a second.

"You two," he says, pointing to Mark and the guy standing in front of him. "Mark and Ramirez, you're going to check out the first floor with me." His eyes move to Jim, and Dax frowns. "You and your pal take two."

Dax turns toward the first floor with the other two men, and it doesn't escape my notice that he put himself in the larger group. Figures.

Jim and I head toward the stairs, each of us holding a knife and a flashlight, and I can't help feeling like we don't have a clue what we're doing. There's no confidence in me like there was when we were clearing the streets or the day we spent in the dark hospital. Back then, we knew what to expect and how to tackle it, but we're going into this thing totally blind.

"You wanna take the back?" Jim whispers.

I nod, glad that we're on the same page. "Yeah. We'll do it just like in the hospital. I'll light the way and you take out anything that comes after us."

"Perfect," Jim mutters, but his tone tells me he thinks this plan is anything but perfect.

When we reach the door leading to the second floor, Jim and I stop. I put my knife away, leaving the clasp on my sheath open so it's easy to get to if things get bad. In front of me, Jim replaces his flashlight while taking a few deep breaths, working to steady his heartbeat the way he always does before we go into an unknown environment. When he's ready, he nods my way. I return the gesture as I flip on the flashlight and aim it at the door, my body stiff with tension and my heart pounding like crazy.

"Here we go," Jim says, then jerks the door open.

He raises his knife as I pan the beam of my flashlight around, surveying the area. But the hall is clear. When nothing moves, Jim takes a step in, with me right behind him. Just like we've done dozens of times while clearing the streets of Hope Springs. It only takes one step into the hall to realize that someone's already been through this building. All the doors are wide open—a few have even been knocked down—and the floor is covered with trash and other debris.

"This place is gonna be cleaned out," Jim says, his voice echoing through the empty hall even though he's whispering.

"Yeah," I mutter, shaking my head. "We aren't going to find anyone or anything here."

Jim heads down the hall, and I follow. When we reach the first apartment, I shine my light in while my partner lets out a low whistle. Nothing moves, so we go in, but just like we thought, the kitchen doesn't turn up a thing. Most of the cabinets are wide open, and mice or other rodents have chewed through the few things left—like a bag of rice and a box of Lucky Charms.

"Let's check the bedroom," Jim says, shaking his head.

I stay silent as we move, keeping my ears open and working to focus on the present. It isn't easy, though. The knowledge that Jim has serious questions about the leadership, coupled with the uneasy feeling Dax gave me on the drive into town, has my head reeling. Then there's Vivian and Axl and what I'm going to tell Ginny. She's going to freak out.

The rest of the apartment, just like the kitchen, has been picked over. The only thing we end up taking is a *Playboy* Jim finds in the nightstand, and I have a strong suspicion that won't be going into the town inventory.

"Really?" I say, raising my eyebrows as I fight back a grin.

"The apocalypse is a lonely place," Jim says, folding the magazine in half so he can stuff it in his backpack.

I chuckle and shake my head as I follow him back out into the hall.

We head into the next apartment only to find more of the same, and each one we search leaves me feeling more empty-handed than I did when we got here. We're looking for survivors, and any supplies we find are a bonus, but with the way this place has been cleaned out, we're not going to find even one battery. What's more, the only people we come across aren't moving.

"Looks like somebody did a number on this place," Jims says.

I nod and follow him down the hall, headed for the last apartment. He's still armed and on alert, and I'm still using my flashlight to keep the place nice and lit up even though nothing—not even a mouse—is moving.

We're just about to step through the door of the last apartment when the pop of gunfire makes me freeze.

Jim glances my way, and a split-second later we're off. Running down the hall and into the stairwell, pausing when we hear the sound of shouting and more gunshots.

CHAPTER SEVENTEEN

JON

"Up!" Jim calls, jerking his head toward the stairs. I'm still on flashlight duty, so I stay behind him, keeping the beam focused on the stairs to make sure he doesn't get tripped up. The higher we get the louder the voices become and the more foul the air turns. It isn't death, either. That's something I've almost gotten used to. This is the stench of feces and urine, and it's so thick it almost chokes me. Breathing out of my mouth doesn't help, and before we even make it all the way to the top, I'm forced to cover my nose with my free hand. I'd feel like a pussy except Jim does the same, coughing when he sucks in a deep breath.

"Shit," he mutters.

Literally.

"Get up here!" Dax shouts, and I can only assume he's yelling at Jim and me.

We make it to the top and find Dax in the stairwell by himself, holding the door to the third floor shut. Another shot rings through the air, and someone on the other side of the door screams and swears. Then there's pounding, like they're trying to get out.

"Did you lock them in there?" I ask as Jim shoves Dax aside.

Our fearless leader stumbles away, his back slamming against the wall just as Jim rips the door open. I'm right there with him, shinning my light into the hall. The beam illuminates the dark space, and I catch sight of an old man at the end of the hall. He covers his eyes when the flashlight hits him and lets out a howl of pain, dropping the gun he has clutched in his hand.

"Keep the light on him!" Jim yells as he charges forward.

I run after my partner, keeping my flashlight steady and the beam aimed at the man's face. Everything moves fast, but two things stick out. One, the man has a beard so scraggly it looks like he hasn't shaved in months, and two, the stench is so bad it makes my eyes water and my nose burn.

"Get down!" Jim yells. "Flat on the ground!"

"We won't let the cannibals take us," the old man growls but drops to the floor.

His hand moves across the carpet, and it only takes me a second to realize he's going for his gun. Jim must realize it too, because he runs forward and kicks the weapon aside with the toe of his boot. The thing slides across the floor, hitting the wall with a bang much louder than I expected.

"Don't move," Jim says, his voice thick and threatening. "Who else do you have up here with you?"

"Just me," the old man says, keeping his face pressed to the floor and making it impossible to get a good look at him.

"Bullshit," I say, stepping closer. "You said we."

"Just eat me and leave the others alone."

Jim looks my way and I shrug, but our attention is drawn to the door when I a woman steps out with a rifle in her hand. It's pointed right at us.

"I'll shoot," she says, her arms shaking as she moves the barrel back and forth between Jim and me. "Just back on out of here and leave us alone. There has to be someone else out there you can eat."

None of us say a word for a few seconds, and I use the silence to try and figure out exactly what's going on here. The whole floor reeks and the apartments below have been ransacked. The man on the floor screamed like he was in pain when I pointed the flashlight at him, and the woman holding the gun is filthy and so thin she reminds me of a Holocaust survivor. I take a second look at the man, who has turned his head toward the woman and finally given me a chance to see his face. He's younger than the beard makes him look, probably only in his late twenties.

"Shit," I mutter, shaking my head. "Have you been hiding here since this whole thing started?"

The woman jumps at the sound of my voice and turns the gun on me, her arms shaking more than ever. "Shut up," she hisses. "We've seen what the other survivors have been up to, and we don't want any part of it. We'd rather die than turn cannibal."

Jim lets out a whistle as he lowers his gun. "Lady, you've got it all wrong. We aren't here to eat you."

The woman's eyes get big and round when they go back and forth between Jim and me, but she doesn't say anything.

On the floor, the man shifts so he can look up at us. "You're not one of them? We saw it happen after everyone died. The people out there went crazy and started eating each other, so we hid in here. Haven't been out in months."

Jim kneels down, his eyes on the man while I keep my gaze on the woman. Her rifle is still pointed at me, but she's watching my partner.

"There are no cannibals, not that I know of anyway. What you saw was something else. Something we've been fighting for months." Jim takes a deep breath and says, "The virus killed everyone, but they came back. Just like in the movies. Zombies."

The man's eyes get huge, and he glances toward the woman, who has finally lowered her gun. "Desi?"

"Can't be," she says, shaking her head. "It's crazy."

"It's true," Dax says from behind me, coming out of nowhere now that the woman has finally calmed down. "We've got a city cleared out though, and we're looking for survivors to bring back. We can help you."

The man stares up like he isn't sure Dax is real, blinking a few times before finally letting out a deep breath. He climbs to his feet, and I'm able to get a good look at him for the first time. Just like the woman, he's filthy. His skin is caked in dirt, and his hair is so greasy it's matted to his scalp. Holes cover his jeans, and the shirt on his back is threadbare and ripped. Guess they gave up on trying to stay clean.

"You believe them?" the woman, Desi, asks. She twists her body so she's facing her friend like she's trying to keep us out of their conversation.

The man scratches his head, and something drops to the floor. I'm not positive because it was so small, but if I had to take a guess, I'd say it was a bug. "They haven't attacked."

The woman looks back at us, but she still doesn't seem totally convinced we aren't dying to cut her into pieces and serve her for dinner.

"We're not going to hurt you," I say as my stomach rolls.

Now that the adrenaline has worn off a little, the stench is really starting to get to me. My stomach jumps and I have to swallow down the bile that rises in my throat and my eyes won't stop watering. I'm not sure how these people have been able to live like this, but I know I need to get the hell out of here before I lose my breakfast.

Jim spits and shakes his head. "I hate to break up the party, but if we could take this conversation outside, or at least to another floor, I would appreciate it. It smells like shit in here."

The man turns toward the apartment behind him instead of heading toward the stairs. "We've been using the other apartments as toilets."

"Wait," the woman says, grabbing his arm. "You're going to trust them?"

The man looks us over once more, and his eyes hold mine. They're dark blue and intense, and there's so much pain in them that it overshadows the stench.

When he looks back at the woman, he says, "We can't keep going on like this. I'm not sure how much more fight I have in me, and if it comes to staying here or taking a chance on being eaten, I'd almost rather take the chance."

She drops his arm but doesn't argue, which I can only assume means she agrees. The man once again moves toward the apartment at his back. The woman in front of us still hasn't moved when he's disappeared from sight. She just stares at the floor. Unblinking. Maybe she's in shock?

"He called you Desi?" I say, trying to get her to talk.

She looks up, and her brown eyes move from me to Jim to Dax, then back to me. "That's right."

"I'm Jon, and this is Jim and Dax," I say, jerking my head toward the other men.

She nods, but before she has a chance to say anything, the man comes back out of the apartment. Three people trail behind him. Another woman and a man, just as dirty but older than the first, and a kid who can't be more than six. Seeing them after knowing what they've been living in for the past few months is shocking enough, but nothing can prepare me for the sight of the second woman's swollen belly.

"Shit," I mutter, stepping toward her.

Desi lifts her rifle just a bit, and both men step closer to the pregnant woman while the little boy cowers behind her legs.

"Sorry," I say, putting my hands up. "I'm just surprised. How far along are you?"

I don't have a ton of experience—only my first wife and Ginny—but if I had to guess I'd say she's ready to drop that baby any day.

"Not sure," the woman says, rubbing her belly. She's so thin that her eyes appear huge in her gaunt face, and her arms look like they would snap under the smallest strain. "What month is it?"

She doesn't even know what month it is? Shit.

"March," I tell her.

"My due date is the twenty-third. I thought it was getting close."

"We need to get these people back to town," Jim says, and I nod in agreement.

"Right." Dax's authoritative voice booms through the hall, and I turn to face him. "Let's get them downstairs and out of this stink. We'll have a couple people run over to get the trucks and load up any supplies the other group found." He looks over his shoulder and sighs. "Need to get these guys down too."

My gaze moves past him to the end of the hall, and I find the other two men who came up here with Dax. Mark isn't moving—if he's dead, Gretchen is going to lose it—but Ramirez is holding a bloody arm, sweating like he's about to pass out while he glares at Dax. That's when I remember the way the big man was holding the door shut when we came up.

"Shit," I mutter, heading down the hall with Jim right behind me.

I kneel in front of Mark, and I look him over. Blood has soaked through his shirt, but there's so much that it takes me a moment to figure out where it's coming from. His right side. Hopefully, it isn't too bad. I press my fingers against his neck and let out a sigh of relief when his veins thump against my fingertips. His pulse is weak, but it's there.

"We need to get this guy to a doctor," Jim says from behind me, and I turn to find him tying something around Ramirez's arm.

"Mark too," I say.

I don't have any extra clothing, so I remove my jacket and pull my shirt over my head, using it to apply pressure to the hole in Mark's side. Luckily, I have more than one on. Mark groans, but doesn't open his eyes. At least he's alive. If we can get him to a doctor fast enough, he might have a chance.

"We'll head down," Dax says, opening the door to the stairwell and motioning for the still-shaky survivors to head out. "I'll send a few guys up to help you."

Jim and I don't say a word. I keep pressure on Mark's wound while pulling my jacket back on, watching Dax lead the group we just found into to the stairwell.

When the door has clicked shut, I turn toward Ramirez. "Dax lock you in here?"

The man nods, breathing through the pain. "We were taking a look around when the guy with the beard freaked out. He started shooting and Dax made a run for it, slamming the door in our faces so he could save his own ass. Mark got hit and I banged on the door, but that bastard wouldn't let us out."

Somehow, I'm not that surprised, but it still makes me sick.

"Prick." Jim gets to his feet and takes a deep breath, cringing when the foul air fills his lungs. Then he drags the sweating and bleeding Ramirez up after him. "You need help with that guy?"

I shake my head and lift Mark up, throwing him over my shoulder and earning another groan from the half-conscious man. For Gretchen's sake, I hope he pulls through.

"Let's get out of this shit hole," I grunt as I move toward the door.

Jim helps Ramirez, stopping to hold the door open so I can step into the stairwell. We head down, and with each step it gets easier to breathe despite the extra baggage. The odor of feces fades, replaced by the faint scent of death I'm used to. It's odd how refreshing it smells after being up there.

We've already passed the second floor and are halfway to the first when a couple guys finally jog up to help us. Donovan, Dax's right-hand man and the guy who was with Richard when they picked Ginny, Gretchen, and me up, takes Mark from me, and I'm finally able to really fill my lungs with air.

"He alive?" Donovan asks, barely batting an eye when he slings Mark over his shoulder.

"For now," I say, shaking my head.

Donovan heads down, while Jim and I follow. We hit the first floor, and I catch sight of the rest of our group through the open door. Dax is hovering over the survivors like he's the difference between them living and dying, and the second I set eyes on him, my blood heats up until it threatens to burn through my veins.

We step outside, and I push past Donovan and head toward Dax, grinding my teeth. "You asshole," I yell when I'm less than six feet away. "You locked those guys in there!"

Dax turns my way, his blue eyes getting wide like he's shocked or has no idea what I'm talking about or some shit like that. Too bad the hardness in his expression gives him away.

"What the hell are you talking about?" he says, shaking his head and playing the part perfectly.

Behind us, not too far away, a few moans fill the air, but I ignore them and take a step closer to our leader. "You know what I'm talking about—"

"You ran out and left us!" Ramirez shouts.

All eyes are on us, but I don't bother looking away from Dax to figure out if they're on his side or mine. Frankly, I don't give a shit. I was there and I know what happened, so whether these people choose to believe him or me, doesn't really matter.

"I didn't leave you," Dax says, "I went to get help."

"You locked the door!" Ramirez winces and grabs his arm, but he doesn't back down.

Dax's expression turns cold. "There's no lock on that door, so I don't know what you're talking about." He looks around and shrugs. "Go check if you don't believe me."

More zombies moan, and I glance back to find a small group of them headed our way. Even though most of the guys around us aren't involved in this confrontation, nobody moves to stop them. They're all too busy gawking. I half expect them to form a circle around us as they start chanting "fight, fight, fight!" over and over again.

Next to me, Ramirez is fuming, but he doesn't say a word, and when I take a good look at the guys around us, I realize why. Everyone is glaring at him like he's the asshole, not Dax. It takes me all of two seconds to figure out why. This man has not only been their leader out here since the beginning, but he's the one who found most of them. Who brought them back to Hope Springs and gave them something they never thought they'd have again: a home.

Dax lets out a deep breath and shakes his head. "Everything happened so fast, so I don't blame you for being confused, but let me clear it up for you. Allen opened fire." Dax jerks his head toward the bearded guy, who's sitting at the edge of the group with his friends. His eyes are huge as he looks back and forth between the incoming zombies and us. "You went down right away. Mark and I were going for help when he got shot. I thought he was dead, I even checked his pulse, and in the middle of all the gunfire I thought you were too. So of course I left. I thought I was leaving two dead guys behind, not running out on my men." Dax steps forward and puts his hand on Ramirez's shoulder. "I never would have left you if I had known."

"I banged on the door and called for help," Ramirez says, sounding less convinced than he did a few seconds ago.

More moans break out, and I look back once again. The zombies are close now. Six feet from the edge of the group, heading right toward the survivors we just saved. The newcomers drag themselves to their feet and huddle together. Dax glances their way. His eyes then move to the approaching zombies, and something flashes in them. Something that makes what just happened in that apartment seem insignificant.

Dax shoots a look Donovan's way, then turns back to Ramirez without addressing the incoming zombies. "I thought it was Allen. I never would have kept the door shut if I'd known it was you."

Dax shrugs, and everyone around him nods like they were there and saw exactly what happened. They weren't, but Jim and I were. We didn't see what went down in the hall, but we did see Dax holding the door shut. There's no way in hell he thought the man banging on the door and calling for help was the guy shooting at him. Why would he?

"Where's your gun?" Allen, the man we just saved, hisses.

I turn to find him shaking and backing away from the approaching zombies. He's unarmed, and so are his friends.

"Shit," Ramirez says, running his hand through his dark hair. "I guess I got confused in all the craziness."

"It happens," Dax replies. "Don't sweat it. I'm just worried that you would think I'd leave you behind."

"No," Ramirez says quickly. "No way. I know I can count on you Dax."

Dax smiles and lets out a deep sigh that is way more dramatic than it should be. "Good." He chuckles and turns toward the group. "Now that we have that taken care of, I should probably take care of these assholes."

He jerks his head toward the approaching dead as he pulls out his knife. By now they're so close that the scent of death has surrounded us. There are around ten of them, but they're slow and shouldn't be much of a match for us. If someone decides to move forward and take care of them, that is. At the moment, though, Dax's men are frozen in place. The crazy thing is, they don't look scared. They're just waiting for their leader to give them go ahead, I think.

Dax steps in front of his men, but instead of heading toward the dead, he moves to Allen's side. "Let me show you how to take these assholes out."

His men continue to hang back. I glance toward Jim, who looks just as confused as I am, and I can't help feeling like we missed something big. Whatever it is, I'm not about to let these dead bastards get the jump on me. I pull my knife and when Jim sees me, he does the same.

Before we can do anything Donovan steps in front of us. "Give it a second," the big man says.

Dax drags Allen, who isn't fighting him but doesn't seem too thrilled by the idea, toward a zombie covered in frost. The dead man chomps his teeth, but I don't have time to focus on what's going on.

The other zombies are closing in, and we're still just standing around like they aren't a threat, which is crazy. No way I'm going to let these assholes take me down without a fight.

I push past Donovan, and Jim is right behind me. Allen lets out a cry, but I stay focused on the dead in front of me. It's just Jim and me heading into the dead. The others, Dax's men, are still waiting.

"Come on!" Jim yells as he slashes his knife into the zom in front of him.

I do the same, and two go down while behind me the women we just saved shriek.

"That's right," Dax says on the other side of the horde. "Make sure you get him in the brain."

There's a grunt and a moan and more screams from the women. The little kid starts crying, and someone, a man, lets out a howl of agony.

Even though my heart is pounding like crazy, I don't look away from the zoms in front of me. Finally the other men move forward to help, but something about the timing bugs the hell out of me. Still, I don't look anywhere but in front of me, keeping my focus on the job I have to do.

When the last zombie has hit the ground, I'm panting and my body is slick with sweat under my leather pants. I step back and glance around to find the other men in the group just as out of breath as I am. When I look at Jim, he's frowning and his eyes are focused on something behind me. I turn, only to find Dax standing above Allen, who's sitting in the snow. Holding his bloody arm against his chest.

"It's okay," Dax says slowly. "You could be immune."

No one else says a word, but when I look around none of Dax's men seem be surprised by what just happened. Almost like this was planned. My gaze meets Donovan's for a second, and suddenly I get why he stopped me from helping.

"We need to move out," Dax calls, stepping away from a sobbing Allen. "We have a few people who need to get to a doctor."

ON THE WAY BACK TO HOPE SPRINGS, I RIDE IN THE back of the truck with Jim and Mark, who moans every time we drive over a bump. Allen and the other survivors are in the back of the other truck, and I'm glad. I have a lot to say about what just happened, none of which they need to hear.

"This is some bad shit," I whisper to Jim, who's crouched beside me.

My partner looks around, but none of Dax's men seem to be paying attention to us. "You think they had this planned before we even left?"

"Not sure, but it's obvious Dax and Donovan did."

"It makes sense. We're looking for people who are immune, but the only way to find out if they're immune is to have them get bitten." Jim shakes his head. "I'm surprised I didn't think of it before we left."

"It doesn't surprise you that he did this?" I'm shocked but until today I haven't had much interaction with Dax.

"Not at all," Jim says slowly.

He pulls out a cigarette and pops it in his mouth, looking around the truck. The other men are at the front, while Jim and I sit with Mark close to the tailgate. No one seems particularly worried about their friend, which makes me wonder what these men are really like. No wonder Corinne has been concerned about things.

"And this?" I ask, nodding toward Mark. "You think he ran out on them on purpose?"

"Sure. His number one priority in this thing is to save own ass."

I exhale when it hits me that this could have been me. I could be the one bleeding out in the back of a truck, not Mark. If Dax hadn't been pissed off when we went into that building, he could have put Jim and me in his group. I could have been the one who got shot.

"Shit," I mutter, leaning back.

"This isn't going to happen to you," Jim says. "You're smart enough to see through him."

"We don't know that. Anything can happen out there."

"Not this."

I shake my head, thinking about Ginny and the baby and everything that could go wrong in Hope Springs. Especially if Dax decides he wants to take over. The gleam in his eyes when he asked about what I'd seen out there is fresh in my mind, and for the first time since arriving in Hope Springs, it hits me exactly how fast things can go from good to bad.

If something happens to me, Ginny will be alone.

I push myself up and twist to face Jim. "I need you to do something for me."

"Don't do this, man." Jim shakes his head and blows out a mouthful of smoke. "This is dumb. Nothing's going to happen to you. Not like this."

"We don't know that and I won't be able to relax until I know I've made some plans for the future."

Jim exhales again but nods. "Fine. What do you want?"

"If something happens to me and this whole thing goes bad…" I glance back toward Dax's men one more time to make sure none of them are listening. "If Dax takes over. Promise me that you'll get Ginny out of here. Take her somewhere else and keep her safe. She can't go through that kind of thing again."

Jim presses his lips together, his cigarette forgotten between his fingers. "You trust me like that?"

"I do," I say, realizing for the first time that he just might be the only person here I can actually depend on.

He's one of us. Someone who would have fit into our old group. No matter who he was before all this, Jim isn't that person anymore. He was right when he said this thing has changed all of us, but unlike most of the world, Jim has allowed this thing to change him into someone better.

Someone who is going to work to shape this world into something new and strong, not rip it apart. Like Axl.

"Will you do it for me?" I ask when he hasn't answered.

Jim nods once, then looks away. "I'll do whatever it takes to keep her safe."

"Thanks." I lean back, staring at the ceiling as we bump down the road toward Hope Springs. For the first time ever, I don't feel like the name is fitting.

CHAPTER EIGHTEEN

GINNY

Gretchen can hardly sit still, and it's starting to get under my skin.

"I told Mark not to go," she says, shaking her head so hard her red hair swishes around her shoulders. "It's stupid. Going out there to look for survivors. What's the point?"

"Because we might find the person who will save us all. A vaccine means we can have a normal life. That a bite won't mean death for any of us."

Gretchen huffs and throws herself on my couch. She and Mark have a house two streets over, but she's been here since the group headed to Duncan this morning. Bright and early. The fact that I was sleeping when she showed up didn't seem to bother her.

"Whatever," she says, staring at the ceiling.

Sometimes it's hard to remember that Gretchen is so young. There are so many aspects of this new life that have made her stronger and more mature, but every now and then she does something like this that shows her teenage side. Maybe it should irritate me—teenagers are notoriously a pain in the ass—but I'm glad. It tells me there are some things about the old world that will never disappear. That teenagers will always have a selfish side. That there are parts of human nature even zombies can't erase.

"They'll be back soon," I say, trying to hold in my smile and failing miserably.

I get to my feet and head to the kitchen, wincing when my swollen ankles protest the movement. Three months to go, but I'm already looking forward to the end.

I've put a lot of weight on. Even more than doctors would typically recommend. If I hadn't been so thin to begin with or gone so long with almost no food, maybe my doctor would be concerned. Instead he just smiles when I step on the scale, as thankful as I am that we've managed to thrive despite our circumstances. I have a strange feeling that if society manages to rebuild itself, we'll go back to the old way of thinking. Back when being a little plump was a status symbol rather than a reason to be mocked.

As for me, I'm glad to have the extra weight. I spent years in Hollywood keeping track of every crumb that passed my lips. Knowing that if I gained even one pound my face would end up on the cover of some tabloid. The eyes of the world were constantly on me, and I didn't realize until it was gone how stressful it had all been. And how unnecessary.

Now that I have a second chance, all I want is to be normal.

"Coffee?" I call from the kitchen.

"Ugh," Gretchen groans from the other room. "Not unless you can get me Starbucks. I'd kill for a Caramel Macchiato right now."

"Seems like a silly thing to kill someone over," I say.

"Not a person." I can practically hear Gretchen's eyes roll. "A zombie, of course."

I laugh but decide not to mention the fact that if Starbucks were still around, there would be no zombies to kill.

I pour myself a cup of coffee, dumping a few teaspoons of sugar into the dark liquid while I stare at the clock. Even though I keep telling Gretchen to calm down, I can't help wondering what's going on out there. The zombies have started to thaw, and more and more show up at the fence every day. They're still slow, but that doesn't mean one can't take you by surprise. It's the people, though, that have me really worried.

A knock on the door echoes through the house and cuts through my thoughts, making me jump so high I almost spill my coffee. My heart pounds faster and my hands begin to shake. I put my mug down and suck in a deep breath, blowing it out as I turn and head toward the living room. Trying to ignore the uneasiness inside me. Gretchen's eyes are big and round and she's staring at the door, but she hasn't moved an inch. I freeze a foot from the door and try to give myself a pep talk, but nothing optimistic or encouraging comes to mind. This whole thing is silly. Someone knocked. It doesn't mean a thing and it could be anyone. It's probably just someone stopping by to say hi or ask for help with a project. Hell, it wouldn't surprise me if someone around here wanted to rub my belly for good luck. It happens all the time on the street.

Before I can talk myself out of it, I jerk the door open.

Richard stands on the doorstep with his back to me, and he pulls his hat off as he turns. I'm momentarily too distracted by his messy, gray hair to notice the way he twists the hat between his hands. It doesn't take long to catch on to his nervousness, though, and it makes my heart skip a couple beats.

"What's wrong?" I ask, my voice shaking as much as my hands were a few seconds ago.

Richard gives me a sympathetic smile that does not help me calm down. "You have any idea where Gretchen is? I've been looking for her."

His gaze moves past me before I have a chance to answer, and I turn to find the teen standing in the middle of the living room. Her pale skin has lost even more of its color, and her blue eyes have already filled with tears.

"Is it Mark?" she asks, moving forward a couple inches, then shrinking back when Richard nods. "Is he dead?"

"He was shot. The doctor took him into surgery, but they think he's going to pull through."

Gretchen nods again, but she barely blinks, and I'm not sure how much of what Richard just said she's actually absorbed.

"Was he the only injury?" I ask as a silent prayer goes through my head. Jon can't be hurt or Richard would have mentioned it first. Right?

He slips his hat back on. "No. Ramirez got shot, but it's not as bad."

My gaze goes to Gretchen, who hasn't moved, then back to Richard. "What happened?"

"They came across some survivors who had been hiding in an apartment. The guy was scared." Richard shakes his head like he can't believe it. "He freaked out and opened fire. There were a tense couple minutes, but once they realized nobody was going to eat them, they calmed down."

"Eat them?" Gretchen says, finally snapping out of it a little.

"I know it's hard to believe, but these people actually thought everyone who had survived the virus had turned cannibal. They've been up there since the dead came back—"

"Since September?" I ask, unable to fathom hiding in one place for so long. Not even trying to find other survivors. What's the point of being alive if you're not going to fight?

"Hard to believe, I know, but it makes sense why they'd think everybody had gone cannibal instead of turning into a zombie. They never saw the dead up close."

Cannibal? It's an odd thought, but I guess from a distance it isn't really that far-fetched. Certainly not any crazier than thinking most of the human race had turned into zombies.

214

Richard looks past me once again, his eyes settling on Gretchen. His expression is soft, just like it always is when he looks the teen. It has a lot to do with his granddaughter, who was on her honeymoon when this all started. He doesn't have a clue what happened to her and most likely will never find out. She and Gretchen apparently look alike — at least according to Richard.

"You want me to take you to the clinic?" he asks, his voice low and gentle.

Gretchen nods and heads his way, grabbing her coat off the couch. "I need to be there when he wakes up."

"I'm coming too," I say as I hurry to grab my own coat.

I need to see Jon. Obviously he's okay or Richard would have said something, but knowing he could've been hurt has my insides uneasy. He's been a major part of the healing process for me. Each day that goes by brings me closer to the person I want to be, and each time Jon is there for me to lean on, it helps me feel just a little more secure. A little stronger. I never felt like I needed anyone before, but I've also never been in love. Not like this. Not with every inch of my soul. Jon is something I never expected to find.

I follow Gretchen and Richard, pulling my jacket closer to my body as a cool breeze sweeps over us. The walk to the clinic will take ten minutes or so. Driving would be faster, but we're trying to conserve gas, so unless it's absolutely necessary we stick to walking. The fact that Richard didn't drive tells me Mark isn't too bad off. If he were barely clinging to life, there's no way Richard would have walked.

"Jon's okay," he says after a few minutes of walking in silence.

I brush a few hairs out of my face when the wind whips them forward. "I know, but I still want to see him. Going out there is scary. Risky. I just want to be able to wrap my arms around him and know he's really here and in one piece."

Gretchen cringes and I feel like an ass, but I can't take it back and I wouldn't want to. This is part of what I'm working on: verbalizing how I feel. Letting Jon know that I love

215

him as much as he loves me and that I can picture the future he has planned out for us. This baby, for example. In the beginning, I could go for weeks at a time without talking about it, but now I find myself constantly bringing it up. Discussing names and ways to keep him or her safe in the middle of all this madness. It's progress, even if there are still moments of darkness surrounding this pregnancy. I may never be able to reach a point where I'm not questioning whether or not Jon is the father.

We reach the clinic, and Gretchen hurries inside the second the doors slide open. Richard follows, walking faster to catch up, but I hang back. If she needs me I'll be here for her, but at the moment Richard will be enough. They've formed a father-daughter kind of bond that I didn't see coming, and it's nice. Gretchen never really had much of a dad before all this.

I spot Jon the second I step through the doors, standing on the other side of the room with Jim. He has his back to me, and his leather jacket is slick with what I can only assume is blood. It's on his neck too, and caked in his hair. Seeing it there makes my heart flutter even though Richard told me there was nothing to worry about.

Jim looks up as I head over, and his eyes hold mine for a second longer than normal. It makes the hair on my scalp stand up, and my steps falter. Why do I feel like he knows everything about me? He says something to Jon, who turns, and just the sight of his face allows the worry inside me to melt away. He's whole and well, barely a scratch on him that I can see. The blood obviously belongs to Ramirez or Mark, not Jon. I shouldn't be so happy about that, but I am and I refuse to apologize.

"You okay?" I ask when I stop in front of him.

He wraps his arms around me and presses his lips to the side of my head. "It was tense, but we made it out. Hopefully Mark will pull through and we can say there were no casualties from our group."

I pull back so I can look Jon in the eyes. "How bad is it?"

216

"He was unconscious and seemed to have lost a lot of blood, but other than that I don't know what condition he's in." Jon exhales and shakes his head, his gaze moving away from me and over to where Gretchen stands. "Did Richard tell you what happened?"

"He said some survivors freaked out and shot at you. That they didn't know about the zombies. Had they really been hiding up there since September?"

Jon's eyes move back to mine, and the expression in them makes my stomach tense. Something happened that I don't know about yet, I can tell. No way Jon would look at me like this unless something big had gone down. Maybe Richard doesn't know everything, or maybe he just didn't have time to tell us exactly what happened out there.

"Yeah," Jon says, his voice low. "They haven't showered since the water went off, and they've been using one of the other apartments as a bathroom. The whole floor smelled like shit. Literally. It was disturbing." He blows out a breath as shakes his head, almost like he's trying to erase the images from his mind.

"How many people?"

"Five," Jon says. "A woman and her seven-year-old boy, two men, and another woman. None of them are related to each other except the woman and her son. Apparently they crossed paths after the virus hit and everyone died. They saw the zombies from a window and thought all the survivors had gone mad. So they hid."

"It sounds horrible," I say, thinking back to all our months on the road. It was rough, but nothing like that. We were making a go of it at least.

"The mother is pregnant," Jon says. "She's due real soon, too. The doctor is checking her out, but it's a good thing we found them when we did. I can't even imagine a baby being born in that filth."

Another pregnant woman. We've already had two births, but neither one of those babies lived for more than a couple hours. Each death has scared me a little more.

"Hey," Jon says, pulling me against him again. "Don't think about that. It doesn't have anything to do with us. This woman's husband died from the virus, so whether or not this baby lives won't mean a thing for us. Our baby has two immune parents, and he is going to be okay."

"He?" I say, rubbing my tears on Jon's jacket before I pull back. "So you've decided it's a boy?"

"I know you don't want to find out, and that's fine, but I can't keep calling our baby it. There's something about the whole thing that creeps me out."

I laugh despite the ache in my chest. We've had a few ultrasounds, just to make sure everything looks good, but I wouldn't let the doctor tell us the sex of the baby. *Being surprised will be more fun.* That's what I told Jon, anyway. The truth is I'm afraid of getting too attached. If I find out what this baby is. If I give it a name and an identity, make it real, I'm not sure I'll be able to hold it together if everything goes bad.

Jon's hand moves up and down my back, but after a few seconds, I get the feeling he isn't really thinking about me or the baby or the pregnant woman they brought in anymore. I look up to find him staring across the room at Dax, and the expression in Jon's eyes sends a shiver through me. I haven't forgotten the things Corinne told me about the other man or the way he acted when we elected our committee last month. He made a play for a position of power, something Corinne called from a mile away. Thankfully, everyone seemed to be happy with the way she was running things. I don't know Dax well, but I've been uneasy about him since my discussion with Corinne.

"How's Mark?" Dax's voice booms through the room, and I turn just as a nurse walks through the door.

"Still waiting to hear," she says.

Dax nods, and I look back to find Jon and Jim in the middle of exchanging a look I can't quite figure out. Something else went on when they were out there.

"We get everything worked out?" one of Dax's men says.

"Got the man in quarantine. Now all we have to do is wait. Who knows, this could be our lucky day," Dax says, much louder than necessary. He has his chest puffed out, and his eyes move across the room, almost as if he's making sure he has everyone's attention. "This guy could turn out to be the person we've been looking for. We'll just have to wait and see."

"What's he talking about?" I ask, turning back to Jon.

He exchanges a look with Jim again before saying, "One of the men we found hiding in the apartment was bitten on our way out."

"Oh my God." My hand goes to my mouth and for a second, I can't find any words. It doesn't make sense. They're usually so careful when they're out. "I thought the zombies were still slow. How did they manage to get the jump on you?"

Jon licks his lips, this time his gaze moving past me to where Dax stands. "There was a lot happening."

It obvious he's leaving some of the details out, but I don't press him. We're in the middle of the clinic, and there are so many people around. If it has something to do with Dax, Jon may not want to tell me right now.

The three of us stand in tense silence while on the other side of the room, Dax and his men celebrate like they've already discovered a cure. It isn't only premature, it's inappropriate, considering they still don't know if Mark is going to make it. I'm glad Gretchen went in the back with Richard. She doesn't need to see these men carrying on like this.

By the time the door opens and the doctor comes out, I'm so irritated that I'm ready to throw something at Dax.

"Give me some good news, doc!" Dax calls. The smile on his face is so big it makes him look creepy.

Dan—Dr. Murray—frowns. "Mark is going to pull through. He lost a lot of blood, but we've given him a transfusion and he's awake. He's in pain, but he's talking and there doesn't seem to be any damage he's not going to recover from. He got lucky."

"Great day!" Dax says, clapping his hands together. "We got supplies and some new survivors. No one died." He turns to face his men, grinning. "We're heroes! Let's get a drink."

The men around Dax cheer. They're all laughing and joking, carrying on as they head for the door. I wait for Dax to ask Jon and Jim to join him, but he just barely glances our way as he walks by. The expression in his eyes is cold. What the hell went on out there?

The second Dax and his men are gone and the clinic is once again silent, I turn to face Jon. "What's going on?"

Jon runs his hand through his hair, and Jim's mouth curls up in disgust. They're both staring at the door Dax just disappeared through.

"He let that guy get bitten on purpose," Jon says, his voice low despite the fact that we're alone.

I blink, and I can't for the life of me think of a thing to say. "What? Why?"

"He's looking for somebody immune," Jim says, pulling a pack of cigarettes out of his pocket. Just like Angus and his dip, Jim seems to have a never-ending supply. "The only way we're going to know for sure is if somebody gets bitten. Just finding survivors isn't enough."

"But that's crazy," I say, shaking my head. "He has to realize the odds of this one man being immune are slim. He's just killed a man for nothing."

Jim's blue eyes hold mine, and for some reason, I find myself taking a step back. I don't know Jon's partner well—he isn't exactly into socializing—but there's always been something about him that's seemed…dangerous. He's always watching. Observing. Being around him is like living under a microscope.

"Some men don't hold morality in the same light as the rest of us. Now that there's no one for them to answer to, there's nothing to stop them from doing what they want."

A shiver runs through me, but instead of stepping back,

this time I'm frozen. Jim's gaze holds mine, his eyes searching my face until every inch of my skin is covered in goose bumps. Only it has nothing to do with him. It's more about what he just said and what I know he can see when he looks at me. Not just who I really am, but everything I've gone through and who it's made me. He knows that I get men like Dax more than most people. That I understand the kind of threat he poses to us and the new world we're trying to create.

"We can stop them," I say firmly. "As long as there are people like us out there, they aren't going to be allowed to get away with doing whatever they want. I won't live in a world like that."

Jim smiles, and for the first time, I feel like I really understand the man standing in front of me. Jon's told me a little about him, but we've barely spoken other than a hello here and there. Now though, I can see who Jim really is, and I know with certainty he's someone who would be there to help us if we needed it. He's someone we can really count on. The first person I've been totally confident in since getting separated from our old group.

CHAPTER NINETEEN

GINNY

Third trimester," Dr. Murray—Dan—says when he walks into the room, and his smile is stretched so wide that you'd never know this whole pregnancy might be horribly doomed. He sits on the wheeled stool, looking my chart over for a second like he hasn't been seeing me every single week since Jon and I arrived in Hope Springs. When he finally looks up, his smile has grown even wider. "Has the baby been nice and active?"

"Enough to keep me awake at night," I mutter, trying to hold on to my bitterness. It's a defense mechanism, I know, but it will help me cope if this doesn't turn out the way Jon and I want it to.

The doctor smiles as he sets my chart aside. "That's good news."

"You're not the one who feels like a zom—"

I stop myself before the word is out completely, and the doctor's smile fades. We sit there for a few seconds staring at each other like neither one of us knows how to respond. It's weird. The saying has been around for as long as I can remember and I've probably said it a million times in my life, but it means more than it used to. Before the virus hit, it was something people said but gave very little thought to because it didn't mean anything. Now it does. It means so much more than I could have ever imagine possible.

"There's one saying that's bound to go out of style," Dan finally says.

"I think it already has. I know I haven't said it since this all started. To be honest, it's a little strange that it popped into my head just now."

My cheeks burn, but I'm not sure why I'm embarrassed. It's such an easy mistake to make, and no one would be mad at me for saying it, but I'm glad it happened here in the privacy of this exam room rather than around a big group of people.

Dan lets out a deep breath, and when it's gone, a smile is back on his face. It's forced though. "Don't sweat it. I'm sure you're not the first person who's said it since this all started."

"Yeah," I say, shaking my head.

"Let's focus on the baby!"

His voice is way too chipper, but I let him have it. My way of dealing with things is to hold on to my anger and sarcasm while his is to act like everything is perfect. Neither one is right and neither one really works, but it's all we have.

I lie back and pull my shirt up, revealing my round belly to the doctor. Holding my breath while I wait. The cold surface of the stethoscope presses against my skin, forcing all the air out of my lungs. The doctor gives me an apologetic smile, barely looking away from my stomach as he listens for my baby's heartbeat. His smile grows after a few seconds, becoming more sincere. It helps me relax. Even though none of the babies have died in the womb, I'm still always waiting for the axe to drop.

224

"Perfect." Dan drapes the stethoscope around his neck and sits back. "Your blood pressure is okay and the heartbeat is strong. Everything is right on track for a perfect delivery."

Everything except the killer virus that may still be clinging to the air.

"Great!" I say, trying to match his enthusiasm. It falls flat, of course. I'm never going to be the cheerleader-esque person I was before all this, and I don't have enough energy to channel the actress I was before either — not to mention the desire.

The doctor sits back and purses his lips. "You're worried."

I push down the urge to throw a *duh* his way and instead say, "A little. Isn't that normal after everything we've been through, though?"

"Of course it is, especially considering the last twenty-four hours."

I almost can't say a thing because I literally have no clue what he's talking about. "What?"

"The woman they found last week in Duncan?"

I shake my head even though I know *who* he's talking about. Jon was on the run when they found the woman and her friends hiding in that apartment. It's been a tense week, and a lot has happened — Mark may have pulled through, but the man Dax allowed to get bitten didn't. He turned and had to be put down, just like every other person we've seen bitten so far. Of course, none of that helps me figure out *what* the doctor is referring to right now.

Dan lets out a deep breath and shakes his head. "Jon didn't tell you."

"Tell me what?" I ask, my voice coming out slightly hysterical.

"She gave birth last night. The baby was full-term, but with her diet and living conditions, we didn't know what to expect. Even after we found out the father didn't die from the virus."

A layer of ice coats my body. "I didn't know that."

"Shit." The laid-back attitude typically surrounding Dan is gone, and in its absence, a fumbling man appears before me. He shakes his head and lets out a half-chuckle that doesn't match the situation in the slightest. "He wasn't immune, or at least we don't think he was. There's no way to know for sure, since he was killed in a car accident when the woman was only ten weeks along. The baby's death could have been for any of a number of reasons: the virus or the lack of prenatal care. Maybe even something the mother picked up in those living conditions. Or it could have just come down to plain old lack of nutrition. It's hard to say."

"So the baby was stillborn?" I ask, my head spinning from all the details and emotions moving through me. I try to grasp ahold of one or two so I can make sense of what I'm feeling, but my insides are too jumbled and confused.

"No." The doctor exhales. "I wish Jon had talked to you about this."

"Maybe he didn't know." It isn't true and I know it, but part of me is hoping Dan will lie.

"He was here last night when she delivered." He shakes his head. "He should have told you. I know why he didn't want to, but there's no way to keep something like this a secret. We're all too involved in each other's lives for that!"

His words echo through the room, or maybe just through my brain. It's hard to say for sure, because I suddenly feel like I'm having an out-of-body experience. I always thought that was a cliché. Turns out, it's not. When your brain is on overload and you can't focus, it literally feels like you're floating above your own body. Like now. I can look down and see myself sitting on the table, staring at the wall while I work to unravel everything I've just learned.

Another baby was born and died. We don't know if the father was immune. This gives my own baby a higher chance of dying.

"Ginny?"

I swallow and blink, forcing my eyes to focus. It takes a few seconds, but when they do, I somehow manage to smile.

226

"Sorry. I just had to think it all through. You're right. There's nothing to worry about. The father probably wasn't immune. He had close to an eighty-five percent chance of being susceptible, right?"

"Right." Dan's eyes narrow on my face. "You sure you're okay?"

"Absolutely," I say as I slide off the table.

Maybe I do have a little bit of the actress I used to be buried inside of me after all.

"Okay..." The doctor gives me another look before nodding.

I almost let out a sigh of relief when he turns away. There's nothing I hate more than being studied. I have too much to hide.

"We'll see you next week," he says, leading me out the door.

I smile and say something that makes him grin, only I have no idea what, then head out. Waving to the receptionist as I go by. Every step is an effort, and my legs are so heavy they feel like they've been filled with rocks, but I don't stop, and I don't let on that anything is wrong as I head through town. Down the street, passing other people who wave and say hello. Two women stop to rub my stomach, a gesture that would make me cringe any other time, but right now I hardly feel it. Hardly even realize it's happening until they're laughing and walking away. Then I'm rounding the corner, moving past the other houses on our street, not even knowing how I got home so fast because it usually takes me a good ten minutes. It hasn't been that long since I left the clinic, has it?

The house is empty when I open the front door and the lights are off. It's only three and the sun is bright enough to light the room, so I don't bother flipping the switch. Light bulbs, like everything else once manufactured in this world, are a precious commodity. Then I'm sitting on the couch, staring at the wall, my hand rubbing my stomach. My baby moves, a foot or an elbow pressing against my side. I touch it, feeling the hard lump and imagining how it will feel when this life comes out of me.

When he takes his first deep breath, filling his newly matured lungs with poison.

Struggling to breathe.

Getting sick.

Dying.

Then someone will put a blade through his skull to prevent him from coming back as one of them.

A shiver shoots through me, shaking my whole body. I can't move. Can barely breathe. Definitely can't force my brain to think about anything other than my baby's death.

I'm still sitting on the couch in the exact same position, thinking the exact same things when the front door opens.

"Ginny?" Jon flips a switch, and I squint when light floods the room. "Why are you sitting in the dark?"

Is it dark? When did the sun go down? I'm not sure, but based on how black the sky is outside, I'd guess it's close to eight o'clock. Jon should have been home hours ago, and I should have fixed dinner.

"I'm sorry," I say as I get to my feet, unable to really focus. "Let me make dinner."

"I don't care about dinner." Jon grabs my arm, forcing me to turn to face him. "What's going on?" He blinks, then narrows his eyes on my face. "Are you crying?"

"Am I?" I wipe my hand across my cheek, but it isn't until I see the moisture on my fingertips that I realize he's right. I am crying. When did I start crying?

"Ginny?" Jon's voice takes on an octave I've never heard before. Like he's going through puberty or just sucked in a mouthful of helium.

I know he's terrified, and even though I want to comfort him, I can't make myself. I should be mad that he didn't tell me about the baby dying, but I can't be because I'm too scared. Not only of what's to come but of all the emotions going through me. I didn't know I'd reached this point until now or that it would all hurt so much when I faced the end.

228

When did the life growing inside me become so important? Just a couple months ago Gretchen told me about another baby dying, and back then I was able to shrug it off. Just part of normal life now. People die, babies die. That's how it is.

Now though, as I think about this pregnancy coming to a tragic end, my insides feel like they're in a vise and someone is turning the crank. Squeezing me tighter and tighter until I can't breathe or function or face the truth of this world a moment longer.

"Why didn't you tell me another baby died?" I finally manage to get out.

The words are almost drowned out by sobs, and even though I want to shake myself until I pull it together, I can't seem to get a handle on my emotions. They're wild and out of control.

"Shit. I was going to tell you tonight. It happened so fast, and when I came home you were in such a good mood. I didn't want to ruin things by throwing this at you."

"I wish I'd heard it from you."

"This doesn't mean anything, Ginny. You know that, right? That baby didn't have a chance. You should have seen the way they were living."

Jon's hands tighten on my shoulders, and I nod, trying to get it together. It doesn't work. Tears stream down my face, and sobs shake my body until I have a difficult time getting air to my lungs. I hiccup like a child, which only makes it all so much worse. I feel like a child. Like a vulnerable, lost child who doesn't have a clue how to find her way home.

"I didn't w-want this b-baby. It w-wasn't my ch-choice."

It's all I can get out, and it isn't what I really want to say to Jon. I want to tell him I've changed my mind. That he *helped* me change my mind. That I fell in love with him and this baby and the life we could have together. I didn't even know it until today when I found out that another baby had died. It snuck up on me, and I didn't even see it coming.

Jon wraps his arms around me, pulling me against him. Cradling me like I'm the innocent life about to be squashed out by this virus. "It's okay," he says, running his hand down my head and over my back. "I'm here. I'll always be here."

The words only make me cry harder because we both know there are no guarantees in this life. Not anymore.

CORINNE IS ON THE RADIO WHEN I SLIP INTO THE room. She smiles when she looks up, but it's fast, and only a second later she's back to writing. Taking notes on the things Hendrix is telling her. I shut the door and head over, listening but not saying a word. They have daily meetings, and even though I have no real right to be in on them, I like being here. I like knowing what's going on in Atlanta and Key West.

"We had a new group come in last night," Hendrix is in the middle of saying. "One woman had been bitten so we put her in quarantine. I told you about the new quarantine measures we've taken, right?"

"Yes," Corinne says into the receiver. "It sounds like you have a good system set up. We've only had the one man get bitten since we found out, and we used the same measures with him."

"Good, good," Hendrix says. "It's worked well for us. I came up with the plan, you know."

"I know."

Corinne gives a little eye roll, and I smile even though I'm anxious to find out what happened with the infected woman. Hendrix loves to hear himself talk—and to be praised for his leadership abilities—which is good for us. He could sit here for hours and tell Corinne about the amazing things he's accomplished in Atlanta, and as a result, I'm sure he's let things slip that other people may not have told us. Like how a group inside the walls tried to challenge the system they'd set up. It didn't go well, and they were forced to make an example out of them. Swift justice, as Hendrix called it.

"Good," he says, and I can hear the pride in his voice. "We, of course, were hoping she wouldn't turn, but only two hours after she was brought in she started showing symptoms."

Corinne frowns. "Did you put her down then?"

This is something we've discussed: the next time someone in Hope Springs gets infected, how long do we let them go before taking care of the situation? When the man from Duncan was brought in, we had no plan in place, and Dax insisted that we wait it out completely. To me it seems cruel to take it all the way to the end, but we don't know how this thing really works. Will they show symptoms before their body fights off the virus?

"We saw the thing through even though we knew it wasn't going to turn out the way we had hoped," Hendrix says. "The virus took the same course as always: lethargy, then the patient bounced back, then sudden death followed by rebirth."

Rebirth. The word makes me shudder. I've heard Hendrix say it before, but it doesn't have any less of an impact this time around. It seems wrong. A birth is the celebration of bringing a new life into this world, but that's not what these things are. They're a distortion of what people really are, and their presence has changed everything. Created a new world that's more horror than hope.

Corinne sighs, and I look up to find her shaking her head. She presses the button on the receiver and says, "Looking for someone who might be immune is a tough job. We have to hope for someone to get bitten even though we know most of the time it will be a death sentence for them."

"There's nothing easy about being in charge," Hendrix says a second later.

"That's the truth," Corinne mutters to herself.

"What else is going on there?" I ask, scooting to the edge of my chair.

Corinne holds the button down. "Any other news? Anything from Key West?"

"Not much. They haven't seen any new survivors recently, but with the hurricane season what it was, we aren't surprised. It didn't seem to knock out the zombies, but it sure as hell took a toll on the survivors." Hendrix sighs. "Things would be better if they'd come up this way, but we're having a tough time convincing them of that."

"People like their independence." Corinne looks my way, and I squirm when her eyes move to my belly. "Two nights ago we had another baby born, but it didn't make it."

All the pain of last night comes back, and I find myself looking away from Corinne. Down at my round stomach. I wish she hadn't brought it up while I was here.

Hendrix comes back over the radio a second later, and my focus is once again on the radio. "Shit! Can't believe I didn't mention it earlier. We had one too. Last night, actually. A little thing, but strong."

I grip the arms of my chair, and Corinne's eyes get huge. She shakes her head, the receiver forgotten for a few seconds as she stares at me in disbelief.

Then she snaps out of it and pushes the button down. "It lived?"

"Sure did," Hendrix says. "Doctors administered some experimental antibiotics during labor, then again after the little guy was born. He had a low fever at first but ended up pulling through. Of course, we have no way of knowing if the virus was the culprit, but we're hopeful."

I exhale and sink back into my seat while Corinne asks a few other questions. The CDC kept a baby alive. It's a miracle, but one that's way too far from Colorado to help my baby and me. Still, it *has* to be good news. There has to be a way to take whatever they've done and apply it here. I just know it.

And if that doesn't work, there's always the possibility that Jon and I can go to Atlanta.

APRIL

CHAPTER TWENTY

AXL

Winston ain't gettin' better, but I can't stop tryin' to get through to him. There's gotta be a way.

"Winston!" I call when I step outside and spot him crossin' the lawn.

He stops but don't turn, and I jog over, cursin' under my breath 'cause I'm to the point where I don't got a clue what to do 'bout all this. I been patient. Waitin' for him to move on. It ain't happened though, and I'm startin' to think it never will. That Winston's lost to us, which is a damn shame. Back when all this first started, I depended on him.

When I stop, Winston finally turns. Don't mean he looks like he gives a damn what I got to say, though.

"Now that it's warmer people have started buggin' me 'bout headin' over to check out Hope Springs," I tell him. "Thought you might wanna come."

"Why would you think that?" Winston asks, not even blinkin'.

"You always been in on the plannin'," I say even though it ain't been true for a long time now. Not since Jess died, really.

Sure, when we first got to Brady's place, Winston pitched in a little. Helped find supplies and get the fence reinforced. Helped keep watch. Now, even when he's out on patrol, he ain't really helpin'. He's just another body I gotta worry 'bout, but I let it go 'cause I knew he needed the space. This is too damn much, though. He's thrown in the towel, and it pisses me off.

"Don't do this," I say, steppin' closer.

Winston flinches like I've hit him, and he backs up. "I'm not doing anything."

"That's the point!" I yell.

My voice echoes through the neighborhood and somebody comes out of the house behind me, but I don't give a shit. I ain't walkin' away 'til I've had my say this time. It's gone on long enough.

"You've given up, and it's pissin' me off. We got a real chance of startin' over here. Especially if them people out in Hope Springs are friendly. It'll mean neighbors and people we can trade with. It'll mean the world can come back!"

"We can't come back from this," Winston says. "We will never be what we were, and I'm not sure I'm equipped to be anything else. Jess was all I had, and now that she's gone it just doesn't seem worth it. All this starving and freezing and constantly trying to dig deep so I can find just a little bit more hope inside me. What's the point in it all? The world we knew is gone. Forever."

I blink, but I don't say a word. I ain't sure what to say exactly. He's right, at least a little bit, anyways. "The world is never gonna be the same, but I'm livin' proof that change ain't bad. Me and Angus. Look who we are! I know you didn't know us before this, but anybody who did would tell you we're different people now. Better people."

236

Winston's brown eyes hold mine, and I suck in a deep breath, waitin' and hopin' he'll get where I'm comin' from.

"Not everyone has changed for the better," he finally says. "Just ask Vivian."

I step back, feelin' like he's punched me in the gut, and he turns away without sayin' another word. He heads 'cross the street to his house and goes inside even though I know he's supposed to be on watch. And we need him now more than ever. Now that the snow has started to melt and the zombies are back on their feet, we can't afford to slack off.

Footstep come up behind me, and I turn to find Angus headed my way.

"Thought he was stronger than this," I say.

"He'll pull through." Angus stops at my side. He spits on the ground and wipes his chin. "Just give him time."

"He's had time," I spit at my brother. "Months. How much longer is it gonna take?"

"He's lost everything. There ain't no time limit on how long it takes to get over that," Angus says.

I tear my eyes off the house Winston just disappeared into and turn to face my brother. Angus ain't said much about Darla since it happened. He buried her a couple weeks ago when the snow started meltin'. Didn't tell a soul 'til it was done.

"What 'bout you?"

Angus puckers his lips. "What 'bout me?"

"You feel like Winston? You gonna give up?"

Angus grunts and spits again, and I hold my breath. Waitin' for him to answer. I thought he was handlin' Darla's death okay, but I never asked. Guess I shoulda.

"Not me, 'lil brother," Angus says. "I'm too mean to give up so fast."

I nod, and I can't help feelin' relieved. "Good. 'Cause I'm gonna need you when we go check out Hope Springs."

"Not a problem," Angus says, slappin' my arm so hard I nearly fall on my face. "Come on."

He heads toward Brady's house, but I don't move. I can't stop thinkin' 'bout Winston. I look back at his place, but I don't know what I'm expectin' to find exactly. Answers, maybe? There ain't none, though. Ain't nothin' I can do or say to change what's happenin' with him or anybody else.

"Shit," I mutter before headin' after Angus.

The door slams behind me so hard a few pictures on the walls rattle 'round. Not that I give a shit. I'm fed up with people throwin' their lives away and poutin' 'cause they lost somebody. We all lost, but we've rebuilt and that's what matters. Parvarti hasn't been much better than a robot since Trey died, and Anne won't stop blubberin'. Now Winston. Pisses me off. Vivian an' me lost Emily, and Angus lost Darla. Shit. Lila and Al lost their damn parents, and they're just kids! They've held on. Coped. Even excelled at livin' in this world.

I stomp through the house in a way that makes me think of Angus, but I'm too pissed off to stop. Everybody turns to stare when I walk into the kitchen. Brady is standin' at the stove, and Vivian is makin' a pot of coffee. 'Round the table, Anne, Sophia, and the kids sit. Angus is leanin' against the wall at Vivian's side, starin' at me like I've gone nuts.

"Where's everybody else?" I snap.

Vivian frowns. "Al and Lila are on watch, Joshua and Parv are sleeping after being on watch all night, and Winston just left."

I wave her off as I shake my head. "Forget Winston."

"What's going on?" Vivian's eyes go to my feet and she frowns even more. "You tracked mud through the house."

I look down and blink at my muddy boots. Thought I'd taken them off, but I guess I was too pissed.

"Shit," I mutter, turnin' to find footprints that lead from the door to the kitchen. "Son of a bitch!"

"Axl," Sophia snaps.

I shoot her a glare before bendin' down to untie my boots. When they're off, I head back to the door, not stompin' any less than I did when I came in. Now I'm pissed at Brady just as much as I am at Winston. Havin' to take my shoes off in the

238

middle of all this is just dumb, and I'm sick of it. Sick of pretendin' things haven't changed with some people while other people cry 'bout how the world ain't never gonna be the same. It's exhaustin'.

"Axl," Vivian says from behind me.

I turn to find her headin' my way. Frownin' down at the muddy footprints. Shit.

"I'll clean it up," I snap.

Vivian looks up and shakes her head. "What's wrong with you?"

"Winston," I say. "He's given up and it pisses me off."

She sighs and reaches out, but I jerk away 'cause I ain't ready to let her comfort me.

"Stop," she says firmly. "I know you care about him, but you have to stop putting so much pressure on yourself. You can't help him when he doesn't want to be helped, and at this point it's very clear he doesn't."

"So I'm just supposed to let it go?" I shake my head and press my lips together, fightin' the urge to spit.

"You have to. We've tried everything. Given him space, support, time. We've let him know we'll be here for him, but if he doesn't accept what we offer, there's literally nothing we can do. Everyone deals with loss differently. Some people use it as an reason to fight harder, but others can't move on."

"I'm afraid we're gonna lose him," I say, and my voice is so quiet that it sounds like a little kid's even in my own ears. Which makes me feel dumb as shit, but I can't help it. The group's fallin' apart, and there's nothin' I can do to stop it from happenin'.

Vivian puts her arms 'round me, and I hug her back. Wishin' we were alone right now. When it's just me and her, things don't seem so bad.

"Come on," she says when she pulls away. "Let's have some lunch."

This time when I walk into the kitchen, nobody looks up except Angus. I'm glad for it. After stompin' 'round the way I was, I can't help feelin' like a spoiled brat. Or a dumbass.

"Have you decided about Hope Springs?" Sophia asks as I'm pourin' a cup of coffee.

"Yup," I say. "We'll head out tomorrow. Get a good look at the place and decide what our next move is gonna be."

Sophia grins, and even Anne looks excited by the idea. Glad I can make somebody happy today.

"Who's goin' with us?" Angus asks.

"Me," Vivian says firmly.

I swear but let it go. I know I ain't gonna be able to talk her outta it, and after what happened last time we went out, I'd almost rather have her with me than sittin' here.

"Parvarti too." I take a sip and look 'round. That don't leave the group here much protection, but I know they'll be careful. "The four of us should be good. Don't wanna take too many people with us."

"You should stop by Duncan on the way," Brady says. "See if you can find some fuel for the generator. We're running low."

"Yeah," I mumble, noddin'.

Findin' it ain't gonna be easy, but Brady's right. We're almost out, and we need it almost as much as we need food.

"Why on the way?" Sophia asks. "Why not after? You go to Hope Springs first and check it out, then stop in Duncan before you come home."

"We gotta find fuel before it gets dark, but who knows how long it's gonna take us to get a good look at what they've got goin' on in Hope Springs."

Sophia lets out a sigh and I wait for her to complain, but she just nods. Good. I ain't in the mood to argue, but I won't back down. We need fuel, and doin' it in the dark—especially now that the zombies are back on their feet—is way too dangerous.

"So tomorrow mornin'?" Angus asks.

"Bright and early," I say.

CHAPTER TWENTY-ONE
VIVIAN

I stick close to Axl's side as he leans over the car, my eyes moving across the empty parking lot. As far as I can see Duncan's main street is free of the dead, but who knows how many lurk just behind these buildings or when they'll decide to pop up. Being on this street, surrounded by the unknown, has me feeling boxed in, but we didn't have any luck finding fuel on the other side of town. The group from Hope Springs probably got it all before we had a chance to get back. They sure as hell made sure the Sam's Club was cleared out.

"We got incoming!" Axl calls, pointing behind me with his free hand.

I shield my eyes from the bright sun as I twist to face the row of stores at my back. Five zombies shuffle from the alley, their movements jerky and awkward. They kick up wet snow with every step they take. It doesn't even look like they're lifting their feet off the ground as they move toward us. I guess they haven't thawed out completely. Not yet anyway.

"I'll take care of it!" I say, jogging forward to meet them.

Axl swears behind me, but he's too busy filling cans with gas to stop me from heading out to meet the zombies.

I'm still five feet from the approaching dead when an arrow slices through the head of one. The thing drops to the ground and I glance over my shoulder long enough to see Angus and Parvarti jogging my way. Angus is pulling a flatbed cart behind him, loaded down with more cans while Parvarti is already notching a second arrow.

"Just in time!" I call as I turn back toward the zombies.

The one in the lead chomps as he moves my way, and I allow myself just a second to get a good look at him. The early morning sun hasn't had a chance to melt the ice crystals clinging to his rotten skin, and they glisten under the bright light. We've hit the low fifties a couple times, helping melt the snow and take the edge off the cold, but the nights are still freezing. Meaning parts of the zombies are, too. The black ooze that usually seeps from every opening on these disgusting creatures' bodies is frozen, masking their stench. The thing in front of me still chomps his teeth, and he still reaches out like he can't wait to sink his fingers into my flesh, but he looks like he's moving in slow motion. Winter was our new best friend, and I suddenly feel like someone who has been abandoned in my greatest time of need.

I sigh but go for it anyway, driving the blade of my knife into the zombie's skull and pulling it out with just as much force. The thing drops to the ground, and the one behind him lets out a little moan. Almost like it knows what's coming. He lurches for me, or tries to anyway, but I slam my foot into his chest before he can get too far. The zombie falls back, hitting the two behind him, and all three tumble to the ground in a tangled mess.

Hoping to get them while they're down, I dart forward just as an arrow whizzes past, barely missing my head. I jerk back so fast my feet slip on a patch of ice, causing me to

242

momentarily lose focus. It isn't long. Just enough time for me regain my footing and make sure I'm not going to fall, but it's also enough time for the zombies on the ground to figure out how to get themselves up. And for the closest one to wrap his rotten fingers around my ankle.

He jerks his arm with more strength than I thought possible, given his half-frozen state, and my foot goes out from under me. This time, there's nothing I can do to stop myself from falling. My body slams into the wet ground, and before I've even had a chance to think about the pain, I'm kicking at the zombie holding me. His fingers only tighten their hold on my leg. Even when my heel makes contact with his nose and a crunching sound breaks through his moans, he doesn't let up.

"Shit," I grunt, kicking harder.

"Hold on!" Angus yells from behind me.

I tighten my fingers around my knife and sit up, still kicking my leg in an attempt to break free. It doesn't work, so I lean forward and jab my knife into the monster's head. He growls but doesn't go down. I must have just missed the mark.

Another arrow flies by me, taking out one of the three remaining zombies. Too bad it isn't the one holding me. I yank my knife out of its skull while bringing my free leg back yet again. This time when I slam my foot into the creature's face, his grip loosens. Angus and Parvarti come running up beside me just as I jerk my leg out of the monster's grasp and stumble back.

Parvarti offers me her hand as Angus rips his knife out of its sheath. His jaw is clenched in determination when he stabs his blade into the skull of the zombie that brought me down, ripping it back out so fast that chunks of gray matter go flying. Before Parvarti even has time to pull me to my feet, Angus has the other one down as well.

He's panting when he turns to face us, and that little vein on his forehead pulsates. "Gotta watch yourself, Blondie."

I ignore him and turn to face Parvarti. "You almost put an arrow through my skull."

"Sorry," she says, but her voice and expression are so blank I have a hard time believing her.

Seeing the vacant look in her brown eyes makes my blood pump so fast it roars in my ears. I've never had much patience with her attitude, but since Darla died, it's been even harder to ignore. We've lost people who were fighting tooth and nail to live, and here Parvarti stands, wasting her life with indifference. Lately, I've had a really hard time not slapping her across the face.

I open my mouth, all ready to tell her to shove her sorrys up her ass, but my words are cut off when Axl lets out a grunt.

"Son of a bitch!" he growls from behind me.

Angus and I spin around at the same time, and in the blink of an eye, all the anger I felt toward Parvarti is gone. A group of zombies has Axl boxed in. Backed up against a car while ten or more of them advance, surrounding him in a semicircle. All of them growling and chomping, clawing as they try to get at Axl.

"Shit!" Angus screams as he takes off toward his brother.

I'm right behind him, not even bothering to give Parvarti a second look as I run after Angus. I replace my knife and pull my gun, too terrified to worry about saving bullets or being inconspicuous at the moment. I'm still three feet away when I start firing, but I have to aim for the zombies furthest from Axl, afraid that I'll accidently get him. My aim is good, but my whole body is shaking and I don't want to risk it.

Axl shoves the zombies back, slashing at them with his knife, but he doesn't seem to be making much progress. None have fallen.

Angus reaches the dead first and dives in, shoving his way through the horde to get to his brother, barely stabbing at them as he does it. I fire again, trying to focus on the creatures I need to take out and not what's happening with Axl and Angus. It's an impossible task when every sound they make

244

has my heart pounding harder.

Two more fall, but my joy is cut short when one of the zombies still standing grabs Axl around the throat. The monster pulls him forward, snarling as he opens his mouth.

"Angus!" I scream, squeezing off two more shots but having no idea where the bullets go or if they hit anything. I'm shaking, and all I can focus on are the zombie's teeth, only inches from Axl's face.

Angus reaches his brother and shoves his arm in front of Axl's face just as he zombie bites down. His teeth sink into the fleshy part of Angus's hand, and his face contorts, scrunching up into an expression that combines agony with fury. Blood seeps from the wound and over Angus's hand, dripping down the zombie's chin.

Angus shoves Axl against the car at his back so he can put his body in front of his brother, acting as a human shield. His hand is still trapped in the jaws of the monster as more of the dead advance, growling and chomping. Angus uses his free hand to stab at them over and over again, his blade sinking into rotten flesh and bone as the zombies close in. Not even trying to free his hand as more of the dead converge on them.

I aim at the head of the zombie using Angus as a snack, but I can't get a good shot from this angle. The brothers are too close.

For the second time today, an arrow whirls past my head, only this time I can't be pissed, because it slices through the skull of the zombie chewing on Angus. The creature drops to the ground, finally releasing his hand, and the second Angus is free, I'm able to focus on the other zombies. I take aim and squeeze the trigger, the gunshot ringing in my ears. My bullet pierces a zombie in the shoulder, and I let out a string of curses.

Sucking in a deep breath, I work to keep my arms steady as I take aim again. This time when I fire, I hit the mark. Black goo sprays across the zombies still standing, and the one I hit drops to the ground.

Within seconds the final two zombies are down, one taken out by Parvarti and the other by Axl, who has somehow managed to break free of his human shield, and we're all finally able to take a deep breath.

"Son of a bitch that hurts!" Angus says, holding his injured hand against his chest as blood soaks into his jacket.

"No shit, Angus." Axl slams his gun in his waistband and shakes his head like he can't believe how stupid his brother is. "Why the hell did you let the bastard bite you?"

"Figured it wasn't gonna kill me," Angus says. "Might as well."

"You're a dumbass," Axl growls.

I step over the bodies and reach for Angus's hand. "Let me see it."

He grunts but doesn't argue when I take his hand. It's hard to see with all the blood flowing from the bite, but it looks like the fleshy part of his hand—right under his thumb—has almost been ripped away.

"You're going to need stitches." I don't let go of his hand but instead pull him away from the pile of dead bodies and over to our SUV. "For now, we need to stop the bleeding."

I open the back door and sift through our supplies until I find the first aid kit Joshua insisted we take. Thankfully, there are bandages inside, because we're going to need them.

"We have to get this clean, then wrap it up until we can get you home," I mutter as I untwist the lid from a bottle of rubbing alcohol.

Angus doesn't even flinch when I pour alcohol over the wound, washing the blood away so I can get a better look at it. The bite is worse than I originally thought. The chunk of flesh the zombie was trying to rip away is barely hanging on. Angus really put himself at risk, and even though it was to save Axl, I can't help thinking he's being a little too reckless with his newfound immunity.

Or is there more to it? He has been different since Darla died. I don't blame him, but I also can't help wondering if maybe he's a little tired of the fight. If he's giving up like

246

Parvarti or Winston or Anne. I hope that isn't true. Asshole or not, I don't want to lose Angus.

I keep my eyes down and focused on wrapping the bandages around Angus's hand. "You only did this to save Axl, right?"

"Why the hell else would I do it?" he mutters.

My eyes flick up, meeting his for just a second before moving back down. "You're not trying to get yourself killed?"

"Fuck no."

Angus grunts and sniffs, and I can't help wondering if there are tears in his eyes. I don't look, though. He deserves some privacy.

I wrap his hand, keeping my eyes focused on what I'm doing so I don't have to look up. What I'm about to say is going to be open for interpretation, and there's no way I want to see the expression on Angus's face when he hears it. "Don't do this again. I know you were trying to save your brother, and I know you're immune, but being reckless is just stupid. You were handed a gift. Don't throw it away."

He chuckles, and despite my better judgment, my gaze moves up to find that classic Angus monkey grin on his face. "You worried 'bout me, Blondie?"

"Don't be an ass," I say, rolling my eyes.

Of course, that just makes him laugh even harder.

"You don't gotta be worried. I ain't plannin' on bitin' it just yet." The amusement is still in his voice, but it doesn't totally mask the pain.

"Yeah well, we aren't always in control of what happens. One bite isn't going to kill you, we know that for sure, but if you get overrun there's nothing we can do about that. It's not like any of us can dive in there to save you, and don't think for a second Axl wouldn't do it if he had to. Is that what you want? Axl throwing his life away to save you from a horde?"

"That's what it'd be if somebody died savin' me?" Angus lifts an eyebrow, his gray eyes focused on me. There's a sincerity in them I hadn't expected. "They'd be throwin' their life away?"

I give him a stern look. He's either reading too much into my words or not enough. The last thing he'd want is for Axl to die for him, and we all know that. After everything Angus said in that cellar when we thought he was about to die, he can't deny it anymore. He wouldn't lift a finger to give a dying stranger a drink of water, but he'd throw himself in front of a train if he thought it might save Axl.

"That's not what I mean, and you know it."

Angus's expression softens, and he nods slowly. "Guess you're right, although admittin' it hurts more than that there bite."

I snort out a laugh as I finish wrapping up his hand. Blood has already seeped through the thin fabric before I've even had a chance to tie it off. We need to get him back to Joshua, and fast.

"Well, there are two things we have in common. We'd both die to save Axl, and we both hate admitting when the other person has a good point."

Angus gets to his feet, cradling his injured hand against his chest. He grins at me though, and the little flash of mischief in his eyes tells me he's already come up with a good comeback. "First time I ever had to do it, though. I can recall a couple times when you had to admit I was right 'bout things."

"You would remember that," I say, smiling.

"A man's gotta commit things like that to memory. Never know when I'm gonna need to throw it in your face."

I shake my head, but I can't help being glad that Angus is still able to find humor in things. It's been hard on him since Darla died, and there were definitely moments right after it happened when I wasn't sure if he'd ever smile or laugh or give me a hard time again. But he's pulled through. Thank God.

I shove the first aid kit into the car, then turn back to find Axl heading our way, dragging the flatbed full of gas cans behind him. They're all different sizes and shapes, some metal and some plastic. The liquid in the containers sloshes back and forth as the wheels thump over the pavement. It's like music to my ears. Fuel has been one of our biggest worries.

"We get enough?" I call when he's still a good six feet away.

Axl's face is red from exertion when he nods. "Should last us a couple more months."

That's good news, so I do my best not to focus on the biggest question going through my mind right now: what are we going to do after that?

"We're going to have to skip checking out Hope Springs today," I say instead of throwing out a question that none of us has an answer to. "Angus is going to need stitches."

Axl exhales. "Sophia's gonna be pissed."

"Nothing we can do about that," I say.

"Let's get this shit loaded, then."

Axl, Parvarti, and I unload the gas cans while Angus smokes. His injured hand is bleeding so badly that the bandages are completely saturated before we're even halfway done with the gas cans. He finds an extra shirt in the SUV and wraps it around the wound instead, but I'm not sure that's going to help either. Every few seconds Axl glances toward his brother, and with each look, the worry in his gray eyes deepens.

When the gas cans are loaded, he wipes his sweaty brow and jerks his head toward the car. "Let's head out."

CHAPTER TWENTY-TWO

VIVIAN

Al and Lila are on watch, and the second the SUV comes into view, Al jogs over to meet us. Even with only one hand, it takes the kid less than a minute to get the gate unlocked and open. It's too long for Axl, apparently. He's practically glaring at the teen while he waits.

"Relax," I whisper, putting my hand on his knee.

Axl sucks in a deep breath and holds it for a second before blowing it out. His hands tighten on the steering wheel like he's trying to crush it.

"Bastard's reckless," he says, just loud enough for me to hear.

I glance over my shoulder anyway, but Angus isn't paying attention to his brother. He's staring down at the nearly soaked shirt wrapped around his hand.

Parvarti's gaze meets mine, and the icy expression on her face sends a shudder down my spine. I'm not sure if she's heartless or she's just trying to make herself seem that way. Whatever it is, her robotic reaction to everything has all those emotions from earlier boiling back to the surface. She needs to make a decision: live or move on. This in-between shit is too much to take.

Axl hits the gas the second Al has the gate open, and we fly through, not slowing until we reach the houses. The tires skid across a sheet of ice when Axl hits the breaks, and I fly forward, my chest slamming into the seatbelt when it locks.

"Shit," Angus growls from the back. "What the hell are you doin'?"

"Tryin' to get you to the doc, you dumb son of a bitch," Axl mutters, throwing the car in park.

"I ain't dyin'."

Axl tilts his head from side to side like he's trying to make his neck crack. He doesn't answer his brother. Instead, he shoves the door open and hops out of the car.

"Come on, Angus," I say, sighing as I hop out after Axl.

He's already headed to Brady's house. The little walkways between buildings that we kept shoveled over the winter are still here, but they're wet and muddy from the melting snow. I'm careful to watch for any patches of ice as I hurry to catch up with Axl.

"Hey," I say when I fall into pace at his side. "Relax."

"You remember the day he got bit?" Axl asks, not even looking my way.

Do I remember? He has to be joking. There are only a handful of days I'll never forget, but that is one of them. Axl and I were fighting, and I wasn't paying attention. I was rushing, and it's part of the reason that horde caught us off guard. Angus got bit, and if he'd died, I would have spent the rest of my life blaming myself, and I would have been right. It would have been my fault.

"Of course I remember," I whisper.

"You told me Angus was reckless, and I thought you was just bein' a bitch. But later, after we found out Angus was gonna be okay, I got to thinkin' 'bout him and the way he is and I realized you was right. He's always throwin' himself into crazy situations, and now that he knows he's immune it's even worse than before. Bastard acts like the zombies can't touch him, and I'm afraid it's gonna get him killed before long."

So that's what this is all about. Axl is more terrified than ever of losing his brother.

I slip my hand into his and give it a squeeze. "Angus has spent his whole life thinking he's worthless. He knows he has value now, and this is his way of contributing. Plus, when it comes to saving you, he was always willing to throw himself in front of a horde. He's going to be okay."

"Not sure 'bout all that," Axl says doubtfully.

"Have some faith."

He lets out a snort. "Right. Not sure I ever believed in God, but I sure as hell don't now."

"I don't know what I believe about God and heaven and hell and all that stuff, I but I do think things happen for a reason." I glance back to where Angus and Parvarti are walking up behind us and lower my voice. I don't want Angus to hear what I have to say. "The whole thing with Darla was proof of that. I'd spent half my life angry at her for running out on me, but if she had taken me with her, I wouldn't have met you. Wouldn't be here. And she probably would have died in Vegas, because we never would have come along to save her. Even though I hated that she was here most of the time, it helped me heal. Helped me feel at peace about my past."

Axl slips his hand out of mine and wraps it around my shoulders, giving me a comforting squeeze. "We still woulda found you in Vegas. If you'd gone with her back then, I mean."

"No," I say. "You wouldn't be with this group. Because of me, we went into San Francisco to meet Trey and Parvarti, which is where we found Mitchell. He led us to the shelter. If not for that, you wouldn't have needed to go into Vegas at all. You and Angus would have found a farm like you originally wanted to. That's where you'd be right now."

"Damn," Axl says, shaking his head.

"I know."

We reach the house, and Axl drops my hand. He shoves the front door open and charges inside, barely pausing to kick his boots off. "Doc! You here?"

Joshua sticks his head out of the kitchen, and his shaggy brown hair falls over his eyes. He shoves it aside as he looks us over. "What's going on?"

"Angus decided to use his hand as a shield," I say as the person in question steps into the house behind me.

"I never did hear a thank you 'bout that," Angus grumbles.

Joshua steps out of the kitchen, shaking his head as he crosses the room. "How bad?"

"It's gonna need stitches for sure." Axl grabs his brother's arm and jerks him forward, shoving him toward the doctor. "Show him."

Angus grumbles again, but he unwraps his hand.

Joshua lets out a low whistle when he sees it. "That's some bite."

"Didn't do it to impress nobody."

"Go into the kitchen and wash it off really well while I get a suture kit," the doctor says.

He grabs his boots while the rest of us head for the kitchen. Angus has the shirt wrapped around his hand, but the thing is covered in blood. Hopefully there isn't any permanent damage from the bite.

Brady's eyebrows shoot up when we walk into the kitchen. "Didn't expect you to be home this early. You have some trouble out there?"

"What's this tell ya?" Angus holds his bloody hand in front of the other man's face.

"It tells me that you should be very grateful you're immune," Brady says, taking a step back.

"Bastard did it on purpose," Axl mutters.

He flips the water on and motions for his brother to come

over to the sink. Once Angus is there, Axl squirts dish soap on his bloody hand and starts scrubbing it.

"Ow, that hurts, you prick!" Angus tries to pull his arm away, but Axl won't let him.

"Hold still."

Brady rolls his eyes, but the corner of his mouth is turned up when he spins to face me. "Joshua go to get supplies?"

"Yeah," I say, leaning my hip against the counter. "He's going to have to stitch Angus up. It's pretty bad. Which is why we couldn't go stake out Hope Springs tonight."

"You can go back out tomorrow," Brady says, heading across the kitchen. "Let me get some light in here so Joshua can see what he's doing when he comes back."

The generator isn't on, and even though it's daytime, the kitchen is cloaked in shadows. With our fuel supply running low, we've agreed to use the generator as little as possible. It's gotten easier now that spring is here — more daylight means fewer candles and batteries being used — but it's still tough to see at times. And it isn't like the candles and batteries are going to last forever.

Silently, Parvarti helps Brady gather the battery-powered lanterns and set them up throughout the kitchen, moving them closer to Angus. They make a huge difference, even if it still doesn't come anywhere close to being as bright as overhead lights are.

Axl is done scrubbing his brother's hand by the time Joshua comes back, but the blood dripping from Angus's hand hasn't slowed. The kitchen sink is so red it looks like someone's throat was slit.

Joshua spreads his supplies out and washes his own hands. Once they're dry, he pulls on a pair of gloves while studying Angus's hand. "You need to be more careful."

Angus lets out a half-chuckle, half-grunt. "Ain't ya heard? I'm invincible."

"Just because you're immune doesn't mean you can't get an infection," Joshua says, his tone stern. "Under normal circumstances, the human mouth is riddled with bacteria. Under these circumstances, who knows what you might catch. The zombie virus isn't the only thing that can kill you."

"Just dose me up with some of them meds we got and I'll be good," Angus barks. He acts like Joshua's concerns are ridiculous.

The doctor looks up, meeting Angus's gaze with a serious expression. "You need to listen to me. This time I can give you antibiotics, but down the road we might not have them. You need to take care of yourself."

"Ain't nothin'," Angus says, still totally unconcerned and utterly oblivious.

Axl crosses his arms as his eyes narrow on Angus, but he doesn't say anything. I'm guessing he's saving his argument for later.

Joshua lets out a deep sigh. "Let's get you stitched up."

I rub Axl's back while Joshua gets to work. It takes longer than I expected it to—although I'm not sure why. It isn't a small injury. It seriously looks like someone put his hand in a blender or garbage disposal.

"I never knew human teeth could do so much damage," I say.

Brady nods in agreement, leaning closer so he can get a better look at Joshua's progress. "Pretty incredible."

"Don't feel incredible," Angus mutters. "We got any vodka?"

"We got something." Axl exhales and pushes himself off the counter. "Hid it from Winston."

Angus grunts when Joshua pokes the needle through his skin for what seems like the hundredth time. Sweat has broken out across his forehead. "Shit. Hurry up."

"How many is that?" I ask as Axl disappears into the other room.

"Seventeen," Joshua says, glancing up at Angus. "We're about halfway done."

"That it?" Angus squeeze his eyes shut and sucks in a deep breath. "Shit. Hurry your ass up, Axl!"

256

"Keep this in mind next time you decide to be reckless," I say even though I feel bad for him. It has to hurt like hell.

Angus doesn't open his eyes when he says, "Did it to stop Axl from gettin' his nose bit off."

"You could have just pushed the zombie out of the way," I reply, softer this time.

Angus swears and grits his teeth when Joshua poke the needle into his skin once again. More sweat has broken out across his forehead, and that famous vein has made an appearance. He doesn't open his eyes until Axl comes jogging back into the room carrying a bottle of vodka.

"Here," he says, unscrewing the lid and shoving it in front of his brother's face.

Angus rips it out of his hand. "Next time I'll let the bastard bite you."

Brady lets out a little laugh, and even though I know it shouldn't be funny, I find myself smiling. There's no way he'd ever do that. Axl just shakes his head, but Parvarti doesn't bat an eye.

The door opens in the other room, followed by the sound of boots being dropped on the tarp. A second, later footsteps head our way. If it's Anne or Sophia, we're going to be in for an argument. Neither one of them is going to be thrilled to find out we had to put off staking out Hope Springs.

"You're back," Sophia says when she rushes into the room.

She glances around, smiling from ear to ear, but it's gone in the blink of an eye. Her gaze moves from Angus to the bloody sink to Joshua.

"What happened? Was it the people in Hope Springs? Did they attack you?" The panicked expression that crosses her face gives away just how much she wants this town to work out. I didn't know how much she needed this until now.

"It's okay," I say, pushing myself off the counter and heading her way. "This didn't have anything to do with Hope Springs. We ran into some trouble in Duncan and Angus needed stitches, so we had to come home. We never made it to Hope Springs."

Sophia relaxes, but it only takes a second for her relief to be replaced by annoyance. "Were you ever really going to check Hope Springs out, or was it all just for show?"

"That's not fair," I say. "We didn't have a choice. Just look at Angus's hand!"

Sophia's gaze moves to Angus, but she doesn't seem to register just how much damage was done by the zombie's mouth. "How convenient. For months we've all been begging you to check out Hope Springs and you've been saying no. I shouldn't be surprised that you found a way to get out of it. There's always an excuse with you people, but you aren't the only ones who can get things done."

She turns on her heel, charging out of the room and leaving the rest of us totally speechless.

"Hormones," Angus mutters. Of course he'd be the first one to break the silence.

"She doesn't really think that's true," I say, turning to face the others. "Does she? She has to know we're trying to keep everyone safe."

"I told you," Angus says. "It's hormones. You may not realize it 'cause you're one of them, but hormones can make a chick go bat shit crazy."

I roll my eyes. "Let's pretend I was asking the more intelligent men in the room."

"I hate to say it." Joshua doesn't look up from his work. "But Angus has a point. Not the bat shit crazy part. The part about Sophia being at the end of her pregnancy and having a lot of hormonal changes going on right now. She's reacting based on her emotions, but give her some time and she'll realize she's overreacted."

Even though I have the sudden urge to slap Joshua upside the head, I can't help it when the truth behind his words hit me hard. Sophia is at the end of her pregnancy, and she's probably spent the entire winter thinking Hope Springs would be there if she needed help. Only we haven't checked it out yet. Right now, as pissed off as she is, I can't help worrying that she's going to hop in one of the cars and drive there herself.

"I'm going to talk to her," I say, hurrying after Sophia.

When I step into the living room, she's just finished getting her boots on—thank God for pregnancy slowing her down. She doesn't even look my way as she heads for the door, and I charge across the room to stop her before she does something dangerous.

"Stop," I say, grabbing her arm.

"No." She rips her arm out of my hand but doesn't leave. Instead she turns my way, glaring. "I've begged and begged, but apparently this just isn't a priority for you. But it is for me. Don't you get it? I'm about to have a baby, and we're in the middle of nowhere!"

She looks away when her eyes fill with tears, and I suddenly feel really bad for not pushing Axl more. He was doing what he thought was best, but it never occurred to me until now how scared Sophia has to be. We have a doctor, but everything else about this delivery will be totally different than her last one. No husband. No hospital. No electricity or operating room if things go wrong. No way to ease her pain during or after her labor. Nothing.

"I'm so sorry," I say, putting my hand on her arm. "You're absolutely right. We should have gone earlier. We should have tried harder. We were being insensitive, and it was wrong."

Sophia's bottom lip trembles. She wipes a few tears away before letting out a sigh. "I'm sorry for being so dramatic."

"You're not. You were right to make a big deal about this. Before now, I didn't think about how you were feeling. I promise we'll go tomorrow. Even if Angus isn't up to the trip I'll make sure Axl, Parv, and I go. We've put it off long enough."

Sophia gives me a shaky smile. "Are you sure?"

"Absolutely!" I pull her in for a hug, feeling only slightly less guilty when she returns it. "I'll make this happen.

Even if I have to use every one of my feminine charms to convince Axl it needs to be done."

Sophia pulls back, laughing a little despite the tears still shimmering in her eyes. "I'm sure you'll hate doing it too."

"Every second of it," I say, returning her smile. "But it will be worth it for you."

She lets out a deep sigh as she wipes the moisture form her eyes. "Thanks. I really appreciate it. I know Axl is just trying to be cautious, but I just can't shake the feeling something bad is going to happen if we try to have this baby here. I'm scared."

"Don't be," I say. "You've done this before."

"But no one else has other than you. And Joshua only has a little bit of experience. He was an ER doctor, which is great when someone needs stitches, but when it comes to something like this, he's having to rely on his one OB rotation." Sophia sinks her teeth into her bottom lip, pausing for a second before saying, "Will you stay with me when the time comes?"

"You want me to be there when your baby is born? What about Anne?" I'm totally taken aback. They two women are always together, taking care of the kids and helping Brady with the food. It never once occurred to me that Sophia would think my company was comforting.

"I love Anne, but she's never been in labor. Plus, you're stronger than she is. You both lost a child, but you've pulled through. I'm going to need someone to lean of if—" She swallows. "You know."

"Of course I'll be there," I say, grabbing her hand. "Don't worry. I'll be there to hold your hand, and if for some reason you need a shoulder to cry on, I can be that too."

"Thank you." Sophia lets out a deep breath before dropping my hand. "I need to get back to Ava. I told Anne I'd be back as soon as I found out what you guys saw in Hope Springs."

She heads out, but for a few seconds I can't move, too overwhelmed both by what she just asked me to do and the fact that we've done such a poor job of considering everyone else's feelings. It should have occurred to me that Sophia would need this. If I were in her position, I would. I can't even imagine giving birth in the middle of nowhere like this.

Axl isn't going to love the idea of us going back out tomorrow, but he's just going to have to get over it. I won't let him talk me out of going to Hope Springs this time.

Joshua is just wrapping Angus's stitched hand when I walk back into the kitchen.

"All done?" I ask, mainly to buy myself some time while I try to figure out how to broach the subject.

"He's good," Joshua replies but gives Angus a stern look. "Be careful with it though. Keep it clean and try not to rip any of the stitches."

Angus grins. "Who you talkin' to?"

Brady snorts.

"Sophia okay?" Axl asks.

He's watching me, and I can tell he's waiting for me to tell him what happened.

"Yeah," I say, nodding slowly.

The front door opens again, and even though I can't see it from here, I find myself looking over my shoulder. Footsteps move our way, and a second later Winston walks into the room. He's wearing his shoes, tracking dirt through the house. He doesn't even bat an eye when Brady frowns his way.

"You're back," he says, looking around. "Thought you'd be out longer."

"Ain't you supposed to be on watch?" Axl asks, his voice more gruff than it used to be.

Winston shrugs. "Yeah. Came to get something to keep me warm."

His moves toward the coffee pot but stops when he catches sight of the vodka in front of Angus. The bottle is still half full. Axl's shoulders stiffen, but if Winston notices, he doesn't let on.

"Coffee pot is full," Brady says.

Winston shakes his head. "Thought we were out."

He moves toward the bottle, but Axl steps in front of it. "No."

Winston narrows his eyes, and Axl glares right back. The mood in the room grows tense. Winston balls his hand into a fist, but Axl doesn't back down. Ever since their last conversation, things have been strained between the two men, but not like this. Now it looks like they're on the verge of fistfight.

"What's your problem?" Winston's tone is cold.

"You," Axl says. "I'm done with this. Done with actin' like this don't matter. It does, and long as I'm here, I ain't gonna stand back and let you drink yourself to death."

"What's it to you, anyway? You're happy with this life, fine. But some of us need a little help to get through the day." Winston's eyes move to me, and the bitterness in them is so sharp it feels like a knife. "Some of us are alone."

"You ain't drinkin' it." Axl swipes the bottle off the counter.

Winston takes a step closer, but before anything can happen, Angus steps between the two men. "No need to get your panties in a bunch. We got plenty of coffee, and that'll keep you just as warm out there as booze will."

Winston looks past Angus, giving Axl one last glare before turning away. "I don't need this shit. You want someone to stand watch, feel free. I'm done."

He stomps out, and I can't think of a single thing to say. Things just keep getting worse, and unless something major happens, I can't see Winston getting better at this point. He needs something to live for, because right now he can't see past our fence, and it's dragging him down.

"We need to go to Hope Springs," I say, turning to face Axl. "I know we had to put it off today, but we need to go tomorrow. For all of us. Sophia wants to know there's a doctor out there in case she needs more help, and Winston needs to see that the world is moving on. It could be the only thing that helps him snap out of this. Knowing other people are out there and life isn't completely over."

"You really think that's going to help?" Joshua asks.

"It could," Brady says.

I nod, then shrug. "Honestly, I don't know. But I can't think of another way. Can you?"

"He's lost." Axl puts the bottle down, and the glass clanks against the stone counter so hard I'm surprised it doesn't shatter.

"He'll be fine," Angus says. "Don't mean we can't check out that town tomorrow. We gotta do it one day, so there's no point in puttin' it off any longer. We'll head out in the mornin'."

Axl nods. "Fine. Let Parv know, and the four of us'll go after breakfast."

Even though I'm worried about Winston, I'm glad it didn't take much to convince Axl. Sophia will be happy too. Hopefully by this time tomorrow, we'll have a good idea of what's going on at Hope Springs and whether or not we can count on them.

CHAPTER TWENTY-THREE

VIVIAN

All my thoughts are focused on Hope Springs, but when I step outside, I find myself distracted by the bright morning sun. Closing my eyes, I lift my face toward the sky. The air still has a bite to it, but the sun's rays are just warm enough to chase away the goose bumps. In the distance, clouds are moving in, but at the moment the sky is bright and clear, and seeing all the blue makes me feel more hopeful than I have in years.

It won't be long before spring is out in full force, and I couldn't be more excited.

The wind blows, carrying voices with it and forcing me to open my eyes. I look around, squinting under the bright sun until I catch sight of Brady. He's across the street, kneeling in his front yard, the little bit of remaining snow soaking through his pants as he stares at the ground. There's almost no grass where he's sitting, and even though the mud under him has been flattened out by the months of heavy snow, it's obvious that he's staring at a grave. And he's talking to himself.

"They've turned out to be a good group," he says as he runs his hand over the ground. His voice is barely audible from the other side of the street. "I was right to bring them here. They've helped me survive. Perhaps even heal a little."

Even though I'm not sure if he'll want to be disturbed, I find myself heading his way. My boots squish against the soft earth as I cross my lawn, but Brady doesn't look up. He's still talking, but his voice is so quiet now that I can't make out the words.

"Brady?" I say when I get closer.

He starts and lifts his head, flashing me a slightly embarrassed smile before dragging himself to his feet. He doesn't even bother trying to brush the mud off his pants.

"You probably think I've gone mad. Sitting out here in the middle of the mud, talking to the ground." He chuckles and pushes his shaggy brown hair out of his eyes. "Maybe I have. Maybe we all have."

"Who are you talking to exactly?" I ask even though I have a good idea who it is.

"My wife." Brady sweeps his hand toward the ground at his side. "I buried her here. I couldn't stand the idea of putting her on the other side of the community. I know it sounds foolish, but talking to her was the one thing that kept me from going insane when this all first happened. Everyone else was gone, and I worked to clean the place up, seeing more and more death as each day passed. Stopping here in the evening to talk to Kristine was the only thing that gave me comfort."

"I don't think you're insane," I say, shaking my head. "We all cope in different ways."

"That we do." Brady turns so he's looking at the ground once again.

Neither one of us says a thing, and I can't help feeling like he has more he wants to say to his wife, so I take a step back.

"I'll leave you alone. I didn't mean to intrude."

"No intrusion." Brady waves but doesn't turn. "Breakfast is ready if you're hungry. Just go on in."

For a second, I watch the small man as he stares down at his wife's grave. The memory of our previous conversation comes back, sending a shiver shooting through my body despite the warmth of the sun. Like the rest of us, Brady has his ghosts, only he hasn't left them behind. Not physically, and I'm starting think not emotionally either. There's a part of him still clinging to the past and an impossible hope, and I can't help wondering if he'll be trapped in this state of limbo as long as he stays here. Especially if his wife is still down there, trapped the way I suspect she is.

When another shiver moves up my spine, I finally turn away. Even though a part of me wants to talk to Brady about the whole thing, I'm not sure if he'll be open to it. Another time might be better.

I turn away but have only taken two steps when Parvarti and Angus come out of the house next door. Like me, they're both dressed for the day, ready to head out to Hope Springs. Even Angus, despite his injury—and it still has to hurt like hell.

"You eat yet?" Angus calls.

Parvarti doesn't say a thing.

"Not yet," I say. "I was just about to head inside."

Angus opens his mouth, but whatever he was going to say is drowned out by a scream.

I spin around just as Sophia comes running out of the house across the street, yelling for help as she drags Ava and Max with her through the muddy yard. None of them are wearing jackets, and tears are streaming down Sophia's face. Ava's crying too, but Max's expression is different. Scared. Angry. It's hard to tell for sure, but the look on his face has my insides twisting and tightening painfully.

It isn't until I realize none of them are wearing shoes that the panic really starts to build inside me, though.

"Angus!" I cry as I take off running.

He takes off after me, passing me as he charges toward the house. Flying by Sophia without pausing to ask her what's going on. He reaches the house, but I stop, torn between following Angus and checking to make sure Sophia and the kids are okay. My gaze moves over them, then back to the house. Then back to the hysterical woman and children in front of me. They don't look hurt though. There's no blood. They're all in one piece.

"What is it?" I ask Sophia, panting and out of breath and more terrified than I've been since those assholes tried to storm our community.

"Winston," she gasps as tears stream down her cheeks.

She shakes her head and Ava cries harder, and the ice that coats my veins is more frigid than the whole winter we just went through. I don't say another word as I turn back toward the house, and the sound of Angus yelling makes my stomach drop to the mud. Parvarti joins Sophia and me, urging her to come across the street and get dry.

I don't have a clue what they do, because I'm running again. Across the muddy yard and into the house, following the sound of Angus's voice.

"Come on, you son of a bitch!" he shouts as I charge up the stairs. "Wake up! Open your eyes."

I reach the first bedroom and stop, almost slamming into the doorframe when I catch sight of Angus. He's on the floor and has Winston turned on his side. Angus is pounding his fist on the other man's back over and over again, but he doesn't make a sound. It only takes one look at the ashy tint of Winston's skin to know we're too late.

"Breathe, you pussy!" Angus grunts. "Don't do this. This ain't the way!"

My legs shake until I find it impossible to stand. I drop to my knees and crawl toward the two men. Trembling so much that I don't know how I'm even able to do that.

"Winston?" It's all I can get out.

My gaze lands on a pill bottle, and I pick it up, but I'm shaking too much at first to be able to read the label. When the words finally come into focus, they still don't make a lot of sense. Where the hell did Winston get it?

"Open your eyes," Angus growls again.

Footsteps pound up the stairs, and a second later Joshua and Axl come running into the room. I move back, giving the doctor room to work even though I know it's pointless. Winston's gone, but none of us will be able to move forward if we don't try everything imaginable to revive him.

"What happened?" Joshua asks, dropping to his knees.

"Pills," I whisper, holding the bottle out.

Joshua takes the little amber bottle, and his eyebrows shoot up. He tosses it to the ground, cursing under his breath as he turns back to Winston. Angus hasn't stopped pounding on his back, but I have no idea what he thinks he's going to accomplish. Hell, I'm not even sure Angus knows.

"Angus," Joshua says, as he presses two fingers against Winston's throat.

Angus finally stops, and I hold my breath, but let it out when a second later Joshua shakes his head.

Angus swears and gets to his feet, making room for the doctor. Joshua starts CPR while the other man stomps out of the room. Axl and I just sit there in silence, not even looking at each other. I can't take my eyes off Winston's lifeless face, and I'm sure Axl feels the same way.

Is this really happening? We all knew he was having a rough time, but I can't believe he did this. It's so wrong. So horrible. It's going to rip our group apart even more than Darla's death did, because this didn't happen at the hands of a monster or men who wanted to destroy us. Winston did this to himself.

A few minutes pass before Joshua stops, and when he sits back the sigh he lets out feels like punch. "He's gone."

The words hurt worse than a dagger to my heart. Sobs that I have absolutely no control over work their way to my throat and eyes, spilling over so violently that it makes my whole body shake. My eyes are so full of tears that the entire room blurs to nothing. In the hall, Angus swears. A violent thump follows, shaking the walls, but I can't make myself move so I can see what's going on. I can barely breathe, and every time I try to, it feels like I'm filling my lungs with lava.

Axl gets up, and I think he's going to come to me, but instead he goes into the hall. Angus is still swearing, and another thump is followed by the sound of breaking glass.

Next to Winston's lifeless body, Joshua hasn't moved an inch.

"Calm down," I hear Axl say.

"Son of a bitch gave up!" Angus growls. "Just threw in the towel. It was weak and stupid and it pisses me off!"

Axl says something I can't hear.

I wipe the tears from my cheeks and peek into the hall to find Axl examining his brother's hand—the one that was bitten yesterday. He must have torn a stitch, because blood has soaked through the gauze and has spotted the wall. Below them on the floor sits a picture, and large pieces of broken glass lay scattered across the gray carpet like icebergs jutting up out of the ocean. The drywall has been pounded in when Angus punched it.

I didn't even think he liked Winston.

Angus shoves his brother away and charges down the stairs. Axl stares at the floor, but I get the feeling he isn't really seeing anything. Like the rest of us, he's in shock. He tried to talk to Winston more than once, tried to get through to him, and knowing Axl, he's blaming himself right now. I can't say I don't feel a little bit of guilt myself. It's impossible not to think that we could have done something to prevent this from happening.

"What do we do with him?" Joshua asks from behind me.

"Ground's gonna be hard still," Axl mutters, finally pulling his gaze away from the floor.

Angus buried Darla a couple weeks ago, but it took him forever to dig the hole. At least the snow has melted more now, making the top layer soft and muddy. A foot or two down, though, it's probably still hard.

"We can't leave him here." My voice shakes so much that it sounds like I'm shivering. Maybe I am. My body seems to be covered in goose bumps.

"Angus and me'll take care of it," Axl says, heading down the stairs after his brother.

When I'm alone with Joshua, I find my eyes filling with tears all over again. "I can't believe he did this."

"He lost everything," Joshua says.

"We all have."

He shakes his head. "No. You lost stuff, but you found something too. Even Parvarti can say that. Trey may be dead, but she got a glimpse of what it meant to be alive. Winston had those things before and they were taken from him, and he lost himself when that happened."

"I just can't—" I shake my head again, unable to find the words.

"I'm not sure I can blame him." When my eyes snap his way, Joshua shrugs. "We've all had these thoughts. You know it's true."

Even though I refuse to say it out loud, he's right. If it weren't for Axl, I'm not sure there would be much of a point in going on. Every day is a struggle, and sometimes when all is said and done, it doesn't seem worth the fight I put up. Axl is the only thing that makes all this worthwhile for me.

Instead of agreeing, I get to my feet. "I can't sit here anymore."

Outside, the streets and yards are empty, and the clouds have moved in enough to block out the sun and all the optimism I felt when I first stepped outside this morning. A breeze sweeps across the yard, and I shiver.

I know my friends well enough to realize they're all gathered at Brady's house, so I head that way. I'm halfway across the lawn when Joshua comes out of the house behind me, but he doesn't run to catch up and I don't slow.

I push the front door open, leaving it cracked for Joshua, then kick my boots off and head into the kitchen. Just like I thought, it's full. Everyone seems to be here but Axl and Angus, but the only sounds are the quiet sobs of my friends.

"He's gone?" Lila asks when Joshua walks into the room behind me.

The doctor nods. "Yes."

"I can't believe it," Anne whispers.

She hasn't been in much better spirits since Jake's death, and if I'd put money on one of them deciding they'd had enough, it would have been her. Winston seemed stronger than this, and even though he'd gotten progressively more withdrawn over the last few months, I really thought he'd be able to pull through. Eventually.

"Axl or Angus come in here?" I ask.

A couple people shake their heads, and I find myself turning away, heading back to the front door. The house is so thick with grief that it's suffocating, plus I want to know what the brothers are doing.

Outside, I stop and listen. The clouds have gotten thicker and darker, and the day is silent other than a quiet clink that I can't place. I follow the sound, heading down the street and into a grassy section of the neighborhood. My boots slosh against the muddy ground, reminding me of a slushie. The metallic clank gets louder the farther I go. When I reach the end of the street, I follow not just the noise but the footprints in the snow. They take me to the edge of the neighborhood, where I find Angus slamming a shovel into the ground while Axl stands off to the side, frowning.

"What's going on?" I ask.

"What's it look like?" Angus grunts, but doesn't pause. "I'm gonna dig a grave."

I take a step closer and watch as he slams the shovel into the ground. He stomps his foot onto the head of the shovel, pushing it a little deeper before pulling the handle back. When it comes away, there's more mud than I expected. A raindrop hits my cheek as Angus tosses the mud aside and goes back for more. I wipe it away, but another one follows. Then more. They fall from the sky and land on my head and arms and face, growing more insistent until I don't see the point in trying to wipe them away.

I close my eyes, standing silently at Axl's side as Angus continues to dig. None of us talks, as water drizzles down on us, running over my hair into my eyes. Within seconds, I'm covered in goose bumps and shivering.

"He's gonna hurt his hand again," Axl says. "Fool won't listen to me, though."

I open my eyes to find his hair soaking wet and his shirt clinging to his arms and chest. He isn't even wearing a jacket. Was probably in too much of a hurry.

"Don't matter," Angus mutters, not looking away from the mud in front of him. "We gotta have a grave, so I'm gonna stay here 'til we got one. It's just gonna take some time. It ain't like we're short on that."

He grunts when he slams the shovel back into the ground. The rain has softened the earth even more, but that doesn't stop Angus from putting all his strength into it. Water drips down his face, and he brushes it away, leaving a streak of blood behind. Axl's right. Angus's hand is bleeding even more than it was inside the house.

"Angus," I say, stepping forward. "It's okay. We don't have to do this right now."

He pauses, and when his gray eyes move up to meet mine, they're darker than usual. Only it isn't rage or anger or any of the other violent emotions I'm used to seeing in them. This is pain. Raw and unchecked. Almost like Darla has died all over again.

"He deserves this," Angus says. "We didn't get to bury his girl, but we're gonna bury him."

I let out a deep breath when Angus goes back to digging, and Axl echoes me. He shakes his head, and I move over to stand at his side, allowing him to pull me in for a hug. We're both wet and cold and covered in goose bumps, but this moment isn't about getting warm.

"We're supposed to be goin' to check out Hope Springs," he says against my head.

"It's fine. We're fine."

It's a lie, and after this, I'm not sure any of us are going to be fine ever again. This is the first person we've lost like this, and it's even more painful than watching someone get ripped apart by a zombie or dying at the hands of madmen. This is like losing Jon and Hadley all over again, and it makes me mad. So mad that I want to scream or throw something.

Spring is on its way, and it was supposed to bring better times with it. A new world we could live in where we could be safe and happy. Where we could start over. But it didn't, and I'm not sure it's even possible anymore.

CHAPTER TWENTY-FOUR

VIVIAN

After days of rain, I'm glad to step outside to a clear morning. The moisture from last night's shower still clings to the breeze, as well as the scent of grass and flowers and all the other smells that come with spring. White, puffy clouds dot the sky above me, and the sun's rays warm my skin even more than they did just a couple days ago.

The longest winter of my life has finally come to an end, and we should be on our way to better times. Summer, which means longer days and warmer temperatures. Growing our own food. Learning to sustain ourselves. Everything on the horizon should be bright and cheerful. Hopeful. Almost like we've been given a fresh start.

Too bad the cloud of Winston's death is still hanging over us.

I exhale, hoping to blow away the weight I've been carrying on my shoulders. It doesn't work, though. Maybe it's too early to feel any real optimism. Now that the weather is warmer, the zombies are more of a threat, and we haven't worked out what we're going to do about fuel and other supplies yet. Plus, everyone is still reeling from Winston's death.

I cross the street and head toward Brady's house when I spot Parvarti in the distance. She waves and I return the gesture, surprised but glad she's showing a little life today.

"Vivian!" Parvarti waves again as she hurries toward me, way more animated than she's been since Trey died.

My stomach clenches, and my feet stop moving on their own. Shit. Will life ever get easier?

"What's wrong?" I call.

Parvarti shakes her head. "Nothing. At least I don't think so." She slows as she approaches, breathing heavily. The soft brown of her cheeks is tinted pink from the cool morning air. "Sophia is in labor."

"Oh."

The word pops out of my mouth, but I can't for the life of me think of what else to say. We knew it was coming, but as to whether or not it's a good thing...only time will tell. I'm also feeling more than a little guilty for not pushing the trip to Hope Springs. After Winston...it just didn't seem like a priority. We needed time to mourn.

"Thought you'd want to know," Parv says with a little shrug.

"I do," I say as I move toward Sophia's house. "Thank you."

When I push open the front door, I'm greeted by an agonized moan, and for just a second, I find myself unable to move. I hold my breath as all the worries I've had about this baby and the future curl into a ball and lodge in my throat. This could be a very happy day or one of the worst we've experienced so far.

"It's okay, Sophia." Joshua's voice floats down from the second floor. "Just breath, you're doing fine."

I kick my shoes off and hurry up the stairs, taking them

two at a time. My heart pounds faster than a hummingbird's wings, but I'm not sure if it's from fear or excitement. The only thing I know for sure is this baby is coming, and I promised Sophia I would be there with her.

She smiles my way when I walk in, but it's twisted in pain.

"I'm here," I say, hurrying to her side.

Sweaty hair has matted itself to Sophia's forehead, and dark circles ring her eyes. I know she hasn't been sleeping well, but she looks even more exhausted now than she did just a few days ago. How long has she been in labor? All night?

"What can I do?" I ask, tearing my eyes off Sophia.

Joshua sits at the foot of the bed, rubbing her leg. "There's nothing we can do right now," he says, pushing his hair back off his forehead. "She just needs time."

The circles under his eyes tell me they've been at this for a while now.

"When did it start?" I sit on the side of the bed and take Sophia's hand, suddenly pulled into the past and remembering my own labor. It feels like a different life now.

"Ava came to get me around two. Sophia's water had broken and the contractions started shortly before that." Joshua lets out a deep breath. "She's only dilated to three. We have a long day ahead of us."

Sophia's hand tightens around mine, and her whole body tenses when another contraction hits her. She groans and squeezes her eyes shut.

"Breathe, Sophia," I say, leaning closer.

She blows out a breath, then sucks another in just as quickly. Repeating it as her body works with the contraction.

When it passes, Joshua grabs his stethoscope and presses it to her round belly. "Good," he whispers. "The heartbeat is still good. We're just going to take our time and we'll get through this."

Sophia nods, but a tear slides down her cheek. I'm not sure if it's from the pain or the knowledge that she might be going through all of this for nothing. Probably both.

"I can get some cold water and a washcloth." I give her hand a pat.

"Thank you," Sophia says.

I get to my feet, glancing at Joshua. "You need anything? Breakfast?"

"That would be nice," he says, giving me an exhausted smile. "Thank you."

I rush from the room and down the stairs, barely pausing to shove my feet into my shoes before heading outside. I'm not even sure why I'm rushing at this point, though. There's no hurry. Sophia and Joshua aren't going anywhere for a while. She's dilated three now, and the general rule—which I know from my own experience—is that you can expect to dilate one centimeter an hour. She has to get to ten, so seven more hours. If she follows that rule. So far, she hasn't. Her labor started around two in the morning, and it has to be close to eight now. Six hours and only three centimeters…that's not great.

Hopefully, things pick up for her.

"Brady!" I call when I push his front door open.

He comes out of the kitchen just as I kick my shoes off. "Something wrong?"

"No. I'm just coming to get something for Joshua to eat."

"You read my mind," he says, motioning for me to follow him.

I step into the kitchen to find a tray of food ready for me to take over. He wasn't joking.

"Joshua is going to be glad to have this."

Brady smiles up at me. "They need to keep their strength up."

"Thank you," I say as I take the tray. "Although I'm not sure if Sophia will eat anything. They generally don't let you eat when you're in labor."

"Is that so? I hadn't reached that part of the book yet." Brady frowns and shakes his head, and not for the first time I'm struck by the thought that he lost more than just a wife

278

when the virus hit.

"Thank you," I say even though I want to tell him I'm sorry. I don't think of Brady as the kind of person who needs apologies from other people to make his life meaningful, though. "Do you have any idea what time Angus and Axl went out this morning?" I say instead.

Axl was up before I was awake, heading out with Angus to do some hunting.

"I believe it was around five. It was still dark, I know that for sure, and Joshua had already been with Sophia for a few hours."

"Good," I say. "They should be back soon then. Assuming they get something."

"One would think."

I turn, steadying the tray as I head toward the door.

"Let me help you with that," Brady says, hurrying after me.

Somehow I manage to get my shoes on without dumping food all over the place, then Brady holds the door open for me. The bright sun seems more cheery than it did earlier, which makes me happy. Even though we know the odds of this thing turning out good are slim, I don't want to leave *all* the hope I have behind. I want to believe the future can be good and bright and happy. To look back on all the pain and loss we've been through and believe we can have a real life.

Getting into Sophia's house without Brady's help is a bit challenging, but somehow I make it without dropping the tray. Honestly, it's enough food for eight people, but since it could be a long day and I plan on being there to lend a hand, it's good to be prepared. Who knows what will come of this.

I drop the tray off for Joshua, then hurry to the kitchen, where I dig out a bowl. It's a good thing the water coming out of the faucet is already cold, but it would still be nice to have some ice right now. I remember eating ice chips during my own labor, and it was comforting.

Joshua and I spend the day at Sophia's side. Holding her hand, wiping her sweaty face with a cold washcloth.

Only taking a break to eat or use the bathroom. People stop in to make sure we don't need anything, but for the most part they leave us alone.

Shortly after lunchtime, Axl sticks his head into the room. Seeing him helps me relax. Between Sophia's discomfort and the unknown looming at the end of this labor, things are tense. Knowing he's here and he's safe will help me.

"I'll be right back," I tell Sophia, giving her hand a pat before heading out into the hallway with Axl.

"Got a deer," he says when we're alone.

"Thank God," I say, leaning into him. "That will feed us for a while. Take off some of the stress of life."

Axl wraps his arms around me, and I inhale. He smells like the woods. Like spring and wet leaves and dirt. Which is nice. It's been a while since I've breathed him in and had to deal with the stink of death. Every time I think about it, I can't help worrying that it isn't going to last forever. That one of these days we'll find ourselves back on the run. Living out of a truck and fighting for every meal and every hour of sleep. Dirty and covered in the stink of rot once again.

"We'll get it butchered today," Axl replies. "How's she doin'?"

"Good. She's tired and she's in pain, but that's normal." I exhale and pull back so I can look him in the eye. "The worst part of this whole thing is knowing how bad it could turn out. It has to make this so hard for her."

Axl exhales and looks at the ceiling, and I get the feeling he's once again putting the blame on his own shoulders. As if *he* has any control over how this virus affects the world.

"Forget it," I say, giving him a quick kiss on the cheek. "Just go take care of that deer so you can get us all fed. That's your job, and you've done it well."

"We'll get it done."

Axl heads off, and I do the same, going back to Sophia's side, where I sit and wait.

The day moves on, and the sun gets higher in the sky, then dips lower, making the room darker. Still, little changes with Sophia's progress. When the sun finally hits the horizon, Joshua and I are forced to light candles. The shadows grow longer as the sky outside turns black, but still the baby doesn't come, and the more time that passes, the more worn out Sophia gets until she acts like she can barely keep her eyes open.

"Let me check you again," Joshua says an hour or so after we've lit the candles.

Sophia nods, and I hold her hand — and my breath — while the doctor does his thing. It's been hours. Surely she's made some progress.

"How far?" Sophia asks in a strained voice as Joshua pulls the blanket back down to cover her legs.

"Five," he says, wincing. "You haven't progressed at all in the last five hours."

I know enough about childbirth to know that isn't good.

"How long can we hold off?" I ask.

"In the real world, hospitals won't let mothers labor for more than twenty-four hours without intervening. Once the water breaks, there's an increased risk of infection, and with lawsuits it wasn't worth the risk. Before all that, women would sometimes labor for days before having the baby or —" He slams his mouth shut, but it isn't like his meaning isn't loud and clear.

"They died," Sophia whispers.

Joshua nods.

"No," I say, getting to my feet. "That will not happen. We can't sit by and let it go on like this when there's a town twenty miles away where they have doctors and medical equipment."

"What do you suggest?" Joshua asks.

I know what he's implying: Axl won't let us go. We haven't staked the place out, and running in there without planning is exactly what he was trying to avoid.

Too bad Axl doesn't always get to be in charge.

"I'm going to talk to Axl. I'm going to make him

understand that this is something we have to do. Even if I have to beat the shit out of him."

Before I've had a chance to take a step, Joshua grabs my arm. "We have time, but you need to let him know that if she hasn't had the baby by morning, it could be very bad."

"I'll make him listen to reason," I say.

Sophia's face scrunches up and she balls her hands into fists, and I know she's having another contraction. They're so close at this point that it's probably impossible for her to get any rest, and I just can't imagine having to go through this with no chance of a break. No medicine to ease her pain or help her sleep. No chance of a medical intervention. She has to be terrified.

I have to get her help.

"I'll be right back," I say, heading for the door.

I go to Brady's house first, relieved when I find Axl in the kitchen drinking a cup of coffee.

"Everything okay?" Brady asks when I hurry in.

I shake my head but don't look his way. I'm too focused on Axl.

"We may have to go to Hope Springs," I say, putting my hand up when he opens his mouth to say something. I'm not going to give him the chance to argue. "I know why you wanted to avoid it, and I understand, but we might not have a choice in this. Sophia's labor hasn't progressed, and if it continues like this she could die."

"Shit." Axl shoves his hand through his hair. "How long we got?"

"Joshua says we can wait until the morning, but not much longer. This is serious, Axl."

"I know."

He gets up from the table, pushing his chair back so violently that it falls to the floor. Brady stands too, but he doesn't say anything. Not even when he bends down and picks the chair up. He just lets Axl pace a few times, shaking his head. The expression on his face tells me he's working through it all, trying to figure out another way. There isn't one though, so I have no doubt in my mind he'll come to the realization that we need to do this.

"We have to go," Brady says finally.

Axl nods. "I know. Don't mean I gotta like it."

"It's going to be fine," I say, grabbing his arm. Stopping him from making yet another loop around the room. "We haven't seen anything that indicates these people aren't trustworthy."

He doesn't look at me. "I got a bad feelin' 'bout it. That's all. I don't know why, but I do."

I don't have time to reassure him, so I give him a kiss on the cheek and say, "It will work out."

Then I turn and hurry from the room, heading back to Sophia and Joshua. Praying that it doesn't come to that. Not because I share Axl's worries, but because it would mean more pain for Sophia. As far as Hope Springs goes, I don't think it's going to be the death trap Axl believes it will be.

"AGH!"

Sophia balls the sheet in her hand, twisting the fabric around her fist while Joshua and I hurry around the room gathering supplies. The contractions are so close together now that she barely has time to relax between them, but she still hasn't made any progress. Outside, the horizon has transformed from black to bright orange, and Axl is loading up the car. He doesn't want me to go, but I refuse to sit here and do nothing when I know I can help.

"Just keep breathing," Joshua repeats. "We're almost ready."

Footsteps pound up the stairs, and Axl appears in the doorway. "You got your shit together?"

"Almost." Joshua shoves one more thing into his bag and zips it shut, then tosses it to Axl, who catches it mid-air. "We'll be down in a second."

Axl hurries from the room.

I sit on the edge of the bed next to Sophia. "We're going to get you some help."

Her hair is so sweaty that when she nods it doesn't move an inch. "Thank you."

"You're going to be okay."

I help her sit up, and Joshua goes to her other side as she climbs to her feet. She's unsteady, thanks to the lack of sleep and food, not to mention the intense pain she's been in for over a day now. I'm surprised she can stand at all.

"Nice and slow," Joshua says as we move toward the door.

We make it five steps before another contraction hits and we have to stop. Sophia squeezes my hand as she pants through the pain, and even though it feels like my bones are about to be crushed, I let her.

"It's okay," I whisper. "Hang in there. Almost done now."

She nods and lets out a deep breath, and then her hand relaxes.

"Let's move," Joshua says.

We make it out the door and down the hall to the stairs. Joshua goes first, walking backward so he can make sure Sophia doesn't lose her balance. I stay at her side, holding her arm. Every step she takes is wobbly, and we only make it part of the way before she has to stop.

"Urgh." Sophia grabs the railing and squeezes. Her knees buckle, and I grip her arm tighter, trying to keep her up.

"Hang on, Sophia. You can do it. This is the last one, then we'll be in the car."

She nods even though she doesn't open her eyes.

When the contraction passes, we move again. Down the stairs and to the front door, then outside. We head down the sidewalk to the waiting car, the door hanging open and the engine idling. Axl stands by the open door, ready to shut it after Sophia has climbed in. We only have four feet to go.

Sophia lets out a wail when another contraction squeezes her body, and this time she ends up on her knees.

"Shit," Axl says, hurrying toward us. "She okay?"

"No!" I snap.

"It's okay," Joshua says, much calmer than I am. "She'll be fine. Just give her a minute. It will pass. Let her breathe through it."

Axl's face is whiter than the snow was, and I'm suddenly afraid he's going to pass out.

"She'll be okay," I say, grabbing his arm.

He nods but doesn't take his eyes off Sophia.

When the contraction has passed, we all move. The three of us haul Sophia to her feet and toward the car. Then she's in and the door is shut. The men hurry around to the other side while I climb into the passenger seat. Axl throws the car in gear the second he has his door shut, barreling toward the fence where Angus waits, ready to open the gate for us. Thank God.

"I'm sorry," Axl says, shaking his head. "Maybe we shoulda gone earlier. Maybe you was right."

I reach over and squeeze his knee. "It's okay."

"No one could have predicted this," Joshua says from the back. "She had a normal labor the first time around, so I'm not sure why her progress has stalled like this."

I haven't been outside the fence since our trip to Duncan, and things look totally different than the last time. The snow is completely gone, and everywhere I look the world has turned green. Flowers bloom on trees and in fields, and the animals seem to have returned. Of course, so have the zombies. I can see them shambling through woods and open meadows as we speed toward Hope Springs. No wonder Axl doesn't want me to go out.

The twenty-minute drive is filled with the moans of Sophia. Joshua sits at her side, constantly reminding her to breathe, while I do the same for myself. Every second that passes feels like she's one step closer to death. I don't know how she's gone on this long.

By the time the town comes into view, I'm on the edge of my seat. The gate is fortified and heavily guarded, and even though it makes me nervous, there's nothing else we can do. Sophia's energy is almost gone.

Axl pulls to a stop in front of the gate, and a few men rush forward, aiming automatic weapons at the car.

"Stay low," he says, wringing his hands on the steering wheel.

A guy moves to the front of the pack, and I recognize him right away. Dax, the man we met in the Sam's Club parking lot last November. He's just as beefy and probably even blonder. Just like last time, everyone seems to follow his lead. Hanging back while he checks things out. Waiting for him to either tell them to attack or to ease up.

He waves as he approaches, smiling, but any comfort the friendly greeting might give me is washed away when his jacket moves aside. He has so many weapons attached to his belt that it looks like he's heading out to war. I slip my hand down my side and onto my knife, but I don't pull it out. I just want to be ready.

"I'm gonna roll the window down," Axl says, then glances in the rearview mirror.

Joshua scoots closer to Sophia as Axl pushes the button on his door. The window slides down, disappearing just as Dax stops at our side. His eyes sweep across Axl, checking out every inch of him.

"Welcome to Hope Springs!" Dax says, moving his gaze to me. He blinks, and his already wide smile grows bigger. "We ran into you folks once, didn't we? I'd remember that pretty face anywhere."

Axl leans forward so he's blocking me from view. "Saw you last fall in Duncan. Sam's Club."

Dax snaps his fingers. "Right. I remember now. You said you had a safe place. Have you come to your senses?"

"We're good where we are," Axl says. "But as you can see, we need a doctor."

Sophia moans, emphasizing Axl's words, and Dax's gaze moves to the back. He tries to lean in, but Axl's body stiffens even more.

286

"You gotta back off. Understand?" His voice is so cool it could freeze the devil in the pits of hell.

Dax steps back, raising his hands. Still grinning. "Sorry. Just trying to help."

"You can help by showin' us where the doctor is."

"I can do that, but we have procedures. The first thing you're going to need to do is pull through the gate and step out." Dax points past the fence, and I glance forward. His men have their guns up but not aimed at us. Doesn't mean they don't look ready to shoot if necessary. "We'll do a quick sweep of the car, just make sure everything is okay. We aren't going ask you to leave your weapons, but we want to know what you have with you. Do you understand?"

Axl's mouth scrunches up, and even though he doesn't look happy about it, he nods. "We understand you got to protect your people, but we got a lady back there who's in a lot of pain. She can't get out. Not right now."

"Please," I say, leaning forward so I can see Dax. "She's been in labor for over a day. We need to get her to a doctor."

Dax's eyes hold mine for a second, and then he exhales and motions to the men in front of us. They back away as another man pulls the gate open. Dax waves us forward. "Drive on through and we'll take care of it. Just know that we *will* open fire if we feel you are a threat. So tread lightly."

Axl slams his thumb against the button, rolling the window back up. "Prick," he mumbles before the window is all the way shut.

"Careful," I say. "You're sounding an awful lot like Angus right now."

Axl just snorts.

He pulls through the gate, following Dax's directions when he motions for us to stop.

After he shuts the engine off, Axl reaches for the doorknob. "Keep your eyes open. Got it?"

"Yeah," I say, opening my own door and climbing out.

Even though they're being cautious, there doesn't seem to be anything overly threatening about the men guarding the gate. Not even Dax. Axl may be overreacting, but I agree with him. It doesn't hurt to be careful. And right now, the most important thing is to cooperate so we can get Sophia to a doctor.

Axl, Joshua, and I climb out, but Sophia stays where she is. I keep close to her open door as a couple men move forward to search the car. They're not holding guns, and they're pretty laid back, but they aren't taking any risks either. They look under seats and in the glove compartment. A guy even pats us down one at a time. Dax watches closely, following the man's progress the whole time. When it's my turn, something about the expression in the big man's eyes gives me the creeps. I'm pretty sure it's all in my head, though. He's just doing his job. Right?

When Dax looks away from me, he focuses on Sophia. "She's been like this for a day and you're just now coming?" He shakes his head like he thinks we're morons.

"I'm a doctor," Joshua says defensively.

Dax snorts. "Well, we have an obstetrician and all the necessary equipment. Including electricity. She'll be in good hands here."

"They're clean," a guy calls from behind Dax.

"Okay, then," Dax says, tilting his head toward the car. "Hop in and follow me."

We pile back into the car while the other man climbs into a souped-up golf cart, of all things. There's so much metal welded to the thing I'm surprised it still drives. You'd think it would be too heavy.

Dax drives off before we've even had a chance to get our doors shut, but it's not like we're going to have trouble catching up. The SUV moves way faster than that little golf cart. Plus, there's only one road open.

"It seems okay," I say once we're all back in the car and the doors are shut.

The men outside have relaxed. Gone back to standing guard, which means not doing much other than being ready. Despite the one creepy feeling I got from Dax, I'm not overly concerned about this place.

"Yup." Axl throws the car in gear and I lurch back. "Don't know if I trust this guy."

"He's a pompous ass," Joshua mutters, but it's almost drowned out by Sophia's moans.

"I don't think you'll ever trust another man after Vegas," I say, putting my hand on Axl's leg. "So I'm sorry if I don't exactly trust your judgment."

"How can *you*?" He glances toward me, his expression pained.

"Because the nice, caring men I've met have had a much greater impact on my life than those assholes ever could." I give Axl's leg a pat, ignoring the way my stomach twists at the memories of Vegas. And Hadley. I doubt I'll ever be able to get over her loss. Or the hope that we'll bump into her again somewhere.

Axl nods slowly as he drives down the street, following Dax through town, but he doesn't say anything. We pass a few people standing on the street, and the normalcy of it is slightly unnerving after all these months of seeing empty, broken towns. They're talking. Just standing on the sidewalk talking to each other like things are totally normal. A young girl with bright, red hair catches my eye, and without thinking, I do a double take. It isn't Hadley—her hair isn't even close to the same color—but I can't stop myself from hoping anyway.

"We should ask about Hadley again," I say after we've passed the girl.

"We will," Axl replies.

Dax turns onto a road that's lined with cute little shops, and Axl follows. We drive until we reach the end of the street, slowing to a stop when Dax pulls up in front of a building. Above the door a sign reads *Hope Springs Women's Health*. An actual OBGYN's office? It's crazy to think such a thing could actually exist in this world still. But it does and we're here, and maybe, with the help of these doctors, Sophia's baby will stand a chance.

CHAPTER TWENTY-FIVE

VIVIAN

Before I've even had a chance to open my door, people have rushed from the building, and Dax is waving them our way. It reminds me of a medical drama I used to love when I was a kid. I'd watch reruns on the little TV we had in our trailer, staying up late at night and losing myself in the drama. Pretending that could be me. A doctor who saved lives and made a difference in the world.

Now that world is gone, though, the only difference I can really make is to keep on living.

Dax's eyes meet mine when I hop out, and he smiles. "I radioed ahead," he says with a shrug. "I'm not a total hard-ass."

Axl steps in front of me. "We appreciate it."

If I wasn't so worried about Sophia, I'd smack him upside the head.

I ignore Axl and his jealousy and instead focus on why we're here. Joshua and one of the women who came out are busy helping Sophia into a wheelchair. Thank God they have one, because with the way her legs are shaking, I'm not she'd be able to stand right now. The second she's settled, we're all rushing into the building. Sophia in the chair and Joshua at her side. Me right behind her. Axl follows, and I'm pretty sure even Dax comes. My heart is pounding like mad, and I get more and more tense with every step I take. This is the moment of truth. The one we've been hoping for and dreading since we found out Sophia was expecting.

A nurse meets us in the lobby, carrying a clipboard. Her eyes are huge, and something about the expression on her face turns the blood in my veins to ice. Why do I get the feeling these people look at Sophia and see a death sentence?

"Do you know how much you weighed before the outbreak?" she asks, her pen poised over a clipboard.

"Around." Pant. "One forty." Sophia grips the arms of the wheelchair and lets out a tortured moan.

The nurse scribbles it down as we hurry through the lobby. Joshua is with Sophia, so I'm not sure if she'll still want me in the room too, and I almost stop. But when she looks up, the terrified expression in her eyes makes the decision for me.

"I'm coming," I say, hurrying down the hall at her side.

We go down a sterile hall, passing offices and a couple exam rooms where the lights are off before stopping in front of one of those old-school scales with the different size weights. I look at the nurse like she's nuts, but she's too focused on Sophia to notice.

"Do you think we can get your weight?" the nurse asks.

Joshua lets out a frustrated sigh. "I'm her doctor, and I'm telling you we need to get this baby delivered. She's been in labor for nearly thirty hours now, and you and I both know it's not just infection we're risking at this point."

"O-okay," the nurse stammers.

She takes us to a room that's been set up for delivery, but I can't help thinking we're wasting precious time. It's obvious by this point Sophia is going to need a C-section.

"Where's the doctor?" Joshua yells when the nurse pulls out a gown.

She yelps and drops the gown, and I rip it off the floor. "We need a doctor now."

The nurse nods and practically trips over her own feet as she hurries from the room. Sophia pants, and Joshua rubs the bridge of his nose. I've never heard him yell before, but I can't blame him. I'm not exactly sure what these people think is going on here, but we need to move fast if we want Sophia to come out of this alive.

"This is bullshit," Joshua hisses.

A clock on the wall ticks, reminding me of the silence that covered my elementary school classroom during tests. I can remember the constant tick of the second hand like it was yesterday. The sound seemed so loud on top of the stillness that sometimes I found it hard to concentrate.

Sophia moans again, breaking the silence, then looks up at me. "Do you think there's any hope?"

I swallow and force myself to meet her gaze. Before I answer, I have to know if she's looking for the truth or false hope. I'm willing to give either one at this point. Whatever helps her get through what comes next.

Her brown eyes search mine, and a lump forms in my throat, growing bigger the longer I stare at her. "I think," I say, finding the words more difficult to get out than I could have ever imagined, "that we will have to wait and see for sure, but they have everything you could need for a successful delivery."

Sophia nods, but anything she was going to say is cut short when the door opens and a doctor rushes in, pulling a portable ultrasound machine with him. He's young and thin, and the glasses he wears are held together by tape. For some reason, it reminds me that we are in the middle of the apocalypse more than anything else we've seen since driving into this town, and that this baby isn't going to survive.

"My name is Dr. Murray, but you can call me Dan. My nurse tells me you've been in labor for over thirty hours?"

"Going on thirty-one," Joshua says.

The doctor nods as he gets his ultrasound machine set up. "And you think you're full-term?"

"I found out I was pregnant—" Sophia grunts. "—right before the virus got bad."

"Very good." The doctor motions for her to lift her shirt, but I do it for her. She's still in the wheelchair, and I have a feeling he's leaving her where she is because he knows he's going to have to operate.

"I want to get a quick look to make sure the baby isn't in any distress, and then we're going to move you to another room. They're prepping for surgery now, and my colleague is scrubbing in."

"Thank God," Joshua mutters.

"You're her doctor?" Dan asks as he squirts gel on the ultrasound wand.

"I am."

"And the heartbeat has been strong?"

"Very," Joshua says.

"Good."

The doctor moves the ultrasound wand across Sophia's belly, and the room fills with the whooshing sound of the baby's and Sophia's heartbeats. One is much faster than the other, but they are both strong.

The doctor squints at the screen for a few seconds, then gives a little nod. "Everything seems to be okay," he tells Sophia as he replaces the wand. "We're going to take you back now. You'll need to say goodbye to your friends."

I put my arms around a shaky Sophia and give her a squeeze that's meant to be encouraging, but I'm sure falls terribly short. "It's going to be okay," I whisper. "Hang in there. You're almost done now."

"Thank you," Sophia says, squeezing my hand when I pull back. "Thanks for everything."

"You're welcome."

I step back, and she gives a similar farewell to Joshua. Then the Hope Springs doctor is gone, rushing Sophia down the hall and leaving us alone in the much too silent room. The ticking of the clock seeming to grow louder and more ominous with each passing second.

"I guess we go back to the waiting room," I say after Joshua and I have stared at the empty doorway in silence for much longer than necessary.

He sighs. "Yeah."

We head out together, my stomach no less tense now that Sophia is on her way to surgery.

In the waiting room, we find Axl pacing and Dax leaning up against the wall. Both men turn our way when we walk in.

"Everything go okay?" the new man asks.

"We hope so," I say. "Thank you for helping."

Dax shoves himself off the wall, smiling. Still. "No worries. She's in good hands, so I don't want you to worry about her. We've been through a lot, and these doctors have helped patch up more people than I can count."

"How many doctors do you have?" I ask.

"Three." Dax's smile finally fades, and he shakes his head. "Maybe I should have told your friend before she went in, I'm not sure. But we've had a few babies born here already."

"Did they make it?" I ask, knowing by the grim expression on his face that they didn't.

"No," Dax says flatly.

"None of them?" Joshua asks.

Dax shakes his head.

Axl's gaze meets mine, and he crosses the room to stand at my side. I slip my hand into his, thankful that he's here with me. There's probably less hope for this baby than we originally thought, which isn't giving it much of a chance. We always knew Sophia's baby was a long shot, but I hadn't totally given up the belief that things could work out. It's like I've been walking around with my fingers crossed for the last few months.

"How many babies?" I ask even though a part of me doesn't want to know.

"Too many," Dax replies.

"How many?" Axl growls.

Dax turns his gaze toward Axl, his expression so raw and hard that I find myself taking a step back. "You want to know how many? Fine. Four. We've had four babies born here since the dead came back, all at different times and under different circumstances. None of them lasted more than a couple hours outside the womb."

Joshua swears, and my hand slips out of Axl's so I can cover my mouth. A feeble attempt at trying to hold in the sobs. We'd been praying for a fifty percent chance, but in the blink of an eye, all the hope I've been clinging to for weeks drains away.

"Shit," Axl mutters.

Dax exhales, and his shoulders slump. "It's been...rough. Every baby was a chance at a new life, and every time one of them died, we felt that hope slipping further and further away. The last one was born just last week, and since then, things have been pretty depressing. We're still trying, but if we can't repopulate it seems like it's all for nothing." He runs his hand across his blond head. "We have one woman who got pregnant after the outbreak, though, so all hope isn't lost. Both the parents are here, so obviously they're both immune. We just have to pray that when she gives birth, the baby will survive."

"When is she due?" I ask.

"June, so we have some time to wait."

That's good news. It's also something we've talked a lot about, whether or not a baby conceived by two immune parents would have more of a chance at survival. It's hard to say, but possible. Of course, we don't know anything for sure. This virus is a total mystery to us. Which means none of us has been in a rush to be the first one to get knocked up. Just in case.

I exhale, and Axl wraps his arm around me. "It's gonna

be okay. Sophia is gonna make it."

I don't know if he's right, but I do know this: if Sophia had been here, she would have had a better chance. We all would have. We were stupid to wait, and if she dies, I'm going to carry the guilt of this with me for the rest of my life. We should have tried harder, done more. We were too cautious this time, and now Sophia might pay the price for our mistakes.

"She should stay here," I whisper.

I want to tell Axl that we all should stay here, but I know he's going to need to ease into the idea. Now that we know the people of Hope Springs aren't a threat, I don't see the point in staying out in the middle of nowhere.

"Can't make her."

"I don't think we'll have to." I turn to face Axl, looking up into his eyes. "I know you like our little town, and that's fine. We've worked hard to get things set up, and it wasn't easy. It's safe, and we have a good shot at turning it into something good and real. But you are going to have to accept that some of our group may want to come here. Sophia and Ava at the very least, but possibly a few of the others."

"We're a family," Axl says, shaking his head.

"We are, but we're also very secluded, and it's terrifying at times. You know it is. If we get attacked again, we could be in big trouble."

Axl grunts but doesn't say anything, and I let it go. I don't expect him to give in right away, but I want to put it out there so he's prepared for what happens next. Eventually, our tight little group will split up for one reason or another.

Joshua drops into a chair and lets out a deep sigh.

"You okay there?" Dax asks him.

"We've been up all night," I say, suddenly feeling the weight of my own exhaustion.

"We can get you a place to stay for the night once we know what's going on with your friend. I'd take you now, but I'm thinking you'd rather wait."

"We would," Axl says stiffly.

Dax's eyes cloud over at Axl's tone, and for a second, I think there's going to be some kind of confrontation. The big man glances my way, looking me over more than necessary before nodding.

"Alright, then," he says.

Dax settles into a chair—as far away from Axl as he can get—and seeing him sitting down turns my legs to Jell-O. I slide out of Axl's grasp and take a seat next to Joshua, who looks like he's barely hanging on. Axl doesn't sit, though. He paces.

A clock on the wall ticks, and my heart pounds. I'm not sure how long a C-section takes, but I know it's going to seem like an eternity in this silent waiting room. None of us are exactly in the mood for conversation, though, and there's nothing for us to do but wait. So we do.

"VIVIAN."

My eyes open to Axl's stormy gray eyes, but it takes me a second to remember where we are. When the memory of driving through the gates of Hope Springs comes screaming back, I bolt upright.

"What is it?"

Axl frowns as he runs his hand through his hair. "Sophia."

"She's dead." My heart almost stops and I can't seem to catch my breath, and all I can think about is little Ava and what she's going to do without her mom. This is an impossibly cruel world to grow up in without parents. Even worse than the one I faced.

"No." Axl kneels so we're eye level. He shakes his head but never looks away. Never abandons me as the heaviness of what he's about to say settles around us. "She ain't. But the baby..."

"The baby didn't make it." It crushes more than I thought it would. Like a piano dropping on my head.

"Lived for ten minutes," Joshua says, and I turn to find

298

him sitting next to me still, his face in his hands. "All that for nothing."

It doesn't seem fair.

"Poor Sophia."

"We're gonna find a place to stay the night," Axl gets to his feet, grabbing my hand and pulling me up with him. "Get some rest before we go back. Sophia wants us to bring Ava."

I'm not surprised by her decision, and I'm also not surprised that Axl seems to take it as a personal insult.

I wrap my arms around him. "It will be okay."

He just nods.

Dax clears his throat, and I look over to find him waiting by the door. "I'm sorry to rush you, but I have work to do."

"It's okay." Joshua stands and stretches. "I could use a bed to lay down in, I'm not going to lie."

"Then you're in luck. We have houses available, and they've all been cleaned out," Dax says, pushing the front door open, smiling. "They're just waiting for someone to move into them."

He sounds way too chipper considering what we just went through. Then again, he didn't know Sophia, and he's been through a few infant deaths already. Maybe he's just gotten used to it all.

Joshua heads across the room. "Perfect."

I can't argue with him. My little nap in the waiting room chair didn't leave me feeling very rested. A bed and some alone time with Axl is just what I need. I never feel like I've processed something completely until we've had a chance to talk it out.

"Come on," I say, taking Axl's hand and pulling him after Joshua.

We leave our car parked in front of the doctor's office and follow Dax through town. It's odd, because walking through the streets of Hope Springs feels a lot like going back to several months ago when life was normal. When kids played in streets and people had jobs. I keep waiting for something horrible to happen, only I'm not even sure what.

Someone to fire a gun at us or a horde of zombies to come rushing around the corner. Maybe even for someone to jump out laughing and pointing, telling me the last few months have been nothing but an elaborate hoax.

If only that were true.

"How many people do you have here?" I ask Dax as he leads us down the street, causing Axl to stiffen at my side.

"Nearly two hundred now," Dax says over his shoulder. He doesn't look back at me, and I'm sure it has a lot to do with all the glares Axl has been giving him.

"Are more people still coming in?" Joshua asks.

Dax shrugs. "On and off, but it isn't as many as it was before winter hit. We spent winter clearing the streets and fortifying our fences, and it paid off. We started sending parties out to look for survivors once spring came, but the zoms moving around again has slowed our progress. We've picked a handful people up since the snow melted, but not many."

"Have you gone far?" I ask, wondering how much ground they've covered. It's a little surprising they never made it our way.

"Fifty miles or so in all directions."

They must have missed us somehow. It's odd but possible. We're pretty secluded.

Of course, there's always the possibility that the men who attacked us were from here. But that couldn't be, could it? This place seems fine. No one's shown any hostility toward us since we got here...

I glance toward Axl, who's even tenser than before. He's frowning and looking around, studying everything we pass like he's thinking the same thing I am. Still, though, nothing seems off or threatening. People smile when we pass. They seem nice. Happy.

There's nothing to worry about. I'm positive.

Dax leads us down streets that have been cleared of debris and bodies. The blood that was most likely here at one point has been scrubbed clean, and many of the stores we pass are not only in use but open. People walk by and wave, and I can't shake the feeling that I've entered *The Twilight Zone*. Especially when we pass a jewelry store filled with people. Like they're shopping or something.

"The jewelry store is open?" I ask, shaking my head.

"Not really," Dax glances back but keeps it brief. "We're taking inventory, then we'll move it all over to the bank. Right now we're preparing for the future. The assumption is that all this stuff will have value again one day, and we want to be prepared. Eventually we'll have a reestablished government, and who knows what will be useful."

He has a good point, and even if I'm not sure the crap we valued before all this will ever matter again in our lifetime, it doesn't hurt to be prepared. And it's smart. Assuming they actually find another town out there, which I have some serious doubts about.

"You're assumin' there are other people out there," Axl says, echoing my thoughts. "You seen anythin' to back that up?"

Dax stops and turns to face us, this time looking Axl right in the eye. "We've more than seen it, we've spoken to people. In Atlanta. They have the city blocked off and they've created a new government."

Axl's mouth drops open, and all I can do is stare at Dax. There are other people? There's a government?

"What?" I say after almost a minute of silence.

"You heard me. We got in touch with them back in January." He turns and starts walking again. "Let's get you a house. There's plenty of time to share all the details."

We start moving again, but it feels so automatic that I start to wonder if Dax has a remote control. My legs move, but it's like I'm watching myself from a distance, because all I can really think about is what this new information means. Help? Maybe. We're so far from Atlanta that I'm not sure how much this will really affect us. A future? Absolutely. The fact that someone out there is rebuilding and reestablishing a government means that the world, that humanity, will have a chance.

"Richard!" Dax yells out of nowhere, and I look past him just as an older man turns our way.

The guy waves and jogs over, huffing by the time he stops in front of us. "What can I do you for?"

Dax nods toward us. "Need to get these guys a house, didn't know if you were headed toward the dorms."

"I'm not," the new guy says, "but it doesn't matter, because Corinne passed that job on to Ginny last week. We're wanting her to take it easy now that she's getting close to the end."

Dax shakes his head, but he's back to smiling. "They never tell me anything."

"Doesn't matter. I can get these people where they need to go so you don't hafta." Richard waves as he turns and starts walking again. "Follow me."

"You heard the man," Dax says, grinning from ear to ear.

Axl takes off after the older man, pulling me with him, but I pause long enough to return Dax's smile. "Thanks for all your help."

"Anytime," he says, giving me a wink that for some reason makes the hair on the back of my neck stand up.

Joshua mumbles his thanks as well, and we both have to jog to catch up with the others. I can actually feel Dax's gaze on me as I walk.

"You just get here?" Richard calls, glancing over his shoulder to make sure we're still behind him.

"We came to see a doctor," Joshua says.

The man frowns and looks us over. "Everything okay I hope?"

"Yes and no," Joshua says. "But there's not much we could have done to change things."

"Shame. Well, welcome anyway. We're happy to have new folks. The more we get the more likely we'll be to survive. I'm Richard, by the way."

"We ain't movin' here," Axl says.

302

"We have a place," I explain. "Thanks for the hospitality, though."

I introduce the others and myself, then fill Richard in on what we're doing here, giving him a little background information. He listens intently, nodding as we walk, and in his presence, Axl relaxes just a little. Maybe there isn't something off about Dax.

"It's good to hear there are other groups nearby who are making it," Richard says when I've finished talking. "That's what we need, after all. We don't all have to live in the same town."

"Exactly," I say, glancing at Axl, who has relaxed even more.

My mind wanders to this town and the people here. Close to two hundred now? If Jon and Hadley are still alive, they have to be here. It makes sense, especially if they've gone out searching for survivors the way Dax said. They could have run into Hadley and Jon months ago. Maybe even right after we split up.

"Have you seen Hadley Lucas?" I blurt out, making Richard stop walking.

He turns to face me, his eyebrows pulled together like he's trying to figure something out. "Hadley Lucas the actress?" He shakes his head when I nod, and lets out a little laugh. "Can't say that I have. It sure would liven things up if she walked through our gates, I don't mind admitting."

My heart sinks. Shit. I was so sure they'd be here. If they aren't here, maybe they are dead. Maybe it's time for me to accept the truth: they never made it out of that town. Either they were shot or the men who attacked us took them. Lord knows what Hadley went through, but I can only hope her death was fast and easy. That they didn't keep her alive to torture her the way the men in Vegas did.

Axl gives my hand a squeeze and whispers, "We'll find her."

I just shrug. I'm not sure I can believe that anymore.

Richard is still chuckling to himself when he turns and starts walking, and the three of us follow.

Less than a second later he says, "Lookie what we have here. It's Ginny's husband. He'll get you to the right place, no problem."

He waves to a man a good twenty feet away, but his back is turned to us. Richard can wave as much as he wants, but he's not going to get this guy's attention. He isn't even looking our way.

When waving doesn't get the guy's attention, Richard sticks two fingers in his mouth and lets out a loud whistle. "Jon!"

The man finally turns to face us, and when his green eyes meet mine, everything around me freezes as I find myself swept back in time. Back to Vegas and the Monte Carlo and a broken man desperate to save his sister from a fate worse than death. To feelings of terror as we tried to escape. To the days following, our group hiding in our underground shelter while Hadley and I licked our wounds. Then the attack and all the uncertainty surrounding us as we spent weeks on the road, struggling and fighting to survive. And the devastation of the loss when he disappeared.

There are so many memories in those green eyes, and they all hit me at once, bringing all the emotions surrounding each event with them. The feelings are so strong that I can't move. Can't breathe or think or react. Not even when the man steps forward. His mouth dropping open as his eyes move from me to Axl to Joshua. I never thought I'd see this face again. Not really, and having him in front of me after all this time makes me feel like I've struck gold.

Sobs shake my body, and before I even know what's happening I'm running toward him. Tears stream down my face, but I can't control them. I'm not even sure I want to. This is the moment I've been praying for.

"Jon," I whisper, still not believing what I'm seeing. Then I run faster, and his name breaks out of me again, only this time it sounds like a cry of joy. "Jon!"

Acknowledgements

A very special thanks to everyone who has read and loved this series. While the number of enquiries I received regarding the release date of book five was at times stressful, it's also a great feeling to know that so many people enjoy my books! Keep sending me emails and telling me how much you love this series, it never gets old.

Thanks, as always, to my best friend Erin Rose. I love being able to shoot you a text with any medical questions I have. Thanks also to Jen Naumann for taking the time to beta read and gush about the book online, and to Scott at Graywolf Survival for clarifying some information about Ham radios. I always want to be sure I at least sound like I know what I'm talking about! And thanks, yet again, to Laura Johnsen who took time out of her life to read *New World* for me and search for typos.

A huge thank you goes to Robert Kirkman and Norman Reedus (AKA Daryl Dixon), as well as everyone working on *The Walking Dead*. Without the popularity and success of the show, my sales wouldn't be where they are now.

And last, but not least, a special shout out to my family. My husband Jeremy and our four kids, who are always patient even when I'm stressed about deadlines and rushing to get everything done. I love you all so much.

About the Author

Kate L. Mary is an award-winning author of New Adult and Young Adult fiction, ranging from Post-apocalyptic tales of the undead, to Speculative Fiction and Contemporary Romance. Her Young Adult book, *When We Were Human*, was a 2015 Children's Moonbeam Book Awards Silver Medal winner for Young Adult Fantasy/Sci-Fi Fiction, and a 2016 Readers' Favorite Gold Medal winner for Young Adult Science Fiction. Don't miss out on the *Broken World* series, an Amazon bestseller and fan favorite.

For more information about Kate, check out her website: www.KateLMary.com